The Beast of Bradhurst Avenue and Other Stories

The Beast of Bradhurst Avenue and Other Stories

George S. Schuyler

MINT EDITIONS

The Beast of Bradhurst Avenue and Other Stories was features
work first published between 1933 and 1934.

This edition published by Mint Editions 2024.

ISBN 9798888975343 | E-ISBN 9798888975497

Published by Mint Editions®

 MINT
EDITIONS
minteditionbooks.com

Contents

The Beast of Bradhurst Avenue: A Gripping
Tale of Adventure in the Heart of Harlem

An Author Forgotten

In 1926, in the midst of a creative revolution known as the Harlem Renaissance, two authors entered a literary debate in the ring of racial politics and only one emerged victorious.

The men were emerging poet Langston Hughes and the Chief Editorial Writer of *The Courier*, George S. Schuyler. The argument? Whether Black art—that is art that came specifically from African American culture—truly existed.

Schuyler, in his now famous essay "The Negro-Art Hokum," would call the idea—or even the possibility of the idea—"foolishness." Hughes, in his defining rebuttal, "The Negro Artist and the Racial Mountain," declared, ". . . I am ashamed for the Black poet who says, 'I want to be poet, not a Negro poet,' as though his own racial world were not as interesting as any other world."

Hughes' essay would become a manifesto for Black creatives of the Harlem Renaissance and help to cement his legacy as one of the defining figures in African American history while Schuyler's essay would be just one of many public statements that would lead him to obscurity.

Whether or not Schuyler was deserving of this fate is not a question this book hopes to answer, rather; it presents the works of a now-forgotten author who, for all intents and purposes, was very much ahead of his time. His biggest successes, *Black No More* (1931) and *Black Empire* (1936–1938) were Afrofuturistic satires that were the first of their kind; both asking what it means to be Black in America while challenging the idea of *what* being Black means and to *whom*.

And it is because those books exist that this book exists.

His more controversial viewpoints aside, George S. Schuyler had proven himself to be a fiercely intelligent, humorous and honest—that is wholly authentic—master of his craft. For his literary contributions(outside of *Black No More* and *Black Empire*) to have seemingly disappeared from the eye of the reading public and the African American literary canon at large is a crime that this book hopes to rectify.

SUGAR HILL: A POWERFUL STORY
OF HARLEM LIFE TODAY

I

Introducing Pretty Melissa Stratford

Where's that brass polish, George?"

"How do I know where it is, stupid! Didn't I give it to you? Boy, you better not be wastin' ol' Alex's brass polish. You know he's a dog when he gits on your trail. Look in your Bible, Billie, maybe you'll find it there."

Billie Smith straightened up swiftly, his long, dark face registering amazement; His eyes like two saucers. With his coat half button and his cap askew, he did not appear nearly as Immaculate as he had been hired to look. Of course, he just got up to make his six o'clock in the morning watch and even plum colored uniforms with gold braid carpet make sleepy colored boys attractive at that hour.

"Look here, George Henderson," he replied, "don't you start making light of the Bible. Don't you start doin' that, son. Speak respectful about sacred things. We sure need the Bible more these days than ever before. Look at all the wickedness goes on in this house! It's a sin, that's what it is."

He glanced around the little basement room, walking over to the clothes closet, He felt up on the shelf for the lost polish, muttering to himself and shaking his head. Then he knelt on the figured linoleum covering on the floor and looked under the gas stove. He scratched his head twice, Then noticing his large Morocco-bound Bible lying open on the table where he had left it the night before, he closed it reverently. Underneath it was the large, flat round box of brass polish.

"There yuh are! There yuh are! Just like I said. And yuh wanted to preach me a sermon just 'cause I put yuh on th' right track." George Henderson smiled broadly and peeled off his plum colored uniform coat in preparation for bed.

"Go on to bed darky," grumbled Billie, a sheepish grin on his face.

"Just what I'm going to do, buddy, an' I don't mean maybe. Son, it was sure busy last night. Why I made three dollars and a quarter in tips!"

"Yeh?"

"Surest thing, that Stratford gal really got away last night, buddy. Why, She threw a party for some ofays up in her apartment and it was just too bad. I had to get them ginger ale twice. Three men went up but I ain't seen but two come down." George smiled cynically, untying his shoes.

"The Lord is gonna punish that young woman," said Billie. "She's too wicked. Sin can never be successful alone. I'm just waiting to see what happens, That's what I'm doing."

"Well, big boy, you'll sure have tuh wait uh long time 'cause that gal is sure sharp an' she's got that wop fooled outta this world," George observed.

"How do you know, smartie?"

"Well he ain't never caught her, has he? An' if she ain't let these ofays bite him in th' back fifty times since I bin here, then my name ain't George Henderson!"

"The devil will desert her some way and leave her to her fate," observed Billie, straightening his cap. "Who else tipped you?"

"Well, Bennie Buford came in about three o'clock. Maybe it was four o'clock. And, boy, was he dressed to th' gills. Gave me four dollars for just openin' th' taxicab door for him! He's sure bin flyin' high since his wife went tuh Florida."

"Yes," Billie observed dolefully, "he's wasting his substance."

"Oh, I dunno," said George quickly, "'bout him wastin' substance but he sure ain't wastin' no time tryin' to make Corrinne, believe me!"

"What Corrinne?"

"Why that slim little black gal with such pretty legs in thirty-four. You know, the bob-haired dame that plays the piano so swell."

"Ain't she married?" Billie inquired. "Ain't her husband that tall light brown-skin fellow."

"Sure," replied George, getting into bed clad in his underwear, "but that dope dunno whut it's all about."

"Well I hate to see so much sinfulness," sighed Billie, button the top button of his coat. "That Charlton seems such a nice Christian man, too."

"He won't be no Christian when he catches up with that wife of his an' that Bennie Buford," George observed. "I sure wouldn't mind seein' him poke that little slick-headed guy. Thinks he's so much just 'cause he's got the orchestra at the Green Gables."

"Well, I wish I had it," said Billie, making for the door of the little green room, the brass polish in his hand.

"You'd do better preachin', Billie," chuckled George, turning over and pulling the covers about his head.

THE LINCOLN ARMS, THE SMARTEST apartment house in black Harlem, adorns like a jewel the crest of the hill along the top of which Edgecombe Avenue runs straight as an arrow from 136th Street to the Polo Grounds. It rises in all of its walnut-colored immaculateness seven stories above the clean, paved street gazing out haughtily across Colonial Park to the shabbier houses and appropriate distance of a block away, and seventy-five feet below.

The Lincoln Arms, with its fresh brown canopy stretched out to the curbstone on a framework of gleaming brass: it's small potted trees and neatly kept strips of flower beds bordering its walk to the great gilded doors with their freshly starched curtains; its courteous uniformed doormen; its elaborate entrance with this formidable array of two hundred electric buzzers opposite as many name cards; its tiled lobby, it's oil painting of the martyred President; its parquet floors and gaudy artificial flowers; its electric refrigerators, intercommunicating telephones, hall incinerators!

The Lincoln Arms, pride of Sugar Hill, that section of Lower Washington Heights, but recently opened up to Negro New Yorkers who are willing to pay for swank, class, cleanliness, and fresh air. What a struggle to get on to Sugar Hill; what sacrifices to stay there! What envy from the black folk Stuffed and gloomy flats. In the canyons below! What speculation from the whites who cruise by in their limousines and wonder how Negroes can afford to live in such apparent luxury! What?

Cynical chuckles from the smart Jewish owner who knows so much that he won't tell!

Billie Smith stopped polishing the brass canopy standards to look at his watch. It was seven o'clock. People would soon be coming out to go to work. He must carry and finish. Colored folks who opened doors downtown didn't relish opening doors. At the Lincoln Arms, especially when there was a doorman to do it for them. He gave the standards a final wipe with his cloth, walked into the lobby and placed the cloth and polish under one of the big red plush sofas.

Billie stood idly by the door. He kept thinking about Melissa Stratford and what George Henderson had said. He tried to dismiss the demimonde from his mind, but he couldn't. From the very first day he had come to work, three months before, he had been captivated by this almost white girl who was so exotically beautiful, so stylishly dressed, and who live so mysteriously, coming and going in taxi cabs, staging wild parties two or three times a week, having so many rich looking white men visit her.

An irresistible longing for this slim, cream colored creature, who tossed her henna-ed curls so naughtily as she tripped across the lobby to the automatic elevator, and almost pulled you to her with that central look in her round black eyes.

Then guilty, he forced her image from his mind. After all, she was a sinner, while he was a Christian, sworn to do the work of the Lord. He reflected painfully that it was sometimes difficult to be a one hundred Christian. This was especially true where sin was attractively garbed.

Oh well! Here was someone coming in from the street. Billie opened the door smartly. A pasty faced little black haired Italian, plumped and well-tailored, half consumed cigar clenched in the corner of his seam-like mouth, walked into the entrance and started to enter the lobby.

"WHO DID YOU WANT TO see," asked Billie, smiling.

"That's alright, Sam," said the Italian, briskly, running his hand into his trousers pocket and extracting a crumpled bill. "I'm

GEORGE S. SCHUYLER

going up to see Miss Stratford in Thirty-Five. She's expecting me. You needn't ring. Get yourself a cigar!"

He winked and handed Billie the crumpled dollar. The doorman took it mechanically, mumbling the usual thanks. He was thinking, thinking, thinking of what George Henderson had said. If there was someone in Melissa Stratford's apartment when Joe Savino got there, who could tell what might happen. What could be done to prevent the Italian from going up there.

"Miss Stratford isn't in, Mr. Savino," he found himself saying. Why he said it, he didn't know. After all, it was none of his business. The woman was a blatant sinner and the man was the owner of the Silver Cup, an illicit dispensary of the hated alcohol. Why should he, the doorman, interfere. And yet he had. Worse, he must help her.

"How you know?" snapped the Italian.

"I saw her go out about an hour ago," lied Billie, praying to the Lord for forgiveness. "Would you like to wait?"

Joe Savino's face clouded, his jet black eyebrows met. Joe hated to be disappointed. It was very seldom that he was, as a matter of fact. Owning a chain of deluxe speakeasies catering to the thirst of black Harlem enabled one to have about what he wanted. But right now, Joe wanted to see Melissa Stratford more than anything else in the world, and she wasn't at home. He tossed aside his crumpled cigar, which caused Billie to frown with disapproval, little fresh one and pluck down on the red plush sofa.

"I wait," he announced grimly. He somehow felt suspicious, but could not think just why he should. And yet he always felt that way about Melissa, ever since he met her, six months before in his "de luke" speakeasy, the Silver Cup. She was always making funny moves. Now what did she mean by going out at seven o'clock in the morning?

Billie wondered what to do as seconds flashed by. He knew Melissa was a Sinner. He knew that she cared nothing for him, a mere doorman who got so little money, and yet he had an irresistible urge to warn her. He looked at the battery of buzzers. There wasn't a chance that way. Joe Savino was too suspicious and alert.

Then suddenly, his heart leaped. He had it! Through the basement, of course. Why hadn't he thought of it before? He buoyed up with the thought.

Slowly he sauntered out the front door. Turning sharply to the left and clattering down the few stone steps to the basement, he ran to the elevator shaft door, and pressing the button, brought the car down. He hastily entered, pressed the button numbered three and the car moved swiftly upward.

He felt so relieved now. He could save her much embarrassment by this. Perhaps she would appreciate it. She was so pretty and white. And yet not really white, so a black boy like him could feel at home with her. You could feel that she was your own, even if she could "pass." Then he felt again ashamed of himself for thinking about this scarlet woman, who violated everyone of the Ten Commandments everyday. And yet something drove him on.

The elevator stopped like a good robot at the third floor. The barred door rolled back with a whirr and a click. He stepped out and hastened down the corridor to No. 35. He pushed the doorbell vigorously for almost a minute before the cover of the eye hole in the door was pulled aside and a big black eye appeared.

"What do you want, Billie?" she said favorably, for it was Melissa.

"Mister Savino's downstairs to see you," he announced.

"Oh, hell! Thanks, Dearie!" she exclaimed. "It was great of you to wise me. You're a sweet boy, I'll see you later."

The eyehole cover snapped back into place. Billie felt joyful, ecstatic. She had called him sweet boy! She, the little princess, so naughty but so nice! He turned to go back to the elevator. Then suddenly his heart caught his throat. Standing there now five feet from him was Joe Savino, a grim, humorless smile, relieving his pasty, sardonic features, his cigar stuck in one side of his mouth, his hands in his overcoat pocket.

"So, she got out an hour ago, Yeh?" he sneered.

There was nothing more he could do now, Billie thought. What lie could he tell, What could he do to save Melissa from her own folly? He stood undecided in the middle of the hall.

The Italian pushed past him and beat with his gloved fist on the door.

"Melissa! Melissa!" He shouted. "Open this door."

"Just a minute, Joe," came Melissa's scared voice, "I haven't got anything on."

II

Pretty Melissa Jilted, But Finds New "Boyfriend"

You lied to me, you little tramp!" hissed Joe Savino, as he stood close to Melissa. "You lied to me! An' I'm tellin' you now, you can't get away with it. Whaddaya take me for, a sap? I knew you was up here all th' time."

"But, Joe, dearie," the octoroon pleaded in a frightened little voice, as she cowered against the door frame, drawing her silken gown about her, revealing her lithe, voluptuous limbs. "I don't get you. I've been here all night, honey. Honest I have."

"Yah," he spat, "you've been here all night, all night, an' you've had somebody here with you too. You put Billie to saying you wasn't here in order to stall me off, but I'm wise to you now, baby."

"Why, I didn't tell Billie anything," she exclaimed, a ring of truth in her voice. "He just ran up here and said you were downstairs, that's all. . ." Her voice trailed off and a light of fear appeared in her big, oval black eyes. Her little ivory fingers plays nervously with the texture of her green robe.

Joe Savino's lip curled in bitter amusement, touched with disillusionment. He glanced around at the room in disorder; the unmade bed, the ash trays heaped with cigarette butts, the stick whiskey glasses, the almost empty bottle of Scotch, the half open window next to the fire escape. Her big scared eyes followed his glance. He strode rapidly across the room to the window and looked out and up from the fire escape. He turned from the window, his eyes narrowing dangerously, and advanced toward her, one hand in this topcoat pocket, a hard cynical smile on his cruel mouth.

The girl cowered. She knew Joe Savino only too well; knew what he was capable of doing. She knew him not only as the owner of the Silver Cup speakeasy around the corner on St. Nicholas

Avenue, but also as the secret leader of a mob of killers. Knowing him, she feared him; feared for her own life.

"Don't, Joe!" She wailed. "Please don't. I haven't done anything. Honest, Joe. I've been level. There ain't nobody but you."

"Shut up!" he snapped. "You dirty little tramp. I oughta plug you, but I don't. Lead is too good for you. You double crossin' me after all I done for you. . . No, I ain't gonna plug you."

He removed his right hand from his topcoat pocket. Melissa breathed more grimly. Still, she wondered what he would do. Then suddenly and with surprising swiftness his clenched fist flew up and crashed against her pretty cupid's bow mouth. She fell backwards, stunned, her mouth bleeding profusely.

The Italian stood over her, an evil expression on his face. Then turning on his heel he went to the door and opened it. He hesitated a moment. He liked this delicate, voluptuous little octoroon plaything on whom he had lavished money and beautiful clothes. He rather hated to leave her. Her beautiful body drew him. . . but, well nobody could double-cross Joe Savino.

"ALRIGHT," HE WARNED HER, AS her eyes opened and she looked dumbly and fearfully up at him. "I go now. Tonight I come back, see? An' if you ain't scrammed I'll rub you out. Get me?"

The door slammed loudly behind him, and Melissa was alone. The tawdry, untidy room seemed vast and lonely and strangely quiet now. Melissa dragged herself limpingly to the bathroom to treat her cut lip.

She thought wistfully of the party she had had the night before, and then, in contrast, of what had just happened. What a rotten break! Under her breath she cursed her stupidity, her flaming passion that would not permit her to be good. Joe Savino was the best man she'd ever had. He had given her everything she wanted. For the first time in her nineteen years, she had almost been happy. And now it was all over. Disgusted with herself, she sagged on the bed, her eyes swelling with tears, and saw violently, passionately.

BILLIE SMITH STOOD AT THE door all morning, resplendent in his plum colored uniform. Mechanically he opened the door, closed it, answer telephone calls, announce visitors and tradesmen, greeted the residents of the Lincoln Arms as they came and went. Apprehensive over the fate of Melissa Stratford, he had blessed her apartment several times during the morning after Joe Savino, grim and dark visaged, had strolled angrily out of the house. He wondered what had happened to the girl who had attracted him so strangely.

At noon, Alex Dangerfield, the little haughty West Indian superintendent, came up from the basement to relieve him for lunch. Alex was black, forty and slender, with a great sense of his importance as custodian of the swellest apartment house in Harlem. He was entered being called the janitor. He insisted, proudly and defiantly, that he was the superintendent. The residents indulged him, although they detested his wife Letitia, a barrel shaped little black woman, arrogant and saucy.

"You may depart for lunch," Alex announced to the eager Billie in his lofty manner, hoping quote, but be back here at one o'clock sharp."

Billie dashed down to the basement, brought down the automatic elevator, and ascended to the third floor. He sped to No. 35. Melissa's apartment pushed the buzzer feverishly a dozen times, getting no response, he tried the door to his surprise. It was unlocked.

He entered swiftly, apprehensively, as he toyed for a moment with the horrid thought that she might be dead. His heart skipped a beat as he noticed her lying outstretched on her disordered bed, her hair loosened. Her robe thrown open, disclosed her beautifully shaped bust. He noted with alarm the bruise on her mouth, and then with relief observed that she was breathing heavily.

SHE WAS IN A DEEP slumber or stupor. How beautiful she was! He bit his lip nervously as an evil thought skipped through his mind and mirrored itself momentarily in his serious, deep set eyes. Yes, he mused, he knew she was a sinner; that she wasn't his kind; that she was a bad woman—not Christian. But the sight of her delicate, delicately molded ivory limbs and her long, loose, silicon brown hair, captivated him—thrilled him.

"Miss Stratford!" he cried softly, standing over her, taking in the rareness of her beauty, "Miss Stratford!"

She stirred fitfully. He reached down with trembling hand and touched her smooth, hot shoulder. An electric thrill ran through him at this contact with the girl. He now frankly confessed to himself that he loved. He shook her now, a little more strongly. Her big, black eyes open with a styled expression, and she sat up, looking wildly at him.

How did you get in here?" she snapped ill temperately.

"The door was unlocked," he replied, contritely. "I rang, but you didn't answer, so I came right in. I thought something might have happened to you."

"Well, how did you guess it?" she mocked, half smiling, touching her lip ruefully.

"Did he hurt you?" he inquired anxiously.

"Take a slant at that wallop on the mouth, will you?" she directed.

"I'm sorry," he blurted. "I could kill him for that."

"Why are you so interested?" She queried, registering surprise, and seeing a new this tall, dark, young fellow, who would always seem so grave and studious—different from the men she associated with.

"We—el," he hesitated, "I just don't like to see a girl hurt."

"Oh!" she replied, attend of disappointment in her tone, then smiling wearily: "I thought you were getting soft about me being hurt."

"Well, I am," he admitted. The words escaped him before he realized what he was saying. He felt his cheeks growing warm and he shifted uneasily in his confusion. "That is," he added, "you're so pretty. I just hate to see anything happen to you." He toyed with his cap and glanced out at the carpet. He felt embarrassed, out of place, somehow, with this pretty white colored girl, bad though he knew her to be.

"Oh!" she exclaimed coquettishly, "so you think I'm pretty, eh?" Then: "Sit down, Billie. You did me a good term this morning. If it hadn't been for you, I guess Joe would have caught me, sure enough and rubbed me out. He's a killer, that guy." She moved over to permit him to sit down. "Come on and sit down," she commanded. "I won't eat you."

"Why don't you give up that fellow?" he asked earnestly.

"Hah! That's good!" she laughed mirthlessly. "Give him up? Why that wop gave me the air this morning and if I'm not out of here by night he says he'll rub me out. . . Give him up? Boy, he's spared me the trouble."

Billie sat down a little gingerly. He was so close to her now that he could feel the heat of her body. The faint perfume on her loosened hair coursed through his nostrils to his brain, intoxicating him, driving away his reason, uncoiling the lashes of his tongue.

"I-I-I'd like to help you if you'd let me," he stammered. "Haven't you got any money to get a place of your own?"

"Not a dime," she said, somewhat bitterly. "Not a lousy dime."

"Well, won't you let me help you?" he begged earnestly. "I'd like to help you, Miss Stratford."

She arched her eyebrows and looked wonderingly, calculatingly at the tall black fellow. "You can call me Melissa," she said coyly, "if you want to."

"Can I?" He asked eagerly. "And will you let me help you?"

"Sure," she smiled, "If you want to."

Melissa recalled to herself that she had never previously dealt in coal" but he was so nice and kind and considerate. And she needed help right through here.

"How much do you need?" he asked, flagging awkwardly in his uniform pocket.

"Well," she replied, eyeing him speculatively through her bewitching smile. "I could rent another apartment like this for forty-five. Could you let me have fifty, Billie?"

The doorman gasped. Fifty dollars! He glanced at her quickly with a look of disbelief. Something within him warned him to stop there and go no further. Then he looked down into her lipid eyes that shone so appealingly into his, and his swift gaze took in rapidly the loveliness of her.

"Alright, Miss Strat. . . er. . . Melissa," he stammered, with difficulty controlling his emotion, "I'll give it to you."

　　　　　　　　　　　　GEORGE S. SCHUYLER

"Oh, you, dear!" She squealed delightfully, kicking her pale bare feet with her pink stained toenails. Then, before he was prepared for it, she threw her plump, warm arms around his neck and kissed him fully, lengthily and passionately upon the lips.

The blissful seconds lengthened into minutes as they clung to each other, engrossed in their new friendship. Billie was giddy with excitement and anticipation; Melissa was gratified that she had so soon solved her difficulties. She observed that his lips were so much softer than the thin hard lips of Joey Savino. He felt his uniform coat, choking him and loosened the top buttons.

"Why don' you take it off, Billie," she cooed softly, her fingers deftly unbuttoning the tunic, and dabbing his perspiring brown with a tiny lace edge handkerchief. Excitedly he withdrew his muscular arms from the sleeve. Now she curled up closer to him.

"I didn't realize it was so hot," he observed, a propose of nothing, drawing her closer to him. She had a way of squirming into his embrace that intrigued him with its catlike, oriental strangeness and willing surrender. Playfully she pushed him. They fell back, launching with abandon as his fingers caught. And the heavy lace of that trimmed her sleeves.

It all seemed like heaven to Billie. That girl, smiling wisely to herself, lay still and quiet, snuggled in his arms.

The minutes flew by swiftly on the wings of passion. Both wondered to themselves how they had grown to know each other so well in such a short while. They whispered nothings in each other's ears.

"I've got to go now," he said. Reluctantly, sitting up.

"I'll have to go, two, before night," she reminded him.

"Oh, yes," he replied, groping in his pocket. "Here's ten dollars, dear. I'll run down to the Dunbar Bank and get the rest."

"You sweet!" she caroled, stretching out luxuriously.

"So long!" He sung out, leaving the apartment.

"What a break!" she murmured, smiling to herself.

III

MARY SUTTON HEARS THAT BILLIE HAS TURNED HER DOWN

There was something so pure, innocent and sweet about little Mary Sutton that almost as soon as men saw her, they honored, respected and loved her. She was a small, a reddish. Dark brown, with long wavy hair and high cheekbones that revealed her Indian ancestry. Although she had occupied a one-room apartment at the swank Lincoln Arms, not a soul in the Edgecombe Avenue edifice had ever pointed the finger of suspicion at her and no whisper of scandal had ever sullied her good name. She went out early in the morning to work for Mrs. Jenny Pinkelbach on Riverdale Drive as a maid of all work, and came back late at night. She saved her money and was a faithful member of the Baptist Church.

Billie Smith had thought that he loved Mary Sutton, but that was before he succumbed to the charms of Melissa Stratford. Mary knew that she loved Billie. She wondered why he had grown so indifferent of late.

"Billie," she said one evening as she came in from work, "what have I done to you? Has something happened?"

"No," the tall doorman replied, shifting uneasily, "Everything's alright, Mary. You're a swell kid."

"But—but, you seem different," she persisted anxiously. She was thinking of several times they had been to the movies together and to church; of how he had brought her ice cream and whispered sweet words to her as they walked through Colonial Park.

"Oh. . . I'm alright," he answered frowning slightly and averting her gaze. "I'm not any different now than I've ever been, Mary. You just think so, that's all."

"Yes, you are Billie. You are different," she continued.

"No, I'm not," he persisted doggedly. His voice grew a little hard. He was really ashamed of himself and sorry for the girl, but then he kept thinking of Melissa. He knew her for what she was or had been and he knew in his heart that Mary Sutton was better. . . cleaner, but there was a witchery about Melissa that bound him in spite of better judgement. He hadn't treated Mary right, but he couldn't help it.

The telephone from upstairs rang and he went gratefully to answer it, glad to escape Mary's accusing gaze. She turned disconsolately and went to her apartment, the tears welling in her deep-set eyes.

Unlocking her door, she threw off her hat and coat and flung herself disparagingly onto her bed. What was the matter with Billie? She liked him so much, even if he was only a doorman and didn't make much money. Why did he not return her regard? What had happened?

She turned the matter over and over in her mind. Had she been too cold toward him? Well, She couldn't be forward, and he had never really pressed his suit in that way. He had always been a gentleman to her.

In the midst of her thoughts, her communicating buzzer rang. It was. Corrinne Charlton on the third floor.

"Hello, Mary," came her clear, bell-like voice. "Can you come up for a little while? I know you're tired, but I'm so damned lonesome. I must talk to someone."

"I'll be right up," Mary also wanted to talk to someone.

Five minutes later she was sitting on the divan in Corrinne's cozy two room apartment.

Mrs. Charlton, statuesque brown woman, in her late twenties, was sitting at the piano, her long, slender fingers moving swiftly over the keys, while classical music filled the well-furnished room. An orange silk robe hung loosely around her, falling carelessly from one well-rounded brown shoulder, while the glow from the subdued light of the floor lamp. It was reflected in the polish of her close crop bob.

"Corrinne," asked Mary, during a lull in the playing, "why are you so dissatisfied? You have everything. Your husband has a good job in the post office, he gives you everything you want, and you have a beautiful home here. If I were in your shoes, I'd be very happy."

"Oh, you just say that because you don't know," said Corrinne, a note of asperity in her voice as she swung around from the keyboard. "Well, I guess all of this might satisfy you, but I'm bored to death. I hate sitting here in the house, going to the movies, playing bridge, never really getting anywhere. I want to do things, Mary—be somebody. What's the good of being what you call an accomplished pianist when I can't put it to any use because Dick won't let me. He just wants me to be an old-fashioned wife. I want a career."

"What would you like to do?" Ask the younger woman.

"Oh," replied Corrinne, enthusiastically, "I'd like to play in a club or have an act on the stage. I can play well enough, and sing too. I'd like to support myself, Mary. I hate to be dependent upon a man. You don't understand how much I want to be my own boss. Of course, Dick is sweet and all that, but he's a fool, too. He thinks the things I love are bad. You ought to have heard him rave the other day after Dorothy King left here."

"Who's Dorothy, King?" Asked Mary.

"Oh, she's that pretty, light Brown skinned girl who lives up on the fifth floor. She's an entertainer at Joe Savino's place around on St. Nicholas Ave. Ashley Dukes, that rich white fellow is her sweetheart. Her husband's a Pullman porter. A big, good looking black fellow. It's really a shame the way she treats him. Everytime he goes off on a run, she throws a big party. Dick has warned me not to have anything to do with her, but she's a really swell kid and I like her lots."

Mary hadn't met people like Dorothy King. Ever since she had come down from Rochester a year before. She had associated with those known to be respectable, but now she had an urge to meet this real woman of the world.

"Would you like to meet her sometime?" asked Corrinne, apparently reading her thoughts. "I'll give her a ring."

"Oh, you mustn't," the girl objected. "Your husband might come in."

"No, he won't," Corrinne spoke with assurance, "He's on a late shift this week." She got up and walked lazily to the house telephone in the vestibule.

GEORGE S. SCHUYLER

"Connect me with Mrs. King's apartment, will you, Billie?" she sang. . . "Oh, Hello, Dorothy! What are you doing? Well, come up for awhile, will you? I want you to meet a little friend of mine. . . Oh, no, he's working late tonight."

Mary appraised Dorothy King with all in admiration. Her clothes were so smart. She was so beautiful. There was a sophisticated cleverness about her that was so much in contrast to her own simple manner. All of the knowledge of the world seemed reflected in her large, heavy lashed eyes. Mary silently compared Dorothy 's beautiful evening gown with her own.

Dorothy draped herself on a big overstuffed chair and lighted a long, slender cigarette, flickering the match stem expertly into a tray on the center table.

"Yes," she chattered, "I won't be in Joe Savino's long now. I'm getting tired of the place. It's too hard on your throat, trying to sing in all that smoke and having to drink all of that liquor. Then, too, he's been evil as hell for the last two weeks."

"What's the matter with him?" asked Corrinne, leaning forward with interest.

"Well," continued Dorothy, with some gusto, "You know he used to keep up that Melissa Stratford, the pretty girl on this floor who looks like white. She pulled the fast one on him and he got wise and threw her out. I think he still likes her, but is too proud to pick her up again. You know how those wops are. He's been biting everybody's head off around the place."

"What's she doing now?" Asked Mary.

"Just what she's always been doing," absorbed Dorothy, "ever since she's been around here; she's got another daddy. And who do you think it is?"

"Who?" Corrinne loved gossip. It was a welcome interlude in her humdrum life.

"Why you haven't heard?" said Dorothy incredulously.

"No, no!" pressed Corrinne. "Who is it?"

Dorothy smiled knowingly, leaning back in her chair and blowing a wreath of cigarette smoke over her head. She enjoyed being able to impart juicy gossip. She derived as a distinct pleasure from tearing other people to pieces. Mary and Corrinne leaned forward expectantly.

"Well," said Dorothy at last, when she had tortured the two sufficiently, "Nobody but Billie, or doorman! . . . Quite a tumble from Joe Savino, eh. But they tell me Billie's git a lot of money saved up. Well, he'll need it!"

Mary sat stunned, expressionless, gazing straight ahead, her eyes blink, her twitching fingers registering her emotions.

"Why, Mary!" Corrinne exclaimed. "What's the matter with you? You look like a mummy."

"Oh, Nothing," said Mary slowly, fighting to regain possession of herself. "I guess I just worked a little too hard today. I . . . I . . . I think. I'll go downstairs and lie down."

She rose quickly, to the amazement of the others, and hurrying to the door, disappeared.

"What's eating her?" asked Dorothy, frowning.

"Oh, didn't you know? Corrinne informed her, turning back to the silent keyboard, a look of exhalation on her face. "The little fool is crazy about Billie. He took her out three or four times and she thought he was liking her."

"Well," observed Dorothy, "She's got lots of competition now."

"Oh, I hate it," exclaimed Corrinne, "She's such a swell kid."

Dorothy puffed thoughtfully on a fresh cigarette and flicked a bit of ashes from her sequin, studied in evening dress. Then she got up, bade Corrinne goodnight and went to the door.

"Listen, Corrinne," She said, pausing with her manicured fingers on the doorknob, "If you're really serious about getting a job, I'll give you a knockdown to Baron Brown. Know about him, don't you?"

"Yes," echoed Corrinne, "I know about him. He wants the green Gables Cabaret, But. . . Well, He's such a character, Dorothy! I'm afraid Dick wouldn't. . ."

"Now, listen here, kid," Dorothy answered in a hard, level voice. "All you good dames are alike; you and Mary. You're afraid to step out and get what you want. If you want to get anywhere, you've got to step out and go, and not let a man stand in your way. . . Why don't you girls be like me? I got a husband, but I don't let it worry me none. . . I mind my business and tell him to mind his. . . I keep him guessing and tell him nothing. . . He can't get me what I want and he knows it, but I get it just the same. She?" She surveyed her lovely draped form and with a knowing smile said, "So long," and vanished.

Corrinne sat for a long time, thinking hard while her slender fingers ran lightly over the keyboard. Then, with sudden resolution she struck a low major chord, then, getting up, she slowly walked to the window and looked out over the housetops toward the Harlem River. Yes, she decided, whether Dick liked it or not, she would meet Baron Brown. She was tired of sitting in the house. She wanted to put her talent to work.

She hummed a catchy tune as she went about preparing Dick's midnight lunch.

Downstairs in her apartment, Mary Sutton lay across the bed, her eyes red and swollen from sobbing, her clothing in disarray. It had been a shock to her, the news about Billie and Melissa. It seemed incredible that a fine fellow like Billie should turn down a girl like her for a woman like Melissa Stratford, and yet she could see it all clearly now; understand why he had grown indifferent to her.

She had felt weak and helpless at first, But the longer she thought about it, the more she felt that Billie was just under this woman's spell and could be rescued before she ruined him. She knew now that she wanted him desperately; that she loved him more than she had thought. Moreover, she was determined to save him. The Indian in her rose to the surface. The thought of surrender was submerged in a wave of anger. She rose, brushed back her hair nervously and went to the inner communicating telephone.

"Billie!" She called. "This is Mary."

"Yes?" came the voice from downstairs.

"What time will you be off? Watch?"

"One o'clock! Why?"

"Well, come up to my place," she requested, marveling at her boldness. "I want to see you."

There was a pause for a moment or two, and ten when he had recovered from his surprise, he replied, "Okeh, I'll come."

Mary hung up the receiver with a satisfied smile and walked to the bathroom, singing softly to herself.

IV

Billie and Mary Quarrel; Melissa Goes Back To Joe

Billie," She began, when he came in. Later, "I understand now why you don't care for me anymore."

He frowned as she spoke. He had expected something like this and had been reluctant to visit her, but he did not want to hurt her feelings. He sincerely liked Mary Sutton. He knew she was better in many ways than Melissa Stratford, and yet he felt within himself that he must continue along the course he had adopted.

"I heard all about you and that Stratford woman," she continued evenly. "I didn't think you were the kind of fellow to have anything to do with a woman like that."

He remained silent, nervously teasing his cap up and down as he sat on the edge of his chair. He resolved that he wasn't going to argue, that he knew what he was going to do and no argument would change him.

"Why don't you say something, Billie? Haven't you got anything to say? After all, I think I deserve some sort of explanation. You remember you said you loved me."

"Yes," he said slowly, "That's true. I did. I still like you a whole lot."

"I know," she added bitterly, "You like me, but you don't love me as you once said you did. What a fool I would have been if I'd have given myself to you."

"Oh, quit seeing the blues, will you," he snarled. "You girls are all the same. . ."

"Yes," she snapped, "That's what you men all think. You don't appreciate a girl who tries to be somebody. I suppose you think that yellow hussy upstairs is even better than I am."

"Keep her out of this!" he snapped.

"Oh, yeah." Her lip curled in anger and disgust, "I suppose she's so precious to you, isn't she?"

He contained himself with difficulty and arose. There was no point in prolonging the agony.

"There is no use of our quarreling, Mary. I really can't help what's happened, I'm sorry. But I hope we can go on being friends."

He moved toward the door, hesitant about going and yet unwilling to stay under the circumstance. What was the use anyway?

She grew alarmed when she saw him preparing to go. The tigress that slumbers in the breast of every woman awakened. Her sudden determination drove back the tears that had begun to dampen her eyes at the prospect of defeat.

"Well," he remarked, apropos of nothing, "it's a little late. I think I'll be going downstairs."

"Not upstairs?" she queried sarcastically.

"I said where I was going," he snarled, "and wherever I go it's none of your business. You don't own me!"

"No, but your Melissa does," she spat, standing close to him and staring straight into his eyes.

"Alright," he muttered, turning the doorknob, "Have it your way."

"Yes, I'll have it my way," she cried, "I'd like to kill her, the yellow—. I guess I'm too black for you."

Stabbed by the taunt, he turned swiftly to face her. "That's just the trouble with all of you dark women," he challenged, "You're always thinking of color. Everytime you lose out, you think it's because of your color."

"Well, I haven't lost out yet, Billie Smith," she flamed, her anger bringing a soft reddish glow to her smooth brown cheeks. "You can't play with me and then go off and give all your money to some yellow—. I won't let you make a fool of me."

Mary was thoroughly aroused now. She hoped to persuade Billie to give up Melissa. His refusal rendered her desperate.

"Alright! Alright!" he growled. "I'm not going to argue about it."

He turned to open the door. Swiftly she reached out and grasped him by the lapel of his coat.

"Please, Billie," she pleaded desperately, "Don't treat me this way. I haven't done anything to you. Give up that woman. She doesn't mean you any good. All she wants is your money, Billie. Please, dear, I—I, well—I love you, Billie, and she doesn't."

She paused, breathless and ashamed at her frank admission. The words had scarcely dropped from her lips. Then she regretted having virtually prostrated herself at the feet of a man who would admit it. He did not love her. She grew angry at herself for her weakness.

"Alright, go on to her," she said resignedly. "I guess I'm a fool to care. There really hasn't been anything between us. Perhaps I could have held you if there had."

Billie thought the same thing, but he didn't say so. He was weary of wrangling. Why was it, he thought to himself, that some women didn't understand that it is often a mistake to hold a man off too long.

"Oh, how I hate her," she flared, with a sudden change of mood. "just when I was so happy, she had to come along. I ought to kill her. . . and you too."

"Don't be a damned fool," he growled irritably. "Goodnight!"

The slamming of the door seemed like a judgment to Mary. So this was the end, was it? This was all that was to come. Of all her dreams. Practically alone in the great city, she had been glad of the friendship with Billie, which had gradually ripened into a clean and beautiful love. Now it was all over. But was it over? Her eyes narrowed craftily. She locked her door and thoughtfully wound her alarm clock.

After the argument with Mary, Billie felt sort of low. He didn't want to go to bed and he didn't feel like seeing Melissa or any other woman. He had that feeling that many men experience at times of wanting only the company of men—of being fed up with women and of all their ways. It seldom lasts very long, If the man is normal, but it comes to all men sometimes.

He walked to the door where his partner, George Henderson, was leaning, peeping out of the side of the curtain doorway.

"Thought you'd gone to bed, Billie," the other remarked.

"Don't feel like it, George. I'm kinda restless."

"Humph! You shouldn't be, as long as you've been in Miss Sutton's apartment."

"Oh, we were just talking. . . Not what you think."

"Oh, yeah!"

"You heard me!"

"Alright, pal, but don't let your high yellow upstairs know that you've been visiting that brown." George snickered.

"Oh, man, I'm not bothering with her," defending himself. "We're just friends."

"Well," observed the other, "all I can tell you is to keep 'em apart."

"What's new?" asked Billie, changing the subject.

"Nothing much, except they're having a big party up in Mrs. King's apartment, I've been out twice now for ginger ale. Made a dollar since one o'clock."

"Any ofays up there?"

"Yeah, that swell dame that comes up here with Baron Brown, she blew in with him about a half hour ago. That Dukes guy has been up there too, for a long time. The party ought to be get righteous pretty soon."

"Gee!" observed Billie, flinging himself down on the red plus sofa in the lobby, "this sure is some house."

OVER AT THE SILVER CUP, in a far corner of the large, garishly decorated black room, sat Melissa Stratford. She was alone, half filled glass of gin before her being turned around and around by her manicured tinted fingers.

Melissa was very thoughtful as she once sat there. She couldn't understand why it was she kept coming back to Joe's place. He had mistreated her, put her out, and yet she couldn't stay away. Once, by virtue of their association, she had been a privileged character here. Now she's another customer and had to pay for her drinks.

She was thinking bitterly of the days not so long ago when she had handled hundreds of dollars of Joe's money. Now she was lucky to get her rent paid. Of course, Billie was a good kid, a real sweet boy, but after all, he had little money. When her clothes became out of style, he wouldn't be able to buy her the kind to which she had grown accustomed. Joe could and had. What a fool she had been to act the way she had. Now, if she had only been discreet—just a little cleverer.

"Hello, kid!" She turned with a start. Behind her stood Joe Savino, suave, impeccable, with that metallic hardness of the polished gangster.

"Whatcha been doin' fer yerself?" he inquired casually, eyeing her.

"Just about makin' it," she replied, looking pleadingly into his eyes. "Honest Joe," she continued. "I can't hardly make it."

It was what Joe wanted to hear. She knew that. He wanted to feel that she had suffered without his care; that she needed him; that she was repentant.

"Well," he said, glancing sharply at her with his beady black eyes, "if you think you can be good, baby, I might give yuh a break."

She brightened visible and beamed upon him. "Oh, Joe!" she gushed, "will you? I'll be good, honest, I will, Joe."

"Well, you'll hafta get rid o' dat darky yuh got, understand?" he warned.

"Oh!" she exclaimed. "That guy doesn't mean a thing to me, Joe."

V

Billie Discovers Melissa's "Double Cross," Fights Joe

"Now yer talkin'," said Joe. He sat down opposite the octoroon and crossed one keenly trousered leg over the other. He unbuttoned his double-breasted coat, drew a long black panatela from a bunch stuffed in his upper vest pocked and bit off the top with his small discolored teeth.

"Have another drink?"

"Yeah," Melissa assented with a gaiety that she had not felt since they had parted. Things were going to be rosy again. She was elated. She wanted to get high. That was always her way of celebrating.

"Hey, Sam, bring us a couple of drinks of that good stuff in the safe."

A bloated Negro waiter shuffled across the room with two well-fitted glasses.

"Well," here's tuh better times," toasted joe, jerking his head back and tossing the fiery fluid down his throat.

Melissa gulped her drink with equal dispatch. She smacked her lips with satisfaction. She smiled as it occurred to her that she would no longer have to swallow cheap gin. She glanced across gratefully at the swarthy Sicilian.

"Gee, Joe, this is just like old times. Remember how we used to get high together."

"Yeah. We sure usta put it away, didn't we, kid? . . . Hey, Sam, bring me that bottle."

The waiter shuffled into the garish room from the bar. Joe poured another drink for himself and Melissa. Now that he and the girl had made up again his irritation that had got on all of his employee's nerves was gone. He was elated and expansive.

"Here," he said, gazing across into her big timid eyes and tossing a twenty dollar bill onto the table, "take this and getcha some chewin' gum." They both grinned.

"Gee, you're a prize, Joe," she murmured. "You're always so good to me."

"He, dat ain't nuthin' tuh whatcha kid. If yuh keep yer self to me alone. All I wanta know is are yuh levelin' wit me."

"Honest, honey, I won't pull anything on you anymore," she promised.

"Well, if yuh do. . ." His voice trailed off ominously and a dangerous look glinted in his close-set dark eyes. "Yuh know me, kid."

They drank and talked. The whisky in the bottle sank lower and lower. Couples began to fill the gaudily decorated room. A pimply-faced, gangling yellow youth in evening dress sauntered in lazily from the dressing room and seated himself at the baby grand piano. There was a stir of interest among the customers. He ran his long, lean fingers over the ivories and swung into an intricate rhythmic blues. The couples forgot their drinks, held spellbound by the witchery of low down music.

The curtains of the dressing room pardoned an out move. Dorothy King, resplendent in a black velvet gown trimmed with rhinestones. Slick-headed gigolos ogled her while their smart women eyed her jealously.

In a full throated, bawdy voice, accompanied by the lewd undulations of her magnificent body, she scanning a scorching parody of the popular song, "I Could Do Most Anything for You." She jerked her body from table to table, leaving an aroma of exotic perfume behind her, detailing the nostrils of her admirers. Occasionally she would swing over and seemed directly into the face of some delighted male, winking roguishly.

She finally came to the table where Joe and Melissa sat. Her eyes spoke volumes as she saw the two together again. Here was a juicy morsel of gossip.

"Come on and have uh drink," he invited, appraising her exquisite form in a manner which momentarily possessive instinct.

"Not tonight, Joe, thanks," she replied. "I'm throwin' a party over my place an' I'm half-high now."

"Who's there?"

"Oh, Just some friends—Baron Brown, Dukes and that Glad dame. I'm going back as soon as I get through. Why dontcha come over."

Joe frowned at the mention of Baron Brown. He was one of the few remaining Negro numbers kings. That had so far refused to bow to Joe's dictatorship of the lucrative gambling racket. He was on the point of refusing the invitation, and then he reconsidered.

"Maybe I will. I wanta see th' Baron, anyhow."

Dorothy and Melissa exchanged swift significant glances. Both knew there was no feeling of commandership between the rival number barons, although there had never been any open hostilities.

Dorothy nodded to both of them, then moved on, warbling her lewd parody.

"She's no sap," Joe commented.

"Oh, she thinks she's so smart," said Melissa, spitefully, as she poured herself another stiff drink.

The piano player swung away from the keys, and the waiters moved among the tables. The hum of voices rose. Accurate cigarette smoke began to fill the low ceilinged room with a blue haze, which the electric blower in the rear world vainly to remove. The odor of cup liquor and cheap gin pervaded the fetid atmosphere. Voices grew louder as the pointed drinks took effect. Melissa and Joe were, as the saying goes in Harlem, "high as a kite."

"Gee, your shweet man," gurgled Melissa. Whisps of her silken brown hair, dampened by perspiration, hung loosely from her coiffure. Her big black eyes were half closed and she nodded her head, drunkenly and tried to look worshipfully into the Italians heavy Lashed orbs.

"Yer, shweet, too, baby," he maundered. His stubby, plump hand pawed over her beautifully shaped ivory arm and move swiftly to her shoulder. The coarse expression of Latin lust pervaded his greasy face. He rose unsteadily and scraped his chair over closer to her, putting his arm possessively around her slim waist. Then, oblivious to the observing customers, he pulled her to him and kissed her long and lasciviously upon her coral pink lips. The fires of passion lighted their eyes as they met.

"Daddy!" she breathed.

"Come on." His voice was hoarse and commanding. "Le's scram over tuh yer place."

He drained the bottle into two glasses and they raised their glasses to drink."

"Melissa!"

The voice rang out, sharp and compelling. It startled the customers and it startled the two lovers. They looked up quickly with sober, guilty alarm. The speaker was Billie Smith. He stood over them glowering with rage.

"I thought you were through with this guy?" snapped Billie, "And here you are, drunk and in his arms. Your promises don't mean a thing, do they? You're just a little double crossing. Tramp!"

There was the extreme bitterness of disillusioned, misplaced affection in his deep voice. He had come in to get a drink and had found this.

"Git outta here!" hissed Joe, frowning darkly.

"Oh yeah?" mocked Billie.

"Yuh heard me didncha?" growled the Sicilian. "Git outta here or I'll t'row yuh out!"

"You and who else?"

"Listen, buddy," warned the Italian, "I told yuh tuh scram an' yuh better be on yer way. I dowanna hurtcha. I ain't got nuthin' against yuh now but I will damn soon. Aintcha got sense enough tuh know when yer washed up? G'wan, scram!"

"Come on out of here Melissa," Billie ordered, ignoring Savino and grasping the octoroon's arm, "and go home. I want to talk to you."

"Take your black hand off me, hear?" screamed the girl, yanking her arm away. "Ain't goin' home 'less Joe takes me. You're through, sucker."

Uncontrollable rage seized the Negro. In the short time he and Melissa have been friends, he had spent all of the money he is saved from his small wages and generous ships to satisfy her endless demands. Now that he was broke, she was quitting him.

He grasped at her arm again. Joe Savino rose unsteadily, upsetting his chair. Customers stood up all over the room. The swarthy Italian swung at the tall black man. Billie step lightly aside, and as the Italian, propelled by the momentum of his blow, past him, the Negro caught him full upon the chin with the crashing right. The white man fell, cursing. Melissa sprang up, screaming. The Negro waiters leaped forward to avenge their boss. A stream of oaths shooting from his evil mouth. Joe Savino rose unsteadily, reaching into his back pocket.

"Get him!" yelled the corpulent waiter, as the three advanced hurriedly on Billie.

"I kill you!" screamed the Italian, yanking a gleaming black automatic pistol from his pocket.

"Get that gun!" yelled a man in the crowd.

Joe Savino aimed the pistol. There was a momentary dead silence. Viciously, he yanked the trigger. There was no report. In his rage, he had forgotten to unlock the safety catch. Before he could remedy his mistake, Billie's foot rose swiftly and sent the weapon spinning. Before he could regain his balance, the three black waiters piled on him, cursing and pummeling.

Several Negro male customers rushed forward to assist Billie, who was being badly handled.

"Git back there!" snapped Savino, baring his rat teeth in a horrible, murderous grimace, snatching a second pistol from an inside holster, and waving it menacingly. "I'm gonna croak dat ——!"

The three perspiring waiters rose from the prostrate form of the doorman and fell back.

"Ah, give 'im a break, Joe," someone intervened.

"Yeh," snarled the enraged Sicilian, "I give him a break right now."

VI

Billie Escapes, Dorothy's Party Get 'Hot,' The Fight

With the cruel grimace on his face, the enraged Sicilian leveled his heavy automatic pistol at the stunned figure of his rival. The low-ceilinged room was quiet as a grave as the crowd of erstwhile revelers stood transfixed.

Suddenly there was a swift movement in the rear, and the room was plunged into darkness. Curses intermingled with screams and explanations of fright and astonishment. The crowd milled around helplessly in the Stygian darkness.

Afterwards seemed eons, but was actually about five minutes, one of the waiters felt his way back to the rear of the place. The lights flashed on. There stood the bewildered crowd. There stood Joe Savino, the ugly automatic dangling on his hand. But Billie Smith was gone.

"Come on!" yelled Joe, his swarthy countenance contorted with rage. "We git 'im." He rushed out at the door bareheaded with the three waiters close behind me.

As the door slammed closed, a massive conversation rose. Questions flash thick and fast about the room. Who had turned out the lights? How had Billie Been revived and escaped so quickly? Would Joe and his men get him?

The last question was answered in the negative with the reappearance of the Italian with his three colored henchmen, their evil faces registering bewilderment.

"He got away, alright," muttered Joe, flinging himself back into the chair opposite Melissa. "Well, let's have another drink. . . Sam! Bring us a couple of drinks of that good stuff!"

Melissa had watched the struggle over her with mingled emotions. She knew Joe had more to offer her than Billie, but her sympathies had been with the handsome doorman in spite of her good judgement. Perhaps it was an awakened feeling of racial solidarity; perhaps it was love. She shook off the mood and picking up her glass carried it unsteadily to her rouge lips. Joe looked across at her and smiled.

"Le's scram," he suggested thickly teasing off his whiskey.

They rose and weaved their way uncertainly out of the Silver Cup up Nicholas Avenue, across to Edgecombe and so to the swank Lincoln Arms.

GEORGE HENDERSON, THE DOORMAN, REVEALED amazement in his staring eyes as he swung open the heavy gilded door for them, Melissa gazed defiantly, fixedly at him. She knew he would tell Billie and she knew Billie was hot tempered, doubly so after what had happened at the Silver Cup. But she was too drunk to care much. Joe Savino, in his usual cavalier manner, thrust a crumpled dollar bill into the itching palm of the uniformed Negro.

"Mrs. King," George finally remembered to say, "says for you to come up to her apartment for a while."

"Wha'ya say?" leered Joe, hanging on to Melissa's arm as he steadied himself. "Le's g'wan up f'while."

Perhaps it might be best, Melissa thought, by the time the party broke up, Billie would be asleep. Then, too, she knew Dorothy King's parties were always so hot.

"Okeh, America!" she warbled, and they made their way unsteadily to the automatic elevator.

As Dorothy admitted them, the pungent odor of "reefers" smoke their nostrils. Wreaths of light blue smoke circled around the chandelier. The serving table was covered with an assortment of whiskey, gin, and ginger ale bottles. The windows were tightly closed and the air was stale, but no one noticed it.

On the floor near the serving table, parked on an enormous pillow, was Baron Brown, a gigantic, black Negro with a bullet head, huge jowls and the torso of a gorilla. Proprietor of the notorious Green Gables cabaret and wealthiest independent numbers banker in Harlem, he bore himself, even in his present state, like a lord. He was clad only in a pair of pink striped shorts and his socks. His clean shaven head reflected the light from a floor lamp behind him.

Lying on the floor with her head across his thighs in her sparkling golden hair, draping his bare black legs, was Gertrude Glad, a slender, big-eyed, pink-skinned musical comedy star from Broadway with "black fever." She was completely nude except for a flimsy pair of step-ins and a tiny brassiere. A "reefer" dangled from her fingers.

Propped up on the sofa was actually Dukes, tall, brown hair, weak-chinned scion of a wealthy Park Avenue family, and "special friend" of Dorothy King. Completely nude except for his socks, he was "refeered" to the skies. Dorothy, draped in a negligee that reached barely to her knees, and was as thin as a mosquito net, returned from the door and fell across the form of her lover, smothering him in kisses.

"Come on and get your duds off," she advised to the newcomers, "and get comfortable. We're all as high as a kite, ain't we Ashley, old boy, old boy?"

"Yes, get undressed and be yourselves," said Ashley, taking another drag on the noxious weed. "The parties just started. Just started!"

"Oh, Daddy!" exclaim the blonde beauty whom tens of thousands of white men would have given their souls to possess, encircling the thick, black, bull like neck of Baron Brown with her shapely pink arms. "I just bet you can love like nobody's business."

BARON BROWN BEAMED AND WING triumphantly at the disapproving Joe Savino as he ran his black paws over the slender body of his admirer.

"Well, baby," he chuckled, "I guess I ain't so bad, I bet you know your stuff, too."

She winked one big blue eye at him, hugged him close again and hummed aloud the chorus of "I Could Do Most Anything for You."

Melissa and Joe rapidly divested themselves of everything but their underclothing and prepared to join the party.

"Hey, Dorothy," yelled Joe above the babble of drolling voices, "got any Bromo Seltzer? Me'n M'lissa wanta start all over 'gin."

"In the bathroom, Joe."

The two late arrivals retired to the bathroom to get their heads clear for a new deal.

Both Ashley Dukes and Baron Brown gasp when Melissa reappeared. She was clad only in her long, black wavy hair, and her ivory colored body brought back visions of "September Morn." Joe Savino, arrayed only in B. V. D.'s, proudly noted their reactions.

"Come on, let's dance," Dorothy suggested, showing off her lovers embrace and going to the radio.

"Nothin' on now, is there?" questioned Baron, looking up from the adoring eyes of the white girl.

"We can get the Green Gables Orchestra now," offered Melissa.

Dorothy twirled the knob. Soon the music began to fill the room. It was the favorite late hour classic, "My Man Rocks Me With One Steady Roll." The nude couples rose and in passionate embrace began to rock about the room, singing the sizzling words as they shuffled.

Oh, I looked at the clock
And the clock struck two;
She said, "Daddy, it's all for you."

Oh, my man rocks me with one steady roll;
There ain't no slippin' when he takes hold.

Oh, I looked at the clock
An' the clock struck three;
She said, "Daddy put that thing on me."

Oh, my man rocks me with one steady roll!

THERE WAS REALLY LITTLE LOVE lost, between the stately Dorothy King and the voluptuous militia Stratford, although they both had much in common and had no reason to be jealous of each other. Both were "kept" by white men of wealth; both sneered at everything, clean and good; Both wore gorgeous clothes and were haughty to black men—unless, like Baron Brown, they had plenty of money. Perhaps the two girls were friendly enemies because of fundamentally different natures. Melissa was hotly passionate, while Dorothy was cold and calculating.

"Say, Dorothy," asked Melissa, when they all stopped dancing to return to smoking and embracing, "where's King tonight?"

"Out on his run, of course." She had not failed to note the slight malicious tone in Melissa's voice.

"It would be just too bad if hubby should come in right now, wouldn't it?" plagued Melissa, enjoying Dorothy's annoyance.

"It wouldn't mean a thing to me. Anytime he don't like what I do, he can clear out. We pay the rent for this apartment anyway, don't we, Ashley, old boy?" Dorothy snuggled her little marcelled head on his bare chest.

"And how," that worthy retorted.

"You'd better look out for that Billie Smith," warned Dorothy, "and don't bother about my business. He was mighty hot tonight if you ask me."

"Well, nobody asked you," snapped Melissa.

"Then, if you can't take it, sister, don't try to dish it out. I'll 'tend to King and you keep your men apart." Dorothy enjoyed taunting.

"I'll tend to you, too, some day," snapped Melissa, her dark eyes afire, her brain inflamed by the fumes of the "reefer" she puffed.

Dorothy jumped to her feet, her body taut, her fists clenched. Melissa leaped to face her. The two were like spirited wild horses preparing for battle.

The other sat waiting expectantly. Here was a happy diversion to the routine of becoming gradually unconscious from liquor and drugs. Their eyes brightened. The white girl lifted her head from barons, encircling arm and gurgled with glee. The huge Negro grinned broadly. Ashley Dukes winked across at Joe Savino.

With a chorus of curses the two mulattresses leaped at each other, clutching, punching and pulling hair. Like two Amazons they battled around the room, stumbling over pillows, chairs and legs.

Finally, Dorothy with a well-directed blow toppled Melissa over a chair, and the latter lay stunned. Joe Savino leaped to her side, shaking her.

"Melissa! Melissa!" he shouted hoarsely.

Gertrude Glad ran up with a carafe of cold water and dashed its contents on the nude body of the prostrate girl.

VII

Savino Determines to "Rub Out" The Baron After Quarrel

M elissa's eyelids fluttered. Her lithe Yellow body shivered from the shower of icy water. The Italian, Dorothy, Ashley Dukes, and the white girl bent over her anxiously. Perhaps none of them cared particularly what happened to her except Joe Savino, but they did not want it to happen inside the apartment. That could cause all sorts of ugly complications.

They lifted the girl on the sofa. Gertrude Glad anxiously patted Melissa's wrist and cheeks. Slowly she began to revive, her big eyes opening and glancing slowly about the room.

"Give her a shot of that liquor," suggested Ashley.

Dorothy poured a full glass of the fiery stuff. Propping Melissa up on a couple of pillows, they made her drink. The ministration had the desired effect.

"J——! What a wallop!" were Melissa's first words as she straightened up and stroked the back of her head.

"Let me look at it, honey," asked Joe solicitously. He felt beneath the cascades of wavy hair. "Does it hurt there?"

"Yes, right there," she replied, wincing under the rough touch of his hard, stubby forefinger.

"I'm sorry, kid," Dorothy offered. "I'm awfully sorry."

"That's alright, Dorothy," smiled Melissa wanly, "I shouldn't have gone out on a limb. I guess I was a little too high."

"Ah, cut th' Alphonse an' gushy stuff!" jeered Baron Brown, "let's have another drink. It's all over. You couldn't hurt that tramp with a sledgehammer."

Melissa flared up immediately. Joe Savino did not smile.

"Don't you call me no trap, you ——!" screamed Melissa, rising from the sofa and standing up over the numbers king. Clad only in a pair of pink step-ins, the octoroon was a gorgeous fury. Her disheveled hair hanging partly down her exquisite back while few strands fell over one breast.

"Ah, sit down!" growled the giant Negro, his low brow corrugating with annoyance. "Sit down 'fore I make you!"

"You're a liar," she shouted back at him, "you won't do a damn thing to me."

The little red eyes of the burly Negro glowed with rage. The group was tense, fidgeting nervously with their glasses. Melissa stood defiantly over the Baron, her fists clenched, her eyes blazing.

"Ah, cut it out," Dorothy admonished, "an' let's be civilized. Drink up an' we'll all take another weed." She was afraid of anymore trouble in the apartment. Neighbors might complain to the superintendent, and he might tell her husband. Dorothy pretended not to care anything about her husband's opinion but she secretly feared him. And so, despite her apparent bravado, she kept her amours secret.

"Yes, let's drink up," added Gertrude Glad, tossing down her drink as an example and reaching for a "refer." She also wanted no fighting or quarrels. As star of the "Broadway Spectacles" the bell of Manhattan, she could not afford to have it broadcast that she frequented Negroes apartments in Harlem. As "high" as she was, she realized that.

"Gwan git f'm over me, woman," boomed Baron Brown at the argumentative Melissa. "I was just playin' with yuh. But if yuh wanna git tight, why alright."

"You're going to take back what you said about me being a tramp," screamed Melissa. "You can't get away with that, Baron Brown."

"Oh, no?" he sneered. "Well, listen here, broad: I ain't takin' nuthin' back and I can git away with anything I want around here, see! Now whatcha gonna do about it?"

In a flash Melissa's little hand shot out and resoundingly slapped the huge, closely shaven jowels of the numbers king.

"That's what I'm gonna do about it!" shouted the octoroon.

"Why you d— little ——!" bellowed the Baron, scrambling to his feet. There was positive murder in his eyes as he swung his huge, ham-like fist back to strike down the angry young girl.

"Git back, Brown!" The cold, level, cruel voice of Joe Savino crashed like a torpedo through the room. "Git back or I'll give it to you."

The Italians automatic was pointed directly at the owner of the Green Gables cabaret, and despite the dissipation of the evening, his hands seemed firm.

"Oh, I see," sneered the Negro letting his arms drop and stepping back, while eyeing the sturdy little Italian gangster disdainfully. "So you're takin' up for 'er eh?"

"Yes, Baron, I'm takin' up for 'er," echoed the sicilian comma his voice grim comma his continence lowering and registering suppressed hatred. "An' if yer thinkin' of enjoin' yer breakfas' you'll be smart an' sit down."

"It's a good thing you got that gat," grumbled the Negro, sitting down in his former position. "Some day I'll git yuh right, an' it'll be jest too bad."

"You'd better hold yer big lip, Baron," warned the Italian, still menacing the numbers king with the automatic, "or that day maybe won't come."

The room was as quiet as a cemetery now. Melissa, Dorothy, Ashley and Gertrude knew the already strained relations existing between the white and black numbers kings. Joe Savino had in various ways eliminated all the other Negro numbers bankers. Some had retired after a gentle warning that the profession might prove injurious to their health; Others had been kidnapped and tortured until they consented to retire and leave the field to the dark-visaged Italian; still others had been double crossed to the police. Only Baron Brown remained, and with scores of runners and a large number of "Stationary stores" as numbers stations, he was Joe's most formidable opponent. Once he was removed, the Italian would be undisputed master not only of the numbers record in Harlem, but the liquor racket as well.

"Come on," begged Gertrude, walking across the room toward the grim Latin, a splendid picture of undraped loveliness, "let's not have anymore trouble, please, Joe. There just be a whole lot of stuff in the papers. And none of us can stand that."

"Shut up!" Thunder Joe, seeming to grow more enraged. "You can't tell Joe Savino what to do. Joe Savino, he tell you what to do."

Gertrude shrank back. Baron Brown, an evil watchful look in his little red eyes, glared painfully at the Italian. Melissa, Dorothy and Ashley Dukes stared in scared silence.

"Ah, put up that cap pistol an' be yourself," grumbled the Negro. "I didn't touch th' gal, did I? What's eatin' you."

"I don't like you, Brown," said Joe slowly. "You remember, long time ago, Joe Savino, he say for you to take ah long trip an' forget all about yer business? Yes? Well, Baron, yuh didn't do it, didja?"

"Naw, I didn't," growled the Negro, "an' whut's mo', I ain't aimin' tuh. You caint scare me, Joe."

"Well, Baron," the Italian mused with cold, cruel significance, "yuh know whut that means, dontcha."

"Yeah I know whut it means," Brown replied, a sinister smirk on his able face, "an' I ain't gonna be sleepin' either. You run all these other colored bankers outta business, but yuh ain't gonna run me, see! Now you better put up that pea shooter an' come an' act like we wuz old friends, 'cause I gotta man outside waitin' fer me an' if I don't show up he knows whut tuh do."

Joe Savino smiled his recognition of frustration. He recalled having seen the palatial limousine of the Negro in front of the Lincoln Arms when he came in, and also remembered that two of Brown's men were lolling up in the front seat.

"Alright, kid," he said nonchalantly, "le's make it a night." He turned to his chair, placing his gun on the seat beside him. He would put on a good face and bide his time. Nevertheless, he was firmly determined now that Baron Brown must be rubbed out.

The tension relaxed. The somewhat sobered group proceeded to quickly attain a state of stupefaction. There was clinking of glass on glass while the ceiling of the room was clouded with "reefer" smoke.

The actress came unsteadily over where Baron Brown was propped up luxuriously on the floor pillows and again reclined across him, her golden hair clothing his bare leg, her pink arms encircling his bull neck.

Melissa sat on Joe's lap, rumbling his jet black hair with her slender pink tip fingers. In between drinks and puffs on their "reefers," they indulged in long, passionate kisses.

Dorothy and Ashley, reclining on the sofa, staged a "circus" that might have astonished or shocked some Parisians.

The stuffy apartment was redolent with a mingled odors of whiskey, beer, "reefers" and bodies. The scene was certainly not different from what might have met the eye in Sodom and Gomorrah, or Babylon, or Rome at the height of imperial debauchery. Here were men and women of both races, with souls lost in sin, meeting in a fraternity of lust, with morals and scruples reduced to an irreducible minimum.

More sober than the rest were Baron Brown and Gertrude Glad. The events of the evening had convinced the Negro that he must keep a clear head; they had convinced the white girl that she must avoid getting in such a position again. Had there been a killing her whole career would have been ruined. Baron realized he had had a narrow escape from death. He knew Joe Savino well enough to understand that.

They conversed in low tones together when the others were too occupied with their debaucheries to notice.

"Baron," asked Gertrude anxiously, "Will he really try to do something to you?"

"Shore. He'll rub me out soon's he can git away with it. He hates my guts, kid. If it wasn't fer me, he'd control all th' rackets in Harlem."

"Aren't you frightened?" She asked, admiringly.

"Nope, I'm jest bein' careful," he said, in a lower tone than usual. "One of us has jest gotta be had, baby, an' somethin' tells me it's gotta be Joe."

"But sweetheart!" continued the blonde, running her pink hand over his shaven head, "isn't he more powerful than you?"

"Yes—yes, maybe he is." The Negro smiled cruelly, one paw patting her golden ringlets, then added significantly. "But only as long as he lives—an' somethin' tells me that ain't gonna be long."

VIII

Love and Revenge Drive Billie And Mary To Enact Tragedy

Billie was stretched across the day bed in Mary Sutton's apartment. With the red in her dark brown sheets heightened by excitement and anxiety, Mary sat beside him, bathing the numerous cuts on his face. For a long time he lay there, resigning himself to her care, because during in the gentle stroke of her soft fingers, wincing ever so often. From the pain as she touched a tender spot, occasionally he opened his unbruised eyes to take in her loveliness.

He wondered now how he had ever been fooling up to succumb to the charms of Melissa. Stratford; Wondered how he could have ever brought himself to rebuff the fine little girl. Who was administering to his care. He raged within when he relived the events of the past fortnight. He had spent all of his hard earned money on a worthless, destitute girl who had not only casually thrown him over for a despicable white man, but had actually gloated over his discomfiture in the very presence of his rival. It hurt him to the quick; hurt him so much that for a long time he remained silent.

"Do you feel better now, Billie?" she asked anxiously.

"Yes," he said quietly. "You've certainly been swell, Mary, after the way I treated you. I can't understand how I could have ever brought myself to do as I did."

She smiled sweetly, with just a hint of sadness. "I forgive you, Billie," she murmured.

"That's mighty fine of you, Mary, but I feel like a dog just the same. What a fool I have been. I should have known better. I knew what she was, and yet I fell for her like a ton of lead." He frowned and then winced.

"I understand, Billie. I have understood all along. I knew it would happen this way. That's why I followed you."

"You followed me?"

"Yes," she answered, her color heightening with embarrassment. "I was so desperate when you left me at midnight that I followed you over to the Silver Cup. I'd never been in such a place before, so I asked George Henderson to go along with me. Please forgive me, will you Billie?"

"Why, of course I forgive you, dear," he said, stroking her hand. "But tell me, where were you when I had that fight with Joe Savino?"

"Well, when we came in, you were arguing with that Italian. All of the people were so busy watching you that they did not notice us entering. We went to the back of the room. When that man pulled his gun and started to shoot you, I reached up and pulled the light switch. George then rushed up front and followed him. We helped you up, rushed you outside, booked a taxi cab and brought you here. We hurried because we feared the Italian would kill you."

"You probably saved my life, dear," he said gratefully. "Savino was mad and drunk—and he's a killer. It was a narrow escape and I don't know how I can thank you. You're wonderful."

"Billie," She murmured, nestling close to him, her honest black eyes casting into his. "I did it because I love you. You know I love you, but you have never known how much."

"I know now, darling, and I'll never forget it."

"Do you mean that, Billie?"

"Yes, I mean it, Mary. I'm through with that girl for good. But I'm going to get even with that Joe Savino if it is the last thing I do. No one can beat me up like that and get away with it." He sat upright, his fist clenched.

"No, you mustn't, Billie," she pleaded. "You'll just get killed. You have had one narrow escape and that ought to teach you a lesson."

"I don't care," he persisted, "I'm going to get even with him. And I'm going to get even with her. I hate her." He spoke with bitterness and vehemence, with the rancor of a man who has been deceived by a woman.

"Please don't bother with those people anymore," she begged. "They're not your kind, Billie. Just forget them, dear, will you?"

"No, I won't, Mary," he declared empathetically. "I won't have them laughing at me because they've made a fool of me, I tell you I'm going to get even."

"But Billie, if you really love me, you'll forget all about those low people. Why don't you turn over a new leaf, dear. I love you, and you say you love me. Now why cannot we go on as before. Remember how we used to go to the pictures? Went to church together? We can be very happy that way again, Billie, if you will."

He rose, and lifting her in his arms, kissed her firmly on her full curved lips while she pretended to struggle in protest, laughing the while.

"I do love you, darling," he said softly, releasing her after a prolonging brace, "and we're going to be just as we were before, but I tell you I'm going to get even with both of them. I hate them, I say."

She surveyed him silently, holding his hands in hers. Then, "Oh, Billie, I love you so. Will you please be careful? Will you promise me not to have anything more to do with these low people. Nothing good can come of it, dear."

He swept her into his arms again, lifting her off her feet and kissing her until she was breathless and flushed with excitement.

"Well," he declared. Finally, "I must be getting downstairs for some sleep. Good Lord, It's three o'clock."

"Billie," she cried, restraining him, "will you promise?"

"I'll be careful," he promised, evading her meaning.

They embraced again. He went out.

FOR A LONG TIME, MARY Sutton stood thoughtfully in the center of her room. She didn't know just what to do. She had seen enough at the Silver Cup to convince her that it was dangerous to fool with Joe Savino, and she greatly feared that Billie would attempt to carry out his threat. She knew from the tone of his voice that he was deeply hurt by the events of the evening or early morning. She knew that he hated Melissa Stratford with all of the hatred one feels upon being spurned. But she also knew that hatred is akin to love. Was Billie Smith still infatuated with his beautiful octoroon girl in spite of himself. If he was willing to give Melissa up and was indifferent toward the girl as he had stated, why was he so eager to revenge himself upon her and her Italian lover? She began to feel that there was some motive behind his determination, stronger than a mere desire to get even. Would he spurn her, as he said, when again the two came together?

The more she thought of it, the more she began to feel that she would have a stronger claim on Billie's affections if Melissa was out of the way. And the more her mind dwelt on this thought, the stronger the feeling grew that in order to safeguard her love, Melissa must be removed from the scene. How could Melissa be removed? She shuddered as the devilish temptation toyed with her imagination. A sinister smile played for a fleeting moment around the corners of her curved lips.

Melissa was drunk. Mary was sure of that. She's probably lying across her bed in a stupor. Suppose something should happen to her mysteriously? Who would suspect Mary Sutton?

"My God!" she exclaimed, passing one hand over eyes, "What am I thinking about?" Tears of repentance sprang to her eyes as she sank down in an easy chair and held her throbbing head.

The more Mary thought over the matter, the more fixed became the conviction that if Melissa Stratford could wield such an influence over Billie Smith, regardless of the happenings of the evening, she might again arouse his infatuation. After all, Mary bitterly soliloquized, Melissa was pretty and almost white, while she, although good looking, was dark, and a dark girl, all things being even, was usually at a disadvantage when competing with a light girl. As long as Melissa and Billie were in the same building, with, there not always be danger of him renewing his infatuation if she gave him any encouragement? Men were so weak and forgetful, and Melissa was a light woman, while Billie was a black man—truly two mutually attractive types.

Yes, there was no way out of it. She must get rid of Melissa Strafford if her happiness was to be assured. So reasoned Mary Sutton. Everything else was subordinated in her mind. She hated the light girl for taking her man away from her, and she hated her for making a fool of him before a room full of people. But she hailed Melissa Stratford most of all because she constituted an ever present menace to the happiness of Billie and her. Once Melissa was out of the way, she would rest more easily and there would be less danger of Billie getting into trouble with the powerful Joe Savino.

WITH A SUDDEN DETERMINATION, SHE rose and prepared to go out. When she was ready, she went to her Bureau and fumbling in a far corner, soon encountered the cold touch of metal. It was the .22 automatic pistol her brother had bought for her protection when she left home to come to New York. Slipping the weapon into her handbag, she opened the door, glanced up and down the silent corridor, and then, spurning the elevator, ran lightly up the stairs to the third floor.

The human soul is a curious mixture and fate plays the strangest pranks. Here was Mary Sutton, embodying all of the finest qualities of Negro womanhood, suddenly transformed by the fire of jealousy and fear, into a vengeful Jezebel, ready to take a human life for the sake of her love. A short time previous she would have been astounded by even the suggestion of such an act. It would have been incredible, in view of her careful home training and her lifelong church membership. Yet here she was speeding up the stairway, face tense, heart pounding, to destroy the one person she felt stood in the way of her happiness.

Coming to the third floor, she hurried down the corridor to No. 35, which she knew to be Melissa's apartment. Taking a final glance up and down, she placed her little hand on the doorknob and turned it to see if the door was locked.

An electric shock ran through her when the door swung inward in response to her gentle push. Her heart pounded. This was great luck! She had not anticipated it. She had rather hastily planned to ring the bell and when Melissa came to the door to force her way in and then settle accounts. With her rival now it would be much easier. Perhaps the girl had come in drunk and forgot to lock the door from the inside when she went to bed. It happened often to sober people. And she knew Melissa was not sober. She seldom was, Mary thought spitefully.

The apartment was pitched dark. Mary entered gingerly, closing the door quietly behind her. She stood still, listening intently. For the first time, she experienced a spasm of fear that cemented her feet to the parquet flooring and prevented her from moving. Her knees felt weak. Her hand shook slightly as she felt along the wall for the switch. Finally, she got up the courage to move a step or two forward toward the room from the foyer, still feeling vainly for the light switch. She regretted not having brought a box of matches along.

Suddenly, she became aware of the sound of heavy breathing coming from the direction of the room, and her alert nostrils caught the faint odor of whiskey. The nearness of her quarry bolstered her courage and reinforced her determination. She moved her hand swiftly along the wall seeking the switch.

Then her heart stood still as she heard the knob turning in the door behind her. Quickly she moved forward into the room and stopped to one side, fright consuming her.

The door opened wider, letting in light from the corridor. She dared not look to see who it was, but froze herself closer to the wall. The door was quietly closed and she felt a presence in the foyer near her. She nervously unfastened her purse and extracted the pistol. Her hand shook. She wondered what she should do now.

She was far from having reached a decision, when suddenly she heard a window being gently raised. The curtain was slipped aside and a hoking figure appeared on the fire escape, dimly outlined by the faint light from the streetlamp. It was a man. He stepped carefully into the room. A flashlight was turned on, the shaft of light sweeping the floor and finally reaching the bed. Mary was frozen to the spot. The person in the foyer had not moved.

There were the figures of Melissa Stratford and Joe Savino, curled in slumber on the bed. The man from the fire escape chuckled wickedly.

Bang! Bang! Bang! Bang! Four shots as loud as mine explosions, rocked the close room, and the acrid odor of gun powder assailed Mary's nostrils. In her fright she squeezed the trigger of her automatic. Before she could tear her finger away, four more shots had added their din to the uproar.

It was too much. She felt the blood rushed to her head, and swaying on her sagging knee. She lost consciousness.

IX

Billie and Mary Flee Following Dual Tragedy

The pleas of Mary had not in the slightest lesson Billie's determination to get even with both Melissa and Joe Savino for the happenings at the Silver Cup earlier that night. He realized full well that he would never have an opportunity to revenge himself on the Italian when he was, as usual, surrounded by his black and white henchman. The best way to get even with the both of them was to confront them in Melissa's apartment, where they would be alone. He was certain they were there together, now.

When he left Mary's apartment, he took the automatic elevator down to the basement and going into the room shared by him and George Henderson, He switched on his light and began hunting for the pistol which he knew George possessed. After ransacking the closet, bureau drawers and suitcase, he finally found the .22 Smith and Wesson wrapped in a large handkerchief. It was completely loaded. He grunted with grim satisfaction as he noted the fact. Shoving the weapon in his coat pocket, he again entered the elevator, and pressed the button for the third floor and was soon standing in front of the door of Melissa's apartment.

The corridor was still as death from a nearby apartment came faintly the sound of a radio playing a late hour broadcast. He glanced at his watch. It was just four-thirty. He paused a moment, hesitantly. And then try the door. He noted with surprise that it was not locked, and turning the knob gently let himself into the foyer.

How often had he entered this apartment with gay heart and feelings of anticipation? What pleasant hours he had spent here with the seductive Melissa! Now what had ended. He grew mad all over as he recalled how he had been double crossed by the girl and beaten up by Savino's men. He would awaken the couple, tell them what he thought of them, and then "give them the works." Who would know? The deed would be ascribed to some of Joe's numerous gangster enemies. No one would ever, he thought, speck, the doorman of the crime. Just three or four well placed shots, then he would. Go to the elevator, descend to the basement, undress, jump in bed and feign sleep. It would all be over in a few minutes and the woman who he feared and the man that he hated would be out of the way forever.

HE WAS STARTLED BY THE sudden swing of the window by the fire escape and the entrance of another person whom he could not distinguish in the darkness. Then came the play of the flashlight and four explosive pistol shots, followed by four more. Through the haze of smoke he saw the assailant disappearing through the window through which he had just came. Before he realized what he was doing, he had raised his pistol and fired four times at the retreating figure.

He turned hastily and was about to leave the foyer when he heard a heavy fall near at hand. He had seen the two entwined figures on the bed and knew immediately that someone else must be in the room. Switching on the light with trembling fingers, he saw with horror and astonishment that the body sprawled on the floor was that of Mary Sutton.

Already there were noises in the corridor as tenants began opening doors and hurriedly exchanging questions. Footsteps were approaching the door of Melissa's apartment. With quick presence of mind, he locked the door and extinguished the light. But before the room was surrounded in Stygian darkness, he noted the couple, Melissa Stratford and Joe Savino, sprawled on the bed nude in a pool of their own blood.

Someone was now knocking on the door. There was a clamor of voices outside, raising louder and louder, more and more insistent. A hand grasped the doorknob. Someone was yelling in a loud voice that the police and the superintendent be called.

There was no time now to lose. Pocketing his pistol, Billie stooped down and picked up the automatic Mary had dropped.

Hastily he breathed upon it, wiped it with his handkerchief and then gingerly threw it on the bloody death bed. Then picking up the prostrate girl in his brown arms, he stepped softly to the open window and stepped out on the fire escape.

Lights were now appearing in all of the apartments and a low hum of excitement was audible. Hurriedly Billie toiled up the fire escape with his heavy burden. The perspiration streamed down his tense face. He finally passed the fourth and fifth floors. Two more flights and he would be on the roof. He could hear voices growing louder and louder below. He toiled steadily upward.

AT LAST, THE ROOF! A great feeling of relief came over him. Perhaps, after all, he might be able to escape. He lifted Mary up to the last two steps and onto the roof. A stiff breeze was blowing. It struck her full in the face and revived her. Billie felt her move.

"Keep quiet, Mary!" he warned in a low voice. "It's me, Billie."

"Where are we?" she said slowly.

"Hush!" He cautioned again. "We're on the roof. Melissa and Joe have been killed. The whole house is aroused. I got you out of there just in time. Come, pull yourself together, we haven't a minute to lose."

Mary recovered quickly at this intelligence. She remembered now all that had transpired. Murder! It was horrible! And she had been there and seen it! She would certainly be accused of it. What did Billie think? What was he doing in the apartment? Was he the murderer? These thoughts flashed through her mind as the two tiptoed to the door leading downstairs into the house.

"Now, if we can just get inside the house without anyone seeing us," whispered Billie, "we're safe."

Hastily, he grasped the knob of the penthouse door and pulled. The door refused to budge, it was tightly fastened from the inside.

"Christ!" growled Billie, "We're sunk now, Sweetheart."

"Wait, dearest, there's another door on the other side."

"That's right. Come on!"

They hurried quietly across the broad expanse of the roof to the other door. Mary reached it first, and tugged and tugged. It too was fastened.

They paused and confronted each other in dilemma. It was absolutely imperative that they get off the roof and down into the house. They did not dare risk either the front or backfire escape, the voices floating up from below told them that. What was to be done now? There was no time to lose. Anytime the police might come piling up on the roof. How could they possibly explain their presence here with the doors fastened from the inside?

Mary began to cry. The strain had been too much for her always acquired girl, whose life heretofore had been spent between her work, the movies and church, she was nonplussed by the terrible predicament in which she was placed. She bitterly reproached herself for letting her jealousy get the better of her good judgment.

Billie sought to console her. "We'll find some way out, honey," he assured her. "There must be some way out. There must be!"

"But can't you see there isn't?" she sobbed. "We're just caught up here, And they'll blame us for everything. We'll go to the electric chair."

"Don't cry, Mary," He soothed. "This is a chance that they'll think it's suicide when they see your gun on the bed. There are no fingerprints on it. I wiped it off. That may stop them for a while, dear. Now get yourself together. We've got to use our heads to get out of this. Wait here and I'll look around and see what can be done."

Leaving the girl near the door, Billie went to one side of the building and looked over the side. A space of six feet separated the Lincoln Arms from the taller building next door. A fire escape ran up the side of that building and so reduced the space to less than four feet. It would not be so difficult to reach across to the neighboring fire escape and to send the six flights to the hanging ladder below, which he knew to reach within five feet of the paved court. But that way, too, was impossible, for there was now a light in every window in both houses, and peering over he could see heads being thrust out of the windows, and tenants conversing with each other. No, that way was impossible. They would be sure to be detected.

He turned and walked across the roof to the other side. Here the building was twelve or fifteen feet lower than the Lincoln Arms, and there was no space whatever between them. There were also no windows. His heart leaped with hope, and he hurried back to the anxious Mary.

"I've got it," he cried exultantly. "I've got it! All we've got to do is get down on the other roof and we're safe. Come on!"

"But we can't jump down that far," Mary objected. "Besides, it's dark and we wouldn't know where we were jumping. We're liable to kill ourselves."

"Well, it's our only chance," he snapped irritably, his nerves rasped to the breaking point. "Any minute now the penthouse doors might open. Then we surely would be lost."

"Will use some of the clothes lines," he suggested. "They'll hold us, alright." He whipped out his pocketknife, ran softly over to the lines and cut them with three or four savage swishes of the blade.

Tying several of the lines together to make a stout rope about fifty feet long, he looped it around a brace of the fire escape, carried it around the edge of the escape doorway, and so over the top of the sidewall to the roof below.

"Quick," he shouted, "over the top, for God's sake, Mary."

Gradually the girl let herself down. When he felt the rope relaxed its tautness, Billie knew she had safely reached the adjoining room. He hurriedly flung himself over, and walking down the side of the Lincoln Arms, holding onto the rope, he was soon beside her. Now, pulling one strand of the loop, he brought the whole rope down to them.

They breathed much easier, but their problems were by no means settled. Both realized that.

Quickly gathering up the robe, Billie carried it to the chimney of the incinerator. There was little odor in the chimney approached by a short flight of the iron steps. Ascending, he opened the rusty door and threw in the rope. Before it could be discovered, he knew it would be burned.

They now hurried to the door leading down into the house. Billie grasped the knob somewhat apprehensively, and tugged. It, too, was fastened!

From above they heard voices, singularly plain in the clear morning air, agitated voices, heavy, brusque voices, inquiring voices, commanding voices! They heard footsteps crunching over the roof, approaching the side nearest them. Their heart sank as they made themselves as inconspicuous as possible, against the side of the penthouse. Suddenly a form, the head and shoulders of a policeman, loomed dimly on the roof above them, peering in their direction.

X

BILLIE IS ARRESTED FOR MURDER
AFTER HE AND MARY ESCAPE

The officer leaned far over the edge of the roof, seeking to penetrate the darkness. It was evident that he did not see them.

"Hey, Sam!" he yelled, turning half around. "Bring your light here. I don't see how anyone could get down without one hearing them, but the fellow couldn't have gone anywhere far."

"Aw, you're all wet," came the voice of another officer, walking across the roof, "there ain't been no murder. That wop and his gal pal about got a snoot full and waged a private war, if you ask me. Didn't yuh see the gat on the bed, you sap?"

"That don't mean a thing," snapped the first policeman. "You're forgettin' that window being open and then eight bullet holes in the wall, ain't you, to say nothin' of the four bullets that plugged them."

"Well, maybe it is a killin' like you say but it's a damn good riddance. That guy that plugged 'em oughtta have a medal."

"Nevermind th' gab," said the first officer, as the head and shoulders of the second appeared beside him, "gimmie that flashlight. I'm gonna see if there's anybody on the other roof."

Billie squeezed Mary's hand. Swiftly and quietly he stepped around the penthouse, drawing her after him. In less than 10 seconds, they had passed the structure beside them and the police.

"Here it is," They heard the second officer say. "I just got a new battery today. That'll let you see a block away."

In a second, the stream of light was playing all over the roof, but Billie and Mary was safe, thanks to the sheltering penthouse. They were far from being out of danger, However, officer number one was more mindful than his partner. He wanted to explore all of the roofs in my colon. The other one is to end the search and go down into the Lincoln Arms. The first officer played the light about the roof three or four times and then shut it off.

"Now is our only chance," whispered Billie. "Not a sound now or we're lost." Mary indicated her understanding by gripping his hand tighter. It was growing less dark with the approach of mourning, and she realized that something drastic must be done immediately if they were to be saved.

With the sound of the arguing officers voices still ringing clearly above them, Billie led the way straight forward until they came to the three-foot wall separating the roof they were traversing from and the next one. Calmly, they stepped over it and knelt down behind it. Then, with Billie in the lead, they crept rapidly on all fours to the back wall absolutely unexposed to the gaze of the two policemen, even as they turned on the flashlight again.

There was now but ten or twelve feet to go straight to the right before the opening of the fire escape would be reached. Billie looked up cautiously and surveyed the situation. He recalled that the fire escape on this particular house was on the corridors of each door instead of the apartments as is the Lincoln Arms. Thus, if they could just reach the fire escaped unobserved, and if the corridor window was not locked on the top floor, they could get in the house and make their way to the street. A lot of "ifs" it was true, but their only chance.

"I think I'll try to get down to that other roof," they heard Officer No. 1 say, "While we're arguing up here that guys liable to get away. I ain't aimin' to get in no trouble with the chief, you know."

"That's a long jump," the other observed skeptically.

"Well, I'm gonna try it, anyway," The first policeman resolved.

Billie knew there was not a single second to lose. He indicated to Mary that they must make a dash for the fire escape. Quickly comprehending, she sped lightly to the opening and began to descend. Billie was close behind her. He had not gone down three steps, however, before he heard the heavy shoes of the policeman strike the adjoining roof.

"Did you make it alright?" He heard the second officer ask.

"Shook me up a heluva lot," the other replied, "but I'm here."

The hearts of the two lovers stood still, escape seem impossible now. In two minutes at the most, the policeman would be above them, throwing the beam of his flashlight accusingly and triumphantly upon them. There was that one chance in a thousand of finding detection. That one chance was on the top floor corridor window.

Mary had reached it. A thrill of mingled hope and uncertainty suffused her slender frame as she pushed upward on the window frame. The window would not budge. Now Billie was beside her. They could hear the policeman walking slowly over the adjoining roof. They pushed and tugged in unison. The window seemed stuck.

"See any signs?" they heard the officer on the Lincoln Arms ask his comrade.

"There's been somebody here, alright," replied the other, "I just found a fresh cut strand of rope. Just a little thread like piece, but it shows I was right. That's the way that fellow got down here. See if the clothes lines were cut, I'll wait here."

"It's no use," whispered Billie. "We're just wasting time here. Go down to the next floor."

Unhesitatingly, Mary sped down another flight. It was getting a little lighter. They must either escape now or go to jail.

"Hey!" They heard the officer on the Lincoln Arms shout, "There's a lot of them. Clothes lines cut. You were right, alright."

"You bet," commented the other. "Come on down with me."

Mary pushed on the window nervously, feverishly. It refused to budge. It was either stuck or locked. Every second now was precious. Billie gained her side. They could hear the heavy shoes of the policemen approaching.

With the last despairing push, embodying all of their strength and frantic desire to escape, they sought to raise the window. It refused to yield. The officers were now not far away. Their voices could be heard very plainly in the clear morning air. Day was fighting back the forces of night.

Without waiting any longer, Mary spread down another flight of the iron steps with Billie close behind her. They descended swiftly, but without a sound. Noise now would have been fatal. They could hear the policeman almost above them now. Any second the two officers might look over the edge. Then there would be no hope.

WITH EBBING HOPE, MARY PUSHED up on the corridor window. Billie, glancing fearfully upward, saw the sweep of the officer's flashlight as he explored the roof. It was now or never.

Mary felt a marvelous thrill go all over her. The window gave easily and rolled noiselessly upward. With great upsurge of the spirit of liberty, she stepped hastily inside, Billie quickly followed her. He lowered and locked the window which some benevolent guardian angel had left unfastened.

"Oh, thank God! Thank God!" cried Mary, almost hysterical now from the prolonged strain.

"Hush!" Billie cautioned. "Hold yourself together, dear. We're not out of it yet, by any means. Get downstairs as quickly as you can."

They made their way rapidly down the stairs, taking two at a time in their haste. When they reached the ground floor, they slowed up and casually walked to the front door as if nothing at all had happened.

Outside was a great crowd of people. The hum of conversation came to them through heavy glass of the front door. It seemed incredible that so many hundreds of people could have assembled so quickly. Some were fully stressed; others wore nothing but shoes and a topcoat over their nightwear. There were many policemen scattered through the crowd.

"Now be careful," Billie admonished. "As the cigarette advertisement says, 'Be nonchalant,'" Mary smiled indulgently, her first smile since many hours before.

"Don't worry," she replied, "all like as if nothing's happened."

"You go first," he advised. "Wait for me on the other side of the street by the park fence. I'll hold back a couple of minutes."

Mary steeled herself in opening the door, watched casually down the three steps to the sidewalk and into the crowd. With some difficulty, she made her way through the mob of the curious to the other side. In three or four minutes Billie was at her side.

A SIREN SCREAMED. THE CROWD parted reluctantly. A huge limousine bearing a bevy of police officials, drew up to the curb in front of the Lincoln Arms. There were already several smaller police cars there. The high officials piled out of the big automobile and marched in the ornate entrance of the of the swank apartment. There were heads at every window of every apartment house down the block.

Up and down the street, throughout the growing concourse of people, could be heard the off repeated refrain in odd tones: "They've got Joe Savino."

"Serves him right," observed one mammoth colored lady in a red dressing gown. "I wish they get all of these dagoes. . . Comin' up here takin' our money."

"Wonder who got him?" a little bowlegged mulatto with topcoat over his pajamas speculated.

"Whoever got him," observed the tall man next to him, "sure got him, and I don't mean maybe."

"An' they got away clean, too," added another fellow.

Mary and Billie looked at each other and smiled grimly. What a narrow escape they had had!

"Well," said Billie. "I guess we can kind of ease over there now and go in, don't you think? I'm just fagged out and I know you must be, dear."

Mary was warned. She had gone through so much in the past five or six hours for the man she loved, and they had escaped by a hair. Now she wanted to rest—to rest with her head on his arm. She looked at him lovingly and gripped his muscular arm.

"Billie, do you love me?" She asked in a whisper.

"More than ever, dear," he replied. "I've been a terrible fool, but I'm cured forever. Come on, Let's go in and get some sleep. It must be after five o'clock. I'd like to get at least half hour's sleep before I go to my watch."

THEY WANDERED THEIR WAY SLOWLY through the milling crowd, finally reaching the opposite curb. Walking under the canopy, they approached the gaudy entrance. Several policemen and detectives were standing around, talking earnestly. Others were smoking and scrutinizing notebooks.

Billie smiled inwardly as he thought how much he could tell them about the murder if he chose. Then he began to wonder himself who had fired the four fatal shots. Well, no matter, he and Mary were lucky to get out of it.

"Hey, you!" The words jabbed themselves through Billie like a sharp sword. He suddenly became short of breath, dry mouth, weak in the knees. Both he and Mary stopped short. He turned his head reluctantly to see who was speaking.

"Talking to me?" He asked the lantern-jawed detective confronting him.

"Yeah, I'm talkin' tuh you," mocked the other, with a snarl.

"What is it?" Billie could scarcely get the question out.

"You're Billie Smith ain't cha?" asked the detective, coming closer as the others gathered around.

Billie's heart sank. A thousand thoughts ran helter skelter through his head. What have they found out? How could they have anything on him?

"Yes, that's me," he admitted, pulling himself together by Herculean effort. "What about it?"

"Lemme see your hands!" commanded the offer in steely tones.

Puzzled, Billie extended his two hands. He hoped they wouldn't search him. George Henderson's pistol was in his back pocket.

Quick as a flash, the detective encircled his outstretched wrist with heavy steel handcuffs.

"That's what it's about," He jeered, yanking Billie along with him toward the elevator, while another officer grabbed Mary's wrist. "We want you for murder."

BILLIE IS ARRESTED FOR MURDER AFTER
HE AND MARY ESCAPE—CONTINUED

Mary Sutton George Henderson sat in the apartment of Walter Terry, the noted Negro lawyer, high up on the sixth floor of the Lincoln Arms. Attorney Terry, a large brown man with graying temples, gazed thoughtfully at the two young people.

"Mr. Smith is in a very difficult position," said the lawyer. "Melissa Stratford enjoys Savino were killed by bullets from a .22 automatic pistol. That is exactly the caliber of pistol which was found on Billie."

"But Mr. Terry," objected Mary, "I'm sure Billie did not kill them. I was right there and I saw the man come in the window and fire at them, I was in the room, Mr. Terry, I couldn't be mistaken."

"It is not what you say that is important, Miss Sutton," contended the lawyer, "But what can be proved. The police have no suspicions that you were there and if you are wise you will not tell them. You say that the pistol comment. A .22 found on the bed was your gun but it was also a .22 automatic with which the two were shot. If you confess that it was your pistol, it will implicate you in the crime, and of course we don't want that."

"But I'm willing to be accused of it, if it will free Billie," said Mary. "I don't care what happens to me as long as Billie is freed, I love Billie."

"I know all of that," agreed the lawyer, puffing on his cigarette. "But it won't help matters any. We don't want either you or Billie to suffer for a crime committed by someone else. What we want to do is clear both you and Billie."

"It was my pistol that Billie had," George interjected. "He went downstairs and got it while I was on duty."

"That is very true," said the lawyer, "but you don't see that only makes it worse for Billie. It proves premeditation, which is playing right in the hands of the police."

"But Billie didn't do it," Mary protested earnestly.

"It is one thing to know the facts and another thing to prove them," contended the lawyer. "Unless we can prove that someone else committed the crime, it will go very bad with Billie. Both of you have been very foolish. You had no business, neither of you, to go into Miss Stratford's apartment. The mere fact that you were in there adds to the assumption of guilt. What we've got to do is prove that someone else committed the murders. Now, who could have done it? We have no evidence as to that so far. I don't believe either you or Billie are guilty, but all of the evidence so far points to your guilt, or rather to Billie's, because they don't think you had anything to do with it. You must not breathe a word about your part. You must say that you and Billie were in the park around the way, making love."

A reddish glow suffused Mary's Indian features. She lowered her gaze. She did love Billie Smith, oh, so latently. It beamed from her very countenance.

"I'll do anything to save him," she murmured.

"I know you will,", commented the lawyer, "But the best thing you can do is keep quiet; to say absolutely nothing; to contend that you know absolutely nothing about it."

"But unless someone does something," the girl objected, "they will send him to the chair. He mustn't suffer for this, Mr. Terry, he mustn't." Her eyes filled with tears at the thought. She reached in her handbag for her handkerchief.

"WELL, WE'LL DO ALL WE can to save him," the lawyer comforted. He lit a fresh cigarette and for a moment lost himself in thought. The two young people watched him anxiously, Mary toyed nervously with the catch of her handbag. George Henderson frowned and looked at his fingernails.

"Now let's see," Attorney Terry continued. "George, you are on the door all night?"

"Yes Sir!"

"What time was it when Miss Stratford and Joey Savino came in?"

"About a little after one o'clock. They were both pretty high, Mr. Terry."

"Do you know where they went when they left the lobby?"

"Yes, They went up to Dorothy King's apartment."

"How do you know that?" Pursued the lawyer.

"Because Mrs. King left word with me for them to come up to her apartment as soon as they came in."

"What did they say when you delivered the message?"

"Well, I remember Joe Savino saying, 'Let's go up there for a little while.'"

"Do you know that they went up to Mrs. King's apartment?"

"Yes, I took some ginger ale up there later."

"Did you actually see them in there?"

"Yes, sir," answered George, "They were there, alright. I saw them with my own eyes. They were having a big time with the rest. All of them were practically naked. It was a righteous party."

"Who else was there, George?"

"Well, there was Mrs. King, Baron Brown, Ashley Duce, Gertrude, Glenn, Melissa and Joe. They were all pretty high, Mr. Terry."

"This Baron Brown runs the Green Gables cabaret, doesn't he?" queried the lawyer.

"Yes, sir, and he's a big numbers banker too."

"Who is this Ashley Dukes?"

"A rich white fellow. He goes with Mrs. King."

"And who is this Gertrude Glad?"

"She's the big white actress from downtown. She's been playing around with Baron Brown."

"Isn't it true that Joe Savino was practically boss of the numbers here in Harlem?" continued Attorney Terry.

"Yes sir, he was the big shot. He controlled everything except Baron Brown up here. The Baron was sort of a lone wolf."

"Do you think Savino and Brown were what you might call rivals in the numbers racket?"

"Sure, everybody knew that," George replied.

"Hummph!" mused the lawyer, a slight smile playing around the corners of his sensitive mouth, "I'll look into that. These gangsters have funny ways of settling their disputes."

"What are you going to do?" asked Mary, unable to contain herself any longer.

"Never mind what I'm going to do," said Terry. "You young folks go on about your business and let me get to work. I'll let you know what's what in a short while."

They all rose and shook hands. Mary and George left the lawyer's apartment and went down together to the automatic elevator.

"Do you think he'll get Billie out of this?" asked Mary as the car descended.

"Well," said George, "He's the smartest lawyer in Harlem."

WHEN THE TWO HAD DEPARTED, Attorney Terry lit a cigar, saying back in his easy chair and lost himself in thought for several minutes. It was a most difficult case. He knew both Billie and Mary were innocent. There was no doubt about that in his mind, but proving it was another matter. And the courts and police would demand conclusive proof. He studied the lengthening ash on his cigar, frowning the while.

Suddenly a light of inspiration glowed in his deep set eyes. He jumped up, buttoned his double-breasted coat, jammed his derby on his head and dashed out of the front door.

Five minutes later he was sitting in the Borough Hall Express of the new 8th Ave. Subway, bound for Broadway, a look of satisfaction and determination on his face. He knew he was making a long gamble, but it was the only chance of saving Billie Smith.

Fifteen minutes later, he emerged from the 42nd Street station of the 8th Avenue Subway and walked rapidly east on 43rd Street. In three minutes, he was standing at the stage entrance of the Manhattan Theater where the New York Scandals were having a long and successful run.

"Who are you looking for?" asked the old Irish doorkeeper.

"Please take this card to Miss Glad, will you?" asked Terry, smiling at the white servitor and squeezing a crisp dollar bill into his calloused palm. He extracted one of his business cards and wrote across the face of it "From the Baron."

"Sure," grinned the doorkeeper. "Wait here." The old fellow hobbled away. Lawyer Terry waited impatiently. In a few moments the Irishman was back.

"She says to come right up," he reported respectfully, stepping aside.

Terry ran up the winding flight of iron stairs leading to the dressing rooms. He stopped in front of the door marked with a large Silver Star. Flimsily clad chorus girls were passing to and fro, chattering and giggling. In a few minutes the afternoon performance would begin.

"Come in!" came the chirping reply to his knock.

Gertrude Glad, gorgeous in a black and red evening dress, sat at her dressing table, putting the finishing touches on her makeup. She looked up, evidently surprised to see a Negro enter her room.

"Well, what is it?" she asked, not without a trace of asperity.

"I'm from the Baron," lied the lawyer, taking a chair, and glancing steadily into her Big Blue eyes.

"Yes?" She questioned, with rising inflection.

"The barons in a little jam," Terry went on, "and he sent me down to advise you to say nothing whatever in the case the cops should happen in and ask a few questions."

The beautiful girl's eyes immediately registered fear bordering on terror. She knew any mention, if even in a whisper, of her Harlem relationships would ruin her career.

"Why, I—I don't understand," she protested insincerely, much to Terry's inward satisfaction.

"Oh, you don't have to stall with me," he said quickly. "Barron and I understand each other, and I know what it's all about between you two. All he wants you to do is to be on your guard."

"Why, what's happened?" She asked, betraying real anxiety. "Did he get into some trouble with Savino?"

Terry felt like shouting. Yes, he said to himself, he was on the right track.

"Well, you know how it was between them," he fished, "what with the numbers and everything."

"What's happened?" she insisted, raising her voice in her excitement and anxiety.

"Joe Savino is dead!" Terry announced solemnly, looking squarely into her frightened eyes. "They are questioning everybody that was in Dorothy's apartment last night. Of course you know what Baron said. . ." He watched her closely, hoping against hope that she would reveal something.

"Well," she said innocently, "He just told me that either he or Joe 'had to be had,' as he put it, and that it wasn't going to be him. But I didn't think he really meant it."

The suave Negro lawyer could have jumped up and danced with enthusiasm. It was the very admission that he had been fishing for.

"The only reason Baron sent me down," he said in a mollifying tone, noting her perturbation, "was just to sort of warn you to say nothing. This will all blow over in a little while. Baron's too powerful for them to do anything with him. Of course he didn't do it himself, you know."

"Of course he didn't," she stated vehemently. "He was with me until a couple of hours ago. . . That is. . . er. . . I saw him."

She smiled coquettishly and he grinned back.

"Of course," he assured her, "I understand. It'll be alright. He just wanted you to put on your guard. Chances are nobody will ever ask you anything, but the Baron is not overlooking any bets."

She smiled with evident relief and rose majestically as a signal for him to go. Just then, the cowboy knocked and opened the door a little way.

Attorney Terry walked to the door. With his hand on the knob, he turned toward the beautiful blonde actress.

"Don't telephone him until tomorrow," he warned. "There's such a thing as wires being tapped."

"You're pretty smart fellow, aren't you?" She complimented him with a broad smile.

"Thank you, Miss Glad," He bowed respectfully. "I have to be on my business."

Outside again, he hurried to the 7th Avenue subway station, chuckling as he strolled along.

XII

Savino Killing Finally Solved, Lovers United

Attorney Walter Terry walked into the office of Captain Brady at the Harlem Police Precinct station.

"Hello, Terry! What's up?" greeted the jovial Irishman.

"It's about that Savino killing, Jack," replied the lawyer, seating himself familiarly. "I'm taking the case for that young fellow you're holding, and I think I've got something real big in the way of a clue that may prove the boy's innocence."

"Hope you have, Walter, but it looks pretty bad for him right now."

"Yes, I know it looks bad, Jack, but I feel sure the boy didn't have anything to do with it. Now here's what I found out."

The lawyer then proceeded to tell about the party in Dorothy King's apartment and what had taken place there between Savino and the Baron Brown. Then he described his visit to the dressing room of Gertrude Glad. The police captain whistled.

"I believe you have got a little something there, Terry."

"I'm sure of it, Jack. If you'll give me a couple of men to help me, I think I can find out something before the afternoons out."

"It's a little irregular, Walter," said the Irishman, hoping quote, but I'll take a chance. We've been wanting to get both Savino and Brown for sometime. Now Savino's gone and if we can get something on the Baron, it'll be a perfect day."

He rang for two of his plainclothes men, and when they came in he instructed them to cooperate with the lawyer, whom they both knew well. After a brief consultation, the three men left the station house together, partying at 135th Street and 7th Avenue.

Attorney Terry held a taxi cab and went immediately to the Lincoln Arms. Five minutes later he was ringing the bell of Dorothy King's apartment.

"Mrs. King," said Terry, when he had been admitted, "I'm not going to take up much of your time. I just want to let you in on something."

"Well?" questioned the girl, gazing shrewdly and not without a feeling of alarm at him.

"I'm sure you didn't have anything to do with the Savino killing," he insinuated, "But certain people whom you know are doing some talking that may hurt you."

"Why, I don't know what damn thing about it," She objected. "They all left here about three o'clock. . ."

"All except Mr. Dukes, I suppose," interrupted the lawyer, suavely, amused at her growing alarm.

"Yes, he stayed," she admitted, somewhat perturbed, "but he don't know nothing about it, either."

"You had a fight with Melissa Stratford," he pursued.

"Yes, but we made-up afterward," she hastened to explain.

"Do you think a jury will believe that?" he quizzed.

"I can prove by Mr. Dukes that I never left the apartment."

"Yes, but will Mr. Dukes be willing to testify? He's a very prominent man, you know. And then there's your husband. What would he say about it?"

Dorothy bit her lip in vexation and frowned darkly. "Well," she said firmly, "what do you want to know?"

"That's right," he said, "It's better for you to tell me all about it than have to tell the police. And I can save you from publicity, if you will be smart. Now tell me what Savino and the Baron said to each other."

After a moment's hesitation, Dorothy detailed the happenings at the "reefer" party. Ten minutes later lawyer Terry left Mrs. King's apartment, after instructing her minutely what to do. Going immediately to his own apartment, he telephoned Captain Brady and conversed for several minutes. Hanging up the receiver with a shrewd smile on his face, he rang Mary Sutton's apartment on the house telephone. "Come up here a moment," he requested, "There may be something doing very shortly."

Three minutes later she hurried into the apartment.

"Sit down, Mary," he said, "all we've got to do now is wait and see how smart I've been. Maybe there'll be something doing, maybe there won't."

BARON BROWN, GARBED IN AN immaculate brown business suit, sat in the room in the back of the Green Gables cabaret that he called his office. On the dark green walls were large photographs of prominent Negro prize fighters, entertainers, musicians and actors. In one corner was a large safe, next to it a steel filing case with a large adding machine atop of it. In the center of a room was a large, flat top desk at which the Baron sat, puzzling over the account books of his widespread, though illegal, business. At a small desk in one corner set a very pretty mulatto stenographer. Overhead an electric fan whirred, its sound mingling with the tap-tap-tap of the typewriter.

The telephone rang insistently. The mulatto girl answered it.

"It's for you, Baron," she purred.

"Who is it?" he growled.

"Miss Dorothy King." The barons frown, relax, and he picked up the French telephone on his desk.

"Hello, Dorothy," he boomed, essential twist to his lips. "What's up?"

"Listen, Baron," came her excited voice over the telephone. "It's about the Savino thing. A cop was just up here. Somebody must have been talking. He knew all about what went on last night. Talk, just like he had the low down. He said something about fingerprints on the windowpane of Melissa's bedroom, and sort of insinuated that they had the goods on one of your boys. Now, it might have been a stall, but I thought I'd better tell you, whether you know anything about the job or not. This bull seemed pretty well healed with information."

"Thanks, Dorothy," he boomed, frowning wickedly and clamping down with his big teeth on the perfecto that tilted from one side of his mouth, "thanks. You're okeh. I'll be remembering you. Don't say anything to anybody until I get my ducks in line. Goodbye!"

He hung up the receiver and scowled at it as though he hated the sight of the instrument. He sat motionless for several moments, drumming on the edge of his desk.

FINALLY, HE PICKED UP THE telephone again and dialed a number. He waited impatiently, frowning darkly. At last, someone answered the 'phone.

"Who's dat?" he growled.

"Corrinne!" came the answer in a plaintive voice.

"Is Spook there?"

"Yes, sir!"

"Well, tell 'im to catch the five-forty. Get me?"

"Yes, sir. Is anything wrong?"

"You heard me, didn't you?" Baron boomed out the words harshly and slammed down the receiver. He puffed thoughtfully on a cigar for a few moments and then an expansive smile came over his face. With a satisfied sigh, he turned back to the perusal of his account book. The office lapsed again into quietness, only broken by the constant whirring of the electric fan and the tap-tap-tap of the typewriter. Once the Baron paused, flicked a bit of cigar ash off his cuff, smiled to himself and muttered, "Perfect!"

Sam Ellington, a tall, muscular, dark fellow, lolled in a chair in the window of the Orgen Barber shop and Shoe Shine Parlor, ostensibly pursuing the daily tabloid. Actually, he was one of the plainclothes men detailed by Captain Brady to cover the Savino murder, and detail to watch the doorway of a certain dingy apartment house across the street. He was on that doorway far more closely than he was the photographs in the tabloid.

After a considerable wait, he was rewarded. From the doorway issued a short, stocky black fellow bearing two suitcases. The man went immediately to the curb, sat down his suitcase and looked up and down the street for a taxicab. Sam Ellington got up hurriedly and hastened across the street.

THE SHORT BLACK MAN FINALLY hailed a yellow cab. The chauffeur got out to help with the suitcases, placing both in the space along his seat.

"Where to, Mister?" he inquired, turning around.

"Penn Station!" commanded the other.

Just then, the door was yanked open and Sam Ellington slid in alongside the short man.

"Police station, boy!" He ordered the chauffeur.

"Hey, what's the idea?" growled the black man, reaching inside his coat.

"Put 'em up, Spook!" commanded the detective, jabbing his service revolver into the other's ribs. "We want to talk to you."

"You ain't got nothin' on me," braved the other.

"Oh, ain't we?" sneered the officer. "Well, you just wait and see. Police station, boy!"

Spook Johnson sat sullenly inside the circle of detectives in the little windowless room in the back of the precinct station. He was sure of himself. He had been through this sort of thing before.

"Spook," Captain Brady began, "You might as well tell us everything and keep yourself out of the chair, if you can. We know that you shot Savino and that girl with that .44 the officer just took off you. We also know that you escaped over the roof afterward. Isn't that so?"

"That's stuff," sneered the stocky Negro, a slight smirk on his face. "I ain't never been on no roof of no place an' that gun ain't never bin shot, see!"

Over and over, first one officer and then another asked him the same question. A half hour passed. An hour passed. Some officers went out, others came in to take their places.

"WELL," SAID CAPTAIN BRADY FINALLY, "We gave you your chance, spooky. We wanted to make it light for you. We have the real goods on you all of the time. See them? Fingerprints? We took them off the fire escape of the Lincoln Arms, near the roof. They're yours, spook, Johnson. They're yours, and you're gonna burn, just as sure as God made little apples."

"That's a lie!" shouted the Negro, shifting uneasily in his chair and licking his dry, thick lips. "That's a lie, I tell you. They couldn't be mine."

"Well, they are yours, Spook Johnson. Any jury will accept them as evidence. You're gonna burn, Spook Johnson, an' you're gonna burn all by your lonesome. Yes, Spook, they're your fingerprints. Got kinda careless, didn't you Spook? Sorta wish you'd worn gloves now, don't you, Spook? Don't you?"

The Negro cringed speechless, hopeless in his chair, with a circle of relentless eyes gazing at him. He rolled his eyes back and forth and moistened his dry lips.

"Well," continued Captain Brady, indifferently, "We don't really care whether you talk or not, spook. We just thought you might tell us who else had anything to do with it, but if you don't talk, then you'll have to burn alone. Too bad the Baron's out of town. That kind of kills your alibi. If you have just worn gloves and not been so careless, maybe you would have gotten away with it. Bare hands are dangerous, spook. They leave prints, Spook, and any jury will accept fingerprints."

"Ha! Ha! Ha!" roared the captain, turning to the other officers and waving the photostatic copy of the fingerprints. "Can you beat that? He still denies it!"

"It's true, I tell you," Well, the perspiring spook, "I was wearing gloves, I tell you. I. . ." He caught himself and clasped his hand over his telltale mouth, but it was too late. He looked hastily at the officers, startled, frightened, appealing. They smiled and grinned knowingly.

"Well, that's all we want, spook," said the captain, rising with satisfaction in gazing down triumphantly at the slump figure of the confessed murderer. "probably you could get bail if the Baron hadn't run out on you. . . Well, you have to take the rap yourself, my boy."

"I'll be damned if I do," shouted Spook, standing erect in his rage and excitement. "He's as guilty as I am. If I burn, so does he. I did it for him."

"Did you get all of that?" asked the captain, turning to the stenographer.

"Say, Captain," asked Spook a little later in Brady's office after he had signed his confession. "How did you get them fingerprints when I was wearin' gloves?"

"They weren't yours, Spook. And we didn't know for sure that you did the job until Baron Brown 'phoned you over a tapped wire."

"Did the Baron leave me holdin' the sack sure enough?" queried Spook.

"Nope, we picked him up five minutes ago in his office," replied the Captain. "We just used psychology on you, Spook. Baron has taken now, so we know we guessed right. After you took him home, you got in the car, grabbed a taxicab and went back to the Lincoln Arms, doing the job and coming down the fire escape and through the basement."

"How'd you know I got out that way?"

"Because there's no other way. The other people went up the fire escape and didn't see you, so you must've gone down."

"You win, chief," said Spook, grinning sheepishly.

It was eight o'clock when the buzzer of Lawyer Terry's apartment sounded. The attorney leaped to his feet and admitted Billie Smith.

"Billie!" screamed Mary, rushing to his arms. She could say no more, but hung there sobbing passionately.

"Mary!" He cried hoarsely, holding her to him.

The lawyer tiptoed into the next room, smiling indulgently, and closed the door. The two lovers who had gone through so much for each other sank down on the setup. They feasted, their eyes gratefully on each other for several moments before they spoke.

"Oh, I'm so glad!" exclaimed the girl. "I love you so much, Billie. I couldn't have gone on. If anything had happened to you. I'd have been alone in the world and I couldn't have stood it, Billie, and I couldn't. I'd have died."

"Mary, will you marry me tomorrow?" he whispered, pressing her to him.

"Right now, if you say so, darling." She ran her hand possessively over his broad shoulders. "Where will we live?" she asked. "In New York?"

"Yes," he said, grinning, "right here on Sugar Hill!"

DEVIL TOWN: AN ENTHRALLING STORY OF
TROPICAL AFRICA

I

WITCH DOCTOR VISITS MISSIONARY ON EVE OF PROPOSED TRIP

From their high wooden stools, the two hissing acetylene lamps shed a brilliant, pale blue light over the wide verandah. A few vagrant stars and a low moon combined to relieve the Stygian darkness of the surrounding African night. Rev. Nasby's droning intonation of the blessing was accompanied by the chirping of lusty crickets in the palm patch and the buzz of numerous insects whirring through the heavy oozing air above bent heads. It was dinner hour at the Ganda Methodist mission.

The missionary finished. A brilliant speckled bug flew in from the darkness and joined the other circling around the bright lights. Mr. Mondo and Mrs. Nasby lifted their gaze simultaneously from their empty plates and soon the evening meal was under way. On the dinner table, spread with a freshly laundered country cloth, was heaping dishes of steaming chicken cooked in the golden palm butter, luscious geese; little saucers of the incredibly hot Liberian peppers, a bowl of big yellow canned peaches and a plate of fresh brown biscuits.

Rev. Nasby helped the plates. A barefoot mission boy, his white trousers and a shirt contrasting sharply with his smooth dull black skin, padded softly about the table, assisting the diners and replenishing the supply of victuals. His assistant, equally black and similarly clad, pumped a Flit gun with great vigor in a futile effort to dispense or dispatch the monstrous insects banking and diving around the lamps, menacing both the diners and the food.

"Sufficient, Reverend! That'll be quite sufficient," protested Mr. Mondo unctuously as each portion of food was placed in his plate. "I know I have difficulty in slumbering at night if I dine too generously."

Mr. Mondo was a short, thicket black man with prominent little eyes that peered observantly from behind horn-rimmed pince-nez.

His kinky hair stood in a bush and a drop of perspiration ran down each side of his shiny jowls as he methodically munched his food. The skin of his neck lapped over his soggy soft collar. His white suit was a bit too tight for his corpulent frame and it seemed as though each additional mouthful would cause his coat to split up the back. He plied knife and fork industriously, the food disappearing with surprising speed. But all of the Mr. Mondo was wondering why he has been invited to dinner. He was only a teacher while Mr. Nasby was in charge of the station. None of the other colored teachers has been asked to come. What could be on this white man's mind?

Save for the clink of silver on plates, the trio ate in silence. Rev. Nasby, a thin, pale little man with straw-colored hair and large watery blue eyes magnified by thick rimless spectacles, ate slowly and absently, gazing straight ahead as he munched, as though to penetrate the mysterious, awesome, impenetrable blackness of the African night. Every so often a vagrant thought caused his narrow brow to corrugate. Rev. Nasby was wondering just how he should begin what he had to say to Mr. Mondo. Secretly he did not think much of Negroes, especially educated ones, but he often took Mr. Mondo's advice.

Mrs. Nasby, a buxom brunette twice the size of her husband, sat in general silence. Her sweaty flushed skin screamed for relief. A rudimentary mustache and large mole on her upper lip strangely enough added a touch of attractiveness to a woman who was quite low in the scale of beauty. She alternately lifted her fork from plate to mouth, brushed back a recalcitrant lock of damp hair and muttered monosyllable orders to the waiter. Mrs. Nasby always felt a bit uneasy when dining with black people. She had not been used to it at home, and three years in Africa had not accustomed her to it. And yet Mrs. Nasby was convinced that it was the Christian thing to do, even if she evaded doing it as much as possible. Jesus would have willingly died with Negroes, she told herself, so why not she? Still, it did not pay to be too familiar. The natives might lose their respect for her.

"Er . . . ah . . . well, Mr. Mondo," the missionary began, clearing his throat "I have been planning an evangelical trip up to the Devil Town. Mrs. Nasby and I thought we might get your opinion about it. Perhaps you would like to come along. We'd just have love to have you, Mr. Mondo."

Mr. Mondo grew perceptibly shy and stared as though he had seen a ghost of some long departed ancestor weaving through the outer darkness.

"Devil Town!" he gasped, his little eyes round with concern, "Why you mustn't think of going up there, Rev. Nasby! Are you white people mad! It's out of the question my friends, out of the question." He gesticulated with his fork and shook his woolly head.

"Why is it out of the question?" snapped Mr. Nasby, belligerently dropping his knife and fork. As a missionary with a reputation for militance and stopping at nothing to propagate the Faith, he hated to be cornered.

"Because it is foolhardy," the teacher replied. "You may be killed. You don't even seem to understand what this Devil Town means to these people. You can preach Christianity to them all you please and they'll listen to you with courtesy and native respect, but you mustn't interfere with the things they hold sacred. If this place were down near the coast I might be persuaded to say go on, but up here, cut off from civilization, in the midst of superstitious and militant pagans, I should call it extremely unwise."

"Well, it's not a matter of compulsion, Mr. Mondo," said the missionary, somewhat contemptuously. "After all, you don't have to go, but *we* do. He will not tolerate any longer this challenge to God. We must carry His Word up there."

Mr. Mondo smiled knowingly, indulgently and avoiding the white man's glance, wiped his thick lips with a white napkin. Ordinarily, he mused, he wouldn't care what happened to two white people, but he knew the mission would be closed if catastrophe befell Rev. and Mrs. Nasby. That would mean the end of his job—and he liked the easy, indolent life at Ganda.

"Reverend," said the Negro in a tone that betokened pride in his command of the white man's language and his assurance that his view was the correct one, "I harbor a premonition that no benefit can possibly flow from this proposed journey. My lifelong experience with these people warns me that it is dangerous to interfere with their religion. You can call it superstition if you like, but whatever you call it, you'll find it dangerous to fool with."

He shot a hasty, appraising glance at the white man and impaled another mouthful of chicken on his fork.

"Pahaw! That's tommyrot!" exploded Rev. Nasby, disdainfully. He removed his blurred spectacles and polished the lens vigorously with a large dark blue bandana handkerchief. "Don't let these native superstitions frighten you, Mr. Mondo. That Devil Town is the fountain of paganism in this district. We can't make much headway here as long as it holds its spell over these people. We must show them that Christians do not take such superstitions seriously and have no fear of their spirits and ghosts. We must show them that God is all-powerful. I sort of thought you might be glad to go with us, but if you won't, why of course, you won't."

"You really ought to go alone, Mr. Mondo," added Mrs. Nasby, beaming persuasively upon their guest. "Think what a great influence it would be for good if the people saw you, a black man, going with us?"

"Does Cotu know of your plans?" Mr. Mondo inquired anxiously.

"No one knows except Davie," answered the missionary, "but we've made no particular effort to keep it secret. We are not afraid of Cotu. We're going up there tomorrow and hold services— whether Cotu likes it or not. We don't intend to permit any witch doctor to interfere with our plans. Cotu's a detriment to Christian work here, Mr. Mondo. This trip will lower his prestige among the natives, I warrant."

"It is all very well for you to go to the Devil Town," said the Negro, "but you must not take Davie!"

"Why not?" challenged Rev. Nasby. "He's a good Christian and he knows the way. We can't go there without a guide that we can trust, and you'll have to admit Davie's the most trustworthy boy we have here."

The missionary mopped his face with his blue bandana handkerchief. Mr. Mondo frowned and pursed his thick lips.

GEORGE S. SCHUYLER

Something, his whole lifelong experience, told him the idea was all wrong. He sighed resignedly.

"Well, you know best, I suppose," he declared.

"Then you're not going with us, eh?" persisted Rev. Nasby.

"No," replied the Negro slowly, "I think not."

THE THREE DINERS ON THE verandah lapsed into silence. The conversation had reached an impasse. Mrs. Nasby dabbed at her neck with a tiny wisp of handkerchief, the only really feminine thing about her. It seemed like swabbing an elephant with a wash rag. The ebony waiter poured their tepid tea. The crickets in the palm thatch almost stilled their chirping. The buzzing of the insects almost ceased. The black boy warring on the bugs laid down his Flit gun and disappeared through the squeaking screen door into the dark interior of the house.

There came shortly from within the strains of "The Blue Danube." It sounded raspy and tiny as the dull needle scratched its way over the worn surface of the record. Into Mrs. Nasby's eyes there floating that wistful, distant, longing look one so often sees in eyes of white women in the tropics and the Orient at the thought of home.

Gone for a time was the missionary zeal, the almost fanatical urge to win all humanity to the worship of Christ. In its place came the depressing feeling of nostalgia. She longed, for a moment, for drifting snow, stately fir trees and glowing fireplaces.

"My! My!" Rev. Nasby exclaimed, wiping the streaming perspiration from his lean, gaunt face, "it's awfully hot tonight, isn't it. Not a breath of air stirring!"

"Our greatest temperatures are always registered just prior to the beginning of the vernal equinox," Mr. Mondo remarked, proudly rolling out the large, mouth-filling words. "On the sea coast, however, the heat reaches its highest point, owing chiefly to the humidity, the very excessive humidity. At Freetown now, one finds the temperature well nigh unbearable."

He raised his teacup in his stubby fingers and noisily sipped the drink. The thought of Freetown always reminded him of cool beer quaffed under the electric fans in the spacious bar of his favorite hotel. He sighed and with a wary face gulped down another swallow of the insipid brew.

The phonograph music ended with a squawk and a metallic clock. The sky was rapidly filling with stars. Higher and higher rose the moon, seemingly expanding in size as it gained altitude. Its ghostly light disclosed the cone-shaped roofs of the huts of a large village a few hundred yards away across a little stream. Looming above them like gigantic sentries were the black forms of huge cotton trees. Here and there a weaving column of smoke issued from the roof of a habitation. A preliminary rumble of a drum caused the three diners to straighten.

"There'll be dancing tonight in all probability," observed Mr. Mondo.

"Yes, I suppose we'll be kept awake 'till all hours," said Mrs. Nasby, testily. The drums made her restless, strangely restless, arousing something wild, uncontrollably primitive within her; something she feared but which fascinated her.

"Ah!" exclaimed the Negro softly, leaning back in the creaking chair, "I love the rhythmic syncopation of the drums and the weird, plaintive monotony of the singing. You know, I delivered a lecture on it once in London when I was studying there. It is the voice of Africa."

"IT IS THE VOICE OF the devil!" rasped the missionary, frowning in disapproval. "Our work would be a lot easier here if it wasn't for these here country devil and witch doctors keeping alive old sinful customs."

The rumble and rattle of the drums quickened: Boom-boom-a-la! Boom-a-la! Boom-a-la! Boom-boom-boom-boom! Boom-a-la! Horns bellowed, pipes screamed shrilly in accompaniment. A full-throated chorus added a few liquid, minor chords, at regular intervals, repeating them over and over with a sort of hypnotic monotony.

"I suppose old Cotu's staging one of his rites," observed the missionary, smiling wryly. "He's certainly got Ganda under his thumb!"

He sighed heavily and drained his teacup.

"They're just children, John," patronized Mrs. Nasby.

"There are singing the praises of Bondu," informed Mr. Mondo, "one of their great legendary heroes. He was a great hunter, a celebrated warrior, a powerful king. He slew huge bull elephants single-handed, laid waste the towns of his enemies, taking their women and children and killing all the boys taller than his walking stick. He owned one hundred pretty young wives. His spirit, ever present, protects these simple folk from evil and brings them good crops."

"Well, we'll have to wean them away from all that," observed Rev. Nasby, grimly. "It may be very picturesque and of ethnological interest but only God can save these poor creatures, not the ghost of a departed murderer and libertine. That's why it's so necessary, Mr. Mondo, for us to go to the very fountain head of these people's superstitious faith and carry there the gospel of Jesus Christ."

"It is a very sacred place," warned the Negro, "and only a few initiates are allowed to enter it. There many of the ancients are said to be buried: kings and wise men who ruled over and counciled past generations of Kpweaat people. If you go up there, Reverend, you'll have to reckon with Cotu. He is powerful, Mr. Nasby, very, very powerful."

His teacher's earnestness drew an indulgent smile from Rev. Nasby.

"I believe you're still something of a pagan underneath, Mr. Mondo," he challenged banteringly.

The Negro stirred uneasily and a momentary flash of fear came into his tiny eyes. Then, composing himself, he smiled ingratiatingly, blinking through his pince-nez. Unbuttoning his cuff and pulling it back, he revealed an arrow-shaped cicatrix. The whites gazed at it curiously.

"I am a good Christian," he explained emphatically, "but when I was a little boy and had not yet found the true God, the Country Devil hit me and I became one of the elect. But now I have forgotten all those things." He sighed regretfully, his eyes searching their faces for any expression of doubt or glimmer of understanding. The couple remained stolidly silent.

The full moon hung now like a great iridescent discover head and the myriad of the stars peppering the dark celestial dome helped to make the scene quite light. A little lizard ran along the porch rail and a faint snarl came from somewhere out of the ominous gloom of the encircling jungle.

The throbbing, wailing music in the village continued. Now it came nearer. Flaming torches bobbed up and down, moving towards the mission.

"They're coming over here!" gasped the woman excitedly. "That's never happened before!"

Rev. Nasby gazed fixedly at the approaching procession, visible now only a hundred yards away. The rumble and throb of the drums was almost deafening; the scream of the pipes blood-stirring.

In the midst of the group four giant blacks carried a striped hammock. In it was Cotu! An elaborate headdress of feathers and teeth sat on a shrunken, hoary head. The man was withered, very black, bony and completely naked, save for a dirty, striped cloth about his loins.

"This must be important," exclaimed Mr. Mondo, moistening his lips and swallowing. "Perhaps he has already heard of your trip. Someone must have told him. Maybe someone overheard you talking, or. . . well, Cotu is a very wise old man, my friends."

"He's an ugly little fiend!" blurted out Mrs. Nasby.

"I wonder what he wants?" her husband mused, almost to himself. For the first time in three years he had been in Ganda, he felt slightly nervous and uncertain.

Fifty feet from the verandah the procession stopped. The drums became mute. Pipes and horns were stilled. The tongues of flame from the torches licked angrily at the darkness. The hammock disappeared as the four carriers stooped. The ranks of the black parted, Cotu emerged, grigri bags about his neck, mace in his gnarled hand. Walking with the stiffness of extreme age and the dignity of station, he approached the Christians.

Author's Note: If you have never been in the majestic African forest, if you have never encountered the black man in his own home, if you have never felt the spell of Africa, the next chapter of *Devil Town* will astound and delight you. And if you know Africa, you will find this tale delighting your memories with its accurate description of the land and its folk.

II

Rev. Nasby Fails to Heed Advice; Heads Out For "Devil Town"

The three Christians arose respectfully as the venerable master of the soil approached. About ten feet from the verandah, Cotu stopped and gazed steadily at the trio, the while fingering a gri-gri back suspended from his gaunt old neck.

Behind him were arrayed the ominously silent mass of his people, the flaming torches licking angrily at the night air and illuminating the serried packs of blacks. The huge moon overhead had grown more brilliant, now hanging like a tremendous light over the scene. The heavens which an hour before had been almost a black void, were now an incandescent mass—a celestial Broadway.

"Good evening, Cotu," greeted Mr. Mondo in Kpwessi, acting by silent consent as interpreter. "What is it that Cotu wants to say?"

"Cotu would have talk with Amecy God-man," began the devil doctor, in a voice that betokened his age. "Tell him that the spirits of our departed ancestors hear all for us and warn us that we may be protected. Tell him to think how the great elephant is often routed by the driver ants. Tell him to think of the mighty leopard that comes to grief because he does not know that the crying goat lures him to his death in the trap. Tell him to think of the sound of the drum which carries the farthest with bad news. Tell him that it is unwise to accept the rice of the host and then spit upon it. I, Cotu, the patriarch of my people, have spoken."

Rev. and Mrs. Nasby stood, faces drawn with apprehension during the harangue. There was a slight murmuring in the assembled mass of natives as if in approval of what the master of the soil had said. Quickly Mr. Mondo interpreted for the white couple. Cotu gazed steadily and quietly at the still handling the mysterious little bag impending from his withered neck.

"What does he mean?" Mrs. Nasby managed to say.

"He is saying," explained the teacher, "that he has heard of the proposed trip to Devil Town and that he disapproves of it. He warns you that no matter how powerful you may think you are you may come to grief, even as the elephant encountering the army of driver ants and the leopard who foolishly permits himself to be lured into the trap. He warns you not to abuse the hospitality of his people and speaks of the drums which carry farthest with bad news."

"Tell him," said Rev. Nasby, "that we thank him for his visit and hope he will come again. Say to him that the God of the American man is Christian and all-powerful and protects his children at all times and in all dangers; that therefore Christian man has nothing to fear; that when he and his people also become Christians, no evil can befall them."

Mr. Mondo translated these words into Kpweasi for the benefit of Cotu. The old man smiled with the ironic wisdom of age.

"Is it true that in Amecy all the white people worship one God, this Christian god?" he asked.

"Tell him it is true," answered Rev. Nasby, doggedly.

"How is it, then," returned the devil doctor, "that evil befalls the white people? For if no evil ever befell the white people, why should there be medicine men like him? And if there is evil to be fought in Amecy, why does him come to Ganda?"

"Tell him," replied the missionary, "that the Christian God is all powerful but that there is a devil, too, that fights him for the souls of the people, and that we disciples of the Lord warn them against the Devil and help them to fight him with God's word."

"Tell white man," said Cotu, "I hear what he says."

With that he retreated slowly backward, the ranks of the natives opened for him and swallowed him, singing again. The four giant blacks lifted him aloft in his canopied hammock. The torches blazed higher into the night air. Once more came the deafening, rhythmic crash of the drums, the bellow of the horns, the squeal of the pipes, the twang of the harps, the mighty chorus of voices.

The procession turned about and marched back to the town, keeping time, capering to the throbbing, wailing music.

The three Christians resumed their seats. Mrs. Nasby dabbed futility at her large, sweaty face with her wisp of handkerchief.

Rev. Nasby noisily blew his nose and smacked a persistent mosquito that had settled on the back of his long thin neck. Mr. Mondo sat silent, uneasy.

"Clever old fellow, Cotu," observed the white man. "Funny, too. Got a keen mind. But of course he's a menace to us with his pagan superstitions."

"He is indeed, a clever man," Mr. Mondo agreed.

"How is it, Mondo, that an old man like him is able to hold power when there are so many young bucks around. He seems to be more powerful than the old chief."

"He is more powerful," explained the teacher. "I think you should devote more time and study to these people, Rev. Nasby. You would understand them much better and you might make more headway with them. No young bucks, as you call them, can superseded Cotu. He is the patriarch, the master of the soil, the oldest living descendent of the first family that settled this land thousands of years ago. He is herefore the living representative, in a sense, of the spirit, the nia of the earth, and the earth is the most sacred thing to the African because it is the oldest thing. He is more powerful than the chief because the chief is merely the political leader, elected to his position by the elders of the four great families. Cotu is the spiritual leader, the master of the soil who once each year assigns each and every man his area to plant; the repository of the ancient lore and mysteries of a people. He holds his position by virtue, not of election, but of birth— and age. He is, to these simple folk, the connecting link between this life and the next; between them and their departed loved ones; between the living present (the breath of life or dia) and the past; the spirits of nias of the ancestors, who freed of their dias, earthly envelopes, still move about invisibly, watchfully, sometimes wrathfully and malignantly. It is to these spirits that the natives render sacrifice. That, my friends, is the religion of Africa. It teaches, if you please, this oneness of nature and the continuity of life."

"Yes," added Rev. Nasby. "It also teaches polygamy and backwardness. It explains why these people are so far behind in the human race for perfection."

"Polygamy is not an unmitigated evil," observed Mr. Mondo, blandly, proud of his superior knowledge of native customs. "It meets a natural need. Man is more promiscuous than woman. His biological function is completed with impregnation when woman's has just begun. His is the pursuit of variety, hers of stability. White society closes its eyes to these facts and as a result you are cursed with adultery and prostitution. Black society faces these facts and adopts polygamy. You throw your discarded women, your surplus, unmarriageable woman, into brothels, prisons, poor houses and paupers' graves; Africa gives its surplus women a good home until death and the honor and place of wives whom the husband is compelled to protect and cannot mistreat."

"You paint a very ideal picture," said Rev. Nasby with a sarcastic smile.

"If I do," Mr. Mondo smiled in return, "it is only because I find life much more simple and beautiful here than I observed it in London, the vaunted capital of white civilization."

The music had died in the town across the creek and the last torch had been extinguished. Not a single sound was audible from that direction. Two or three crickets chirped in the palm thatch. The acetylene lamps sputtered fitfully. A score of big, brilliantly hued insects banked, curved and dived around the lamps and over the heads of the trio of Christians.

"Well, I really must be going," observed the black man. "Mrs. Mondo has been having trouble with her abdomen again."

"What's she doing for it?" asked Mrs. Nasby, solicitously, "Don't you want to take some medicine from our chest?"

"Oh. . . er. . . well, no, thank you," spluttered Mr. Mondo, hastily. "She has some."

"From Cotu?" inquired Rev. Nasby with dry disdain.

"Ah!" sighed the Negro in injured tone. "She is very foolish, of course, but she is a good Christian, my friends, for all her father in Cotu's roots and herbs. . . Well, goodnight. I am exceedingly grateful for a most delightful dinner, and, well, I wouldn't advise you to embark upon that journey."

Bowing, the Negro stepped pompously down from the low veranda, and, electric torch alight, strode down the pathway bordered with whitewashed boulders until he disappeared into the night.

"Do you really think we ought to go, John?" asked Mrs. Nasby, doubtfully, gazing after the retreating figure of the white clad teacher.

"Of course, Martha," her husband replied testily. "You mustn't pay any attention to Mondo. All of these colored people are superstitious, no matter how much superficial education they may have. You know how they are in the states, don't you? Remember how they used to buy charms from that Jew druggist on the corner where we used to catch the downtown car? . . . This Devil Town is a real challenge to us, my dear, and we must meet it."

Day was breaking. The shroud mist lifted from the dark green wall of the jungle. A mighty chorus of birds and insects hailed with rapture the passing of night. Monkeys awoke and added their barks and chatters to the din. From somewhere in the depths of the forest in the back of Ganda came the faint sound of girlish voices in the Gri-Gri Bush greeting with melody the coming of another day.

Gathered in front of Rev. Nasbys' house, a modernized African structure with wide encircling verandas, steep palm-thatched roof and thick mud-wattle walls rubbed with sheep dung mixture to a cool dark gray color, were five young black men. Four, clad only in loin clothes, were grouped around the chair in which Mrs. Nasby would make the journey to Devil Town. The fifth, a tall, slender youth with broad, high forehead, muscular torso, long, slender limbs, and soft, liquid, intelligent, poetic eyes, was dressed in khaki shirt and shorts, heavy brogans, tan golf stockings and a soiled white helmet that had seen hard wear. He sat on the edge of the porch, looking somewhat worried and drumming nervously on a plank with his long, tapering fingers. Besides him was a small bundle of "dash," presents for the inhabitants of Devil Town—leaf tobacco, printed scarfs, salt and matches.

When it was broad daylight the Nasby's emerged. Mrs. Nasby carried a water bottle and a small black bible. From her husband's shoulder hung a big army canteen. The couple was in freshly laundered, immaculate white linen, with dazzling, whitened helmets.

"All ready, Davie?" asked Rev. Nasby cheerily, glancing at his wristwatch.

"Massah!" replied the tall youth, rising from the veranda.

He shifted the black and red leather scabbard of his bush knife further back to facilitate walking and spoke to the four carriers. They each placed a shoulder under the end of the two poles to which the canopied chair was fastened, when Mrs. Nasby had wedged her ample form into the seat. With a chorus of grunts they lifted the chair and, preceded by Rev. Nasby and his black protégé, started with a swinging gait down the pathway toward the town.

Mr. and Mrs. Mondo stood on the veranda of their house as the party passed. They hailed the missionaries and skeptically wished them good luck and the blessings of the Lord. Mrs. Mondo was a tall, thin black woman garbed in an exotically printed Mother Hubbard and wearing a gay handkerchief over her hair. She flashed her splendid teeth in one of those humorless Negro smiles that may betoken delight or derision, merriment or mockery. The two blacks glanced significantly at each other when the whites had passed, and reentered their bungalow.

"Crazy fools, these white people," grumbled Mrs. Mondo, bustling about the little stove, preparing breakfast.

"They have much to learn," Mr. Mondo commented, scrubbing his molars with a tooth stick.

The sun was out now, drying the heavy dew, evaporating the last little clouds of terrestrial mist. The party descended the barren hill on which the half dozen mission buildings sat and, crossing the shallow creek on the swaying native bridge, entered Ganda.

From the dark gray mud-walled huts, women in striped cloths that covered them only from waist to knee, emerged bearing empty earthenware jugs, large gourds and kerosene cans on their erect heads. Young lithe maids, smooth skinned and tight breasted: mothers with swollen, conical breasts and sucking infants astride their hips; withered graying cronies, toothless and bony, all walking erect down the steep path to the stream like figures on the façade of an Egyptian temple.

Men in loin cloths, long sleeves jackets or blue striped robes stirred about, scratching themselves, vigorously plying tooth sticks or making for the half-towns arms with bush knives and hoes. Frisky goats scampered up and down the winding lanes. Little black and tan dogs with ludicrously large, pointed, erect ears, barked alertly from open doorways. Big fat guinea hens strutted about gobbling the morning's banquet of hapless bugs and worms. Naked children with protuberant bellies and big, wondering eyes, stood silently and watched the Nasby party go by. A sleepy eyed cow gazed stolidly, undisturbed.

Cotu, a gaunt, black, withered old man with eyes of keen intensity that belied his great age, hailed them from the door of his hut. Davie paused respectfully to speak to him. The old man talked slowly and smiled cunningly, cynically.

"What did he say, Davie?" asked Rev. Nasby.

"He says the giraffe has a great body but a small head."

"I wonder what he means?" pondered the missionary as they pushed on. Davie frowned thoughtfully. He had neglected to say that Cotu had warned him that the spirits of his ancestors would be angry.

The relentless sun blazed down from a cloudless turquoise sky. A rolling plain covered with low bush extended for a mile or so to the great forest that clothed the great mountain to its summit. The fronds of palms drooped motionless. Already the much trodden trail was growing dusty in the baking heat.

Finally they entered the great forest. It was like stepping from a griddle to a steam bath. The trail narrowed. The carriers grunted as they began to strike the incline. Perspiration steamed off their glistening bodies. The musky, sickening odor of tolling laborers rose from them. Mrs. Nasby sought to waft it away from her sensitive nostrils with a large palm leaf fan.

The deep forest was a place of perpetual twilight, a sinister abode of gloom. Enormous trees, their trunks buttressed by rudder-like roots as tall as a man, and looped together by monster vines, towered over an impassable No-Man's-Land of tangled bushes, palms, poisonous weeds, ferns and creepers. Tiny rays of golden sunshine filtered through the lofty canopy of interwoven branches to the darkness of the silent festooned aisles far below. The forest exhaled a mélange of odors, repellant and attractive; noxious emanations from the dead and decaying mingled with aromatic perfumes and sharp effluvia from the living.

The forest seemed like an Indian temple, at once majestic and terrifying, with a spiritual appeal sharply modified by the feeling of surrounding malevolent physical presence, above, below, on each side, everywhere. The oppressive silence of the place was broken only by the swishing wings of a solitary hornbill cruising unseen above the green ceiling, the snarling of a troop of red monkeys quarreling astride branches a hundred feet aloft, and the rattle of creak of Mrs. Nasby's chair. Once a fat porcupine scuttled across the trail and walk behind her husband, disappeared in the underbrush. Twice brilliantly patterned snakes slithered swiftly across the path.

"Davie!" called Rev. Nasby, when they halted for a drink at the gurgling brook of clear, cold water. "What all do the Devil men do up in this town?"

"I not know, sah," replied the youth. "Nobody know, sah. Nobody go dah, sah. De people de 'fraid too much. It mean trouble too bad. De people dey ain't even palaver 'bout it, sah. It bad business, sah."

Rev. Nasby said nothing. They moved on. Flights of huge insects zoomed perilously about their heads. Thorny branches reached out and tore viciously at black flesh and white garments. Burrs fastened painfully to bare shanks and adhered to clothing. Exclaiming and grunting, the carriers slipped and stumbled over and around rocks, roots, and an occasional decaying tree trunk gutted by industrious armies of red ants. Once or twice vast swarms of the carnivorous driver ants formed the entire party into ignominious flight, wincing at the sharp stings.

Finally Mrs. Nasby had to get out because of the steepness of the trail and walk behind her husband. He was drenched with perspiration and panting heavily. He held one hand to his pounding, painful chest.

Suddenly Davie stopped and pointed to a narrow side trail scarcely distinguishable to an inexperienced woodsman.

"There," he exclaimed, "is Devil Town trail!"

III

Natives Chase Missionary From Jungle Shrine

R ev. Nasby sighed gratefully at this intelligence. He walked close to the very narrow opening and inspected it curiously. Mrs. Nasby leaned forward in her chair to see. She presented a mussy and bedraggled appearance. Her hair was wet and disarranged. Her helmet lay in her lap and her great bosom heaved up and down as she struggled for air. The atmosphere was hot, gloomy, humid.

"Well, well," remarked Rev. Nasby, "I guess this is it, alright."

Two tall sticks joined near the top by a cross bar obstructed the passage. From the bar were suspended three plump, weather-beaten leather gri-gri bags. Below on the ground was a small heap of mud stones on which were two or three bundles wrapped in withered banana leaves and tied with pieces of small vine.

The missionary surveyed it with satisfaction mingled with contempt. It was ample reward for the very arduous trip up the mountain. On several steep inclines he had almost regretted taking the journey. But nothing was to difficult to do in the Lord's service, he told himself righteously. This visit would shake the natives' confidence in their beliefs. The missionaries at the coast stations would be thrilled and jealous when he reported the undertaking. The account of the trip would read extremely well in the missionary magazine. This might win him a transfer to a larger and more important station, and that would mean greater responsibility; perhaps more money. He removed his foggy spectacles and polished them effectively.

Davie and the four perspiring carriers gazed awesomely at the taboo. Rev. Nasby noticed them and smiled contemptuously.

"Come Davie!" he snapped. "We must be getting along. It's growing late. Go ahead! Lead on!"

"I-I-I can't, Reverend," the youth stammered. "I can't go past that. It'll kill me!" His teeth chattered as with malarial chills. He stood frozen to the spot, horror-stricken at the thought, stripped of all his careful missionary training. His sincere belief in the Christian God could not prevail against the deathly fear of violating the ancient taboo.

Rev. Nasby waxed indignant at his prize convert for ignominiously failing to stand the first real test to which he had been subjected. His voice rose harsh and irritable as he argued with the slender lad.

"Give me that knife," he commanded, snatching the machete from the paralyzed fingers of the youth, determined not to be thwarted after coming so far. "It's nothing but a few dead sticks. I'm disappointed in you, Davie."

The mission boy stood rigid and silent, his lips moving, his eyes set. The carriers gabbled together in low, excited tones. The white man swung the bush knife high above his head and brought it down with a sweeping, diagonal blow that sent the dried sticks crackling into a heap.

With a yell of terror, the four carriers turned, bolted down the torturous trail and disappeared around a bend.

"Here! Here! Come back here!" yelled the woman, jumping out of her chair and waving her red arms. "Davie! Tell them to come back! John! How'll I get home?"

Davie stood silent, transfixed. A hopeless fear paralyzed him. His head nodded, his lips moved but no sound came from them. The muscles of his perspiring black face twitched convulsively. He could not move. He saw himself already as one dead, for even though he had not personally destroyed the taboo, he had guided the destroyer to it, and he shared the guilt. Nothing, he believed, could save him. He must die.

Unhindered by the unexpected turn of events, Rev. Nasby ruthlessly kicked the obstruction from the path, his narrow face alight with religious, fanatical zeal.

"You see?" he said mockingly, turning to the speechless youth. "There's nothing to it; nothing happens, nothing can happen. You must have faith in God, Davie. He will protect those who believe in Him. . . Come on Bertha. It can't be far from here. . . Come on, Davie!"

The mission boy looked at him appealingly. Though Rev. Nasby has kicked the taboo aside, to Davie, with his early pagan upbringing, it was still in place, as potentially evil as before.

"It'll kill us!" he finally blurted out.

The white man walked over to him, gripped him by the wrist and tried to pull him in the direction of the forbidden trail. The touch galvanized the boy into action.

With a mad scream that came from the very depths of his soul, he dropped his bundle of "dash" and fled stumbling down the path which they had so recently ascended, following in the wake of the terrified carriers.

The missionary gazed in rage and vexation after his prize pupil. Mrs. Nasby fell back weakly into her chair almost on the verge of tears.

"John, don't you think we'd better go back?" she cried.

"No," he snapped, "we'll go on, I started to go to the Devil Town and I'm going, with the Lord's help. You can stay here and wait for me if you want to, but I'm going on."

She looked around apprehensively at the dismal, sinister majesty of their surroundings. "Alright," she sighed with resignation, easing her bulk again out of the chair. "I'm coming."

She gripped her Bible and adjusted her white helmet. He picked up Davie's bundle of "dash" and holding the bush knife in his right hand, pushed through the narrow opening, closely followed by his wife.

The going was even more difficult now. Seldom trod, the path was frequently indistinct. Even a good woodsman would have sometimes been in a quandary as to which way to turn. Thorns rent their clothing. A half dozen noisy, rushing, turbulent brooks soaked their shoes. Jagged rocks gnawed at their soles. They stumbled over roots, rocks and dead trees. Several times they lost the trail, but they kept doggedly on with true Anglo-Saxon persistence, impelled forward by evangelical zeal.

For two hours they toiled and trudged and clawed their way upward. Mrs. Nasby's white dress was soiled, wet and torn in a half dozen places. Her helmet, now scratched and dented, sat askew on her head. Her Bible, fiercely gripped, was muddy and damp with sweat and water. Rev. Nasby has fared no better.

They were beginning to wonder whether there really was a Devil Town. Then suddenly the trees thinned out and they emerged into a rocky open space on the very top of the mountain. A hundred paces in front of them were three great palm-thatched pavilions or palaver kitchens grouped around a large square and surrounded by a high stockade which revealed only the roofs of the buildings. The space around the enclosure was completely bare except for a surrounding circle of huge boulders about twenty-five yards from the stockade. A magnificent panorama spread out below them. They could see for fifty miles over low, verdure-clothed hills, forested plains, miasmic ferns and jungle valleys to a hazy distant mountain range. A thin coil of smoke ascended here and there from the sea of green, indicating the presence of a village. Far, far below, like a toy settlement, they could see the tiny buildings of the Ganda mission on its low, bare red hill.

"Thank God!" exulted Rev. Nasby. "Come, Bertha, let us go inside and meet the people and hold services. We've accomplished something today! The whole Christian world will know of our feat inside of six weeks. This is the reward of our courage and faith, my dear!"

They started toward the buildings. Then from far below they faintly heard the rhythmic throb of a drum. It seemed to speak. They look questioningly at each other, perturbed, uneasy. Drums talking in the daytime meant trouble. Faster and faster now came the drum beats; an angry boom-boom and rat-a-tat-tat.

"Come on!" he said, with difficulty composing himself. "Let's see who's here. Now, as soon as they come out I'll take the Bible and read a few verses. Then you sing and I'll join with you. Now don't be frightened, my dear."

"Who's frightened?" she rasped. "Go ahead!"

They walked slowly to the circle of great stones, passed through it and approached the gate in the stockade. The beat of the drums came faster now and in spite of themselves their hearts pounded an accomplishment.

"I wonder why the drums are beating?" she asked.

"How should I know?" he snapped, frowning.

He found the ingenuous catch in the gate and unfastened it. He pushed the gate. It creaked gruesomely as it opened. Mrs. Nasby followed closely. When she had entered the little square, he released the gate and it closed with a loud slam.

The two intruders started at the sound. The compound was as silent as a tomb. The palavar kitchens were deserted. The distant drums kept up their boom and rattle. It seemed that the noise grey nearer, but they dismissed that as an illusion. Not a soul was in sight. Rev. Nasby removed his blurred spectacles, polished them as best he could, and then mopped his pale face with his blue bandana handkerchief.

"Hello! Hel-lo!" he shouted at the top of his voice.

The only reply was an echo. He frowned darkly, disturbed.

"Maybe they're asleep," ventured his wife.

"Hello! Hello, there!" he shouted again.

Again there was no reply. They glanced at each other puzzled. They walked slowly over to the largest of the big buildings, facing them directly across the square. Somewhat gingerly now, the missionary walked up the three clay steps and entered the palaver kitchen. Mrs. Nasby stayed in the center of the compound anxiously watching him, her Bible gripped so tightly that her knuckles showed white through her skin.

Boom! Boom! Boom! Boom-boom-boom-boom-boom! Thunderous cacophony! Shrieks of pipes. Screams of horns! Bellows and yells! Right there in the compound! Invisible, but right there! Not miles distant, but right there! They shrank before the deafening tumult. The white man retreated, pale and shaken, to his wife's side. They clasped each other's hands in their terror.

Now from behind the three palaver kitchens filed columns of strange awesome figures; figures covered with rice straw from head to foot; figures with hideous masks; figures with weirdly striped arms and bodies; naked figures, clothed figures; figures clad in the skins of beasts, of leopards, of bush cows, of steers!

Silently they came forth until they had formed a wide circle about the cowering white couple. Then in a chorus they all began to chant a savage, wild song liberally interspersed with growls, groans, and yells, weaving their bodies from side to side, shaking aloft spears, great swords, gri-gri backs of huge proportions, chains of leopards' teeth!

Slowly, a step at a time, they closed in on the missionaries until scarcely fifteen feet away from them. Then the ranks abruptly opened and through the aisle passed a majestic, awesome figure, horrible to look upon. The head was surmounted by a wild headdress of feathers, teeth and rice straw. The hideous face was almost indescribable—an ugly wooden mask painted in brilliant reds, blues, and yellows, with great ghoulish, staring eyes. From the neck to the feet fell a robe of rice straw. The arms protruding from the garment were streaked with white and red; the hands and fingers dripped red, possibly blood!

The monster approached the whites, screaming maledictions on them. He raised his claws above their heads. From somewhere in the closely packed crowd someone threw a huge, naked sword. It was caught with dexterity in the monster's bare hands. He swished it above the heads of the hapless whites until they could hear the blade sing like the warning of an angry insect.

Then all fell silent. The ranks parted again leaving a clear path. At a signal from the monster there was a crash of drums, pipes and horns, accompanied by blood-curdling screams. Horror-stricken, the Nasbys were pushed sprawling from behind.

"For God's sake, run!" he gasped, scrambling to his feet.

Mrs. Nasby had anticipated him. She rose, soiled and torn from the earth and stumbled through the opening toward the gate, her husband close behind her. As they ran the gauntlet, hands and staves struck them across the head and shoulders to the accompaniment of screams of evident anger and hatred.

They gained the gate. Miraculously it opened. Through it they sped, the crowd of fanatical devil men yelling and screaming behind them; the drums booming, the pipes and horns bellowing savagely.

Across the rocky open space the two sped, stumbling and falling, but keeping on, their hearts pounding furiously until it seemed they would burst, fear forcing them on; fear for their lives.

More weird figures rose from behind the great circle of boulders surrounding the stockade; figures in rice straw; figures in hideous masks; figures with striped faces and bodies; yelling, screaming figures, waving medicine staffs and gri-gri bags.

Into the forest the Nasbys plunged, back along the narrow, tortuous trail they had so hopefully traversed such a short time before. They ran, slid and slipped; branches and thorns tore their clothing to shreds, whipped and scratched their faces; stones tore their shoes and bruised their feet.

On and on they fled, and always behind them was the thud of the drums, the screams of the horns and pipes, the shouts of their pursuers.

At last, after an hour of terror-stricken flight, they reached the main trail. There was the chair just where they had left it. They sank down exhausted.

A great silence fell over the mountain. Here and there a cricket chirped, a monkey chattered or a twig broke under the weight of some forest creature, but all else was silence. It became oppressive after the thunderous ordeal through which they had gone.

Slowly, limping painfully, they made their way down the trail to Ganda. The afternoon grew gray. The sun sank lower. In the forest there was twilight already. Footsore, silent, the two whites trudged the last few miles to the mission.

Three hours later after they had arrived back at the station, bathed, treated their numerous cuts and were dining glumly and alone on the veranda, a tall native, swathed in a voluminous striped gown came up the pathway. In his hand he carried a package wrapped in a fresh banana leaf and tied with a bit of vine. He stopped respectfully a few feet from the diners.

"What is it?" asked Rev. Nasby, wearily, wincing with pain as he turned to speak to the man.

"Humph!" the native exclaimed, "Cotu send." He extended the package to the missionary and turning, disappeared in the enveloping darkness.

"What is it?" asked Mrs. Nasby.

Slowly Rev. Nasby unfastened the package. Without a word he laid the contents on the table.

There was Mrs. Nasby's Bible and his rimless spectacles:

The two looked at each other but said not a word. The black attendants winked at each other and grinned.

"Well," boomed the familiar voice of Mr. Mondo from the doorway, where he had been standing for a moment, "I hope and trust you good people had a pleasant and most instructive journey to Devil Town."

"Oh, go to hell!" snarled Rev. Nasby, to his own and everyone's surprises.

GOLDEN GODS: A STORY OF LOVE, INTRIGUE
AND ADVENTURE IN AFRICAN JUNGLES

I

Dying Liberian Gives Treasure Map to Gail; Then It Disappears

Help! Murder! Po—lice!" The cries rang out sharply in the cold wintry night, echoing through the almost deserted streets of Harlem.

Gail Reddick, who had emerged a few moments before from Small's and was walking to clear his head a little before going to bed, stopped short and listened. The cries were coming from 136th street direction.

The tall, athletic Negro, always quick to respond to distress, raced down the street toward the cries. At the corner he and three men scuffing desperately on the sidewalk. It was two on one and the lone defender was obviously getting the worst of it.

"Help! Help!" came his cry again, fainter this time, as he sagged under the fury of the terrible onslaught.

With no unnecessary announcement of his approach, Gail jumped into the fray, both fists flailing with affects. He enjoyed these rough affrays, especially after he had had a few drinks.

The unexpected onslaught took the two men completely by surprise and after receiving several stout wallops, they turned and ran. Gail did not follow them but turned his attention to the man they had been assailing.

"How're you feeling, buddy?" he asked. The man had sagged down on the steps of an undertaking establishment, his head sunk between his shoulders. He made no reply to Gail.

For the first time, then, Gail noticed blood on the sidewalk. Quickly he picked the man up and carried him to a streetlamp a hundred feet away. The fellow was groaning and rolling his eyes in pain. Then Gail saw that he had been stabbed in the stomach. The blood was pouring from between his fingers and splattering on the sidewalk.

Gail whistled to a passing taxi-man. "Harlem Hospital. Quick!" he directed when he had placed the wounded man inside the cab. The hospital was but a short distance away and they were there in a few moments. Willing hands helped carry the man into the institution and in a short while he was being examined. Gail waited to hear the doctor's report.

"Pretty bad case," announced the young colored intern, coming out of the operating room shaking his head.

"Will he make it?"

"Hardly think so. He'll probably be gone by morning. He wants to see you."

"Wants to see me?" echoed Gail.

"Yes. Come right this way."

Gail followed the young intern into the dimly lit ward. The man he had helped was in the third bed.

"I'll leave you with him for a while," said the intern. "Don't let him talk much." He turned and left the ward, whispering something to the nurse as he went out.

Gail sat down by the bed. The man, a huge black fellow with a very intelligent face and a fine head, smiled wanly at him. He shook his head doubtfully when Gail tried to lamely reassure him.

"No, I go soon," whispered the other with apparent effort and pain, "to join spirits of my fathers. Can't talk much. You listen, eh. Ah! Hurt too much! I talk to you. Me Johnny Kpolleh, Liberia man, from Buzi people, see. White mans try to get map. Mean much gold. Maybe twenty thousand pound worth; hundred thousand America dollars. See? Now I die. Yes Johnny Kpolleh die too quick. You black man like me. I give you map. You get golden gods. No want white mans to get 'em. White mans bad. Much bad. Sacred town Winyah up in mountain soon by Voni Jessu, too far up country, soon by Voni Jessu. You go there. Follow map. Be too careful. Devil mans kill you the much. You understand?"

"Well I don't get you very well," Gail admitted, straining to understand. "You see, I know nothing about Liberia. I've never been there."

"Look," said the other, his face distorted in pain. "Doctor man have package with map. Call doctor, quick."

Gail called the pretty young nurse and told her. She came back almost immediately with a package about a half inch thick and the size of a cigar box cover. She handed it to Gail. It was wrapped in brown paper and tied securely with twine.

"Open him up," directed Johnny Kpolleh.

GAIL DID SO. INSIDE THE paper was a rectangle of leopard skin. He turned it over. On the opposite side drawn with red ink was a roughly accurate map of Liberia on an almost minute scale, certainly more than three inches square, on which the location of Winyah, the sacred city, and Voni Jessu, the nearby town, were marked in relation to Monrovia and adjacent rivers and mountains. The remainder of the surface was taken up by a detailed plan of the sacred city showing location of buildings, stockade, palaver kitchen, the shrine and trailing leading to the place. Two trails; the main trail and the smaller secret trail, were marked prominently, Johnny Kpolleh explained with considerable effort, that a stranger could only approach by the secret trail and told of the traps to be avoided. Gail listened intently, his imagination and cupidity fired by the strange tale.

"Me go with white man there. White man make map. We not get golden gods. Bush men chase us. Shoot arrow. Hit white man. Johnny Kpolleh carry away safe. White man get fever bad. Johnny steal map and go for Monrovia. Take job on ship. Come to New York. Johnny figure he go back sometime when all quiet and get gold maybe for himself. Tonight Johnny Kpolleh meet white man in Harlem. You know rest. You black mans. You get golden gods. But take care. Watch out for Ghelleh. He bad witch man." The African's voice grew fainter and his eyes dimmed. "What you name, black brother?"

"Gail Reddick."

"Alright, Gail Reddick," breathed the African, his voice fainter. "You take map. Be careful. Be careful. You go quick 'fore doctor come back. Johnny Kpolleh must go with spirits of fathers. Don't let white mans get map."

"But what is his name? What does he look like?" asked Gail, anxious to get this information before the African passed on. But there was no reply. The man's head sagged. Gail grasped his hand and felt his pulse. They had ceased to beat.

The *SS. Western Hemisphere* made its way slowly through the rough seas of the Bay of Biscay. The decks were practically deserted. Most of the passengers were below in their cabins, ill. In the forward salon, Gail Reddick sat sipping a glass of Madeira and gazing out at the tempestuous sea.

He kept telling himself that in all probability he was a fool; that he should have stayed in New York and taken that job his uncle had offered instead of traipsing off to Africa with his last thousand dollars. But his deep set black eyes lighted up as he thought of the stakes. One hundred thousand dollars in pure gold! A fortune! And no one in the whole world except a few superstitious natives knew where it was. With that much money he could live in leisure for the next twenty years, maybe longer. It was worth taking the risk. And hadn't he always taken risks: in high school, in college and after graduation? He had always had the urge for big adventure. Now he was to satisfy that urge.

He downed the rest of his wine and rose to take a turn around the deck before dinner. He went out. Great seas were pounding the *Western Hemisphere*. She trembled like a mastiff as she lurched and dived from side to side, now on the peak of a watery mountain, now sunk in cavernous troughs. Bending to the wind, Gail made his way with difficulty along the slanting deck, the spray from giant waves making his eyes smart.

He was rounding the corner with head lowered, half-blinded by the salty spume, when he bumped into someone coming from the opposite direction. At that precise moment a huge sea struck the ship and the deck spun from under foot. The two passengers went down together and rolled toward the rail. Gail noticed that the person with whom he had collided was a woman.

"I'm terribly sorry, Madam," he apologized. "I didn't see you."

"And I didn't see you, either," she laughed, as he helped her to her feet. Then for the first time Gail notice that she was a colored girl of unusual light brown beauty; tall, slender, athletic.

His heart skipped a beat. He had been hungry for the sight of a colored person.

"I didn't know you were on the boat," he said, as they continued their walk around the deck together at her invitation.

"I guess not," she said, smiling and displaying two even rows of pearly teeth, "I didn't eat dinner night and I was too sick to eat today, but I'm alright now, I had a package of Mothersill's Remedy and it fixed me right up."

"My name's Gail Reddick," he told her. "I'm going to Liberia."

"And mine's Martha Crockett," she said simply, "and I'm going there, too."

"I'm a missionary," she said, "going to teach at one of the mission schools."

"Devoting your life to the untutored savage?" he inquired in jesting tone.

"No, nothing like that," she laughed, "I just got a chance to come out here for a year or so and I thought I'd take it. You know I've never traveled before, at least not overseas. Now tell me about yourself."

It wasn't hard for Gail to do that. He was smitten by the girl's oriental beauty; captivated by her simple manner and alert mind. He had never bothered much with women save in a casual manner. All through college he had been so absorbed in athletics and his studies that he had paid little attention to girls. He had always felt there was ample time. But toward this girl who was braving the vicissitudes of a jungle assignment with perfect sang-froid he was drawn as he had never been before.

AT DINNER HE LEARNED TO his delight that Martha was seated at his table. She was charming in a Copenhagen blue evening dress that contrasted well with the rich brown of her complexion. The white diners watched the well-dressed couple curiously.

"Our white friends always manage to place our folks together," she said, with a pretty grimace.

"Yes," he replied, "but this is one time I'm not offended." His large black eyes bespoke his satisfaction more eloquently than his words.

"Neither am I," she admitted with disarming frankness. "I was getting awfully lonesome."

The waiter came with the hors d'oeuvres and with him came the wine steward. "Won't you order?" she pleaded softly. "I'm sure you are more familiar with these menus than I, and I'm totally ignorant of wines."

"Does the church allow you to partake?" he teased.

"It doesn't," she grinned, "but I'm going to just the same."

"Gee, but you're regular," he blurted out, compelled to withhold all he would have liked to say for fear of being considered too forward.

It was nearly nine o' clock when they left the dining salon. The sea was still rough but they decided to get wraps and take a turn about the heaving deck.

Afterward they went to the forward salon to chat. For some reason Gail found himself telling Martha his entire history from birth; of his years at school and college, how he won his block letter and graduated at the head of his class the previous June. And then, despite his solemn determination to tell no one of his mission, he found himself recounting to her his strange adventure, of the fight on 136th Street, of Johnny Kpolleh, his murderous assailants and the precious map.

"I don't know why I'm telling you all this," he confessed. "I promised myself I wouldn't tell anyone and now I've been blabbing like a kid. Now you see want a pretty woman can do."

"You can trust me, Mister Reddick," she said, quietly, and he knew by her tone and her expression that he could.

"You may call me Gail, if you wish," he implored, searching her eyes. "I'd love to hear you say it." A dark red tint crept up her cheek toward her hair.

"Gail!" she breathed. "What a strong, romantic, beautiful name!"

"And may I call you Martha?" he begged, leaning toward her.

"Yes, Gail. I feel that we're going to be good friends."

"I wish we could be more than that," he murmured, with a boldness that surprised him. "I've never met anyone I liked more than you."

She turned her eyes hastily away.

"Isn't it strange," she mused half to herself, "that I should be going to the station at Voni Jesu."

"Is that so?" he cried, straightening. "Why I've got to there too! Won't you come down to my cabin a minute? I'd like to show you that map. I don't dare show it in public you know. It'll be alright," he added, reassuringly, noting her momentary hesitation, "I keep it locked in my steamer trunk in a strong iron box."

She nodded in agreement. They rose and descended to Gail's cabin. He took out his key and opened the door. He switched on the lights and then started back with a gasp. The little room was in wild disorder. Bed clothing was scattered in all directions. His clothes had been taken from the closet and were cast about on chairs. His steamer trunk had been broken open and on the wash basin he saw with sinking heart the shattered remnant of the little iron box in which he had locked the precious map.

"My God!" he cried. "It's gone! It's gone!"

II

GAIL REGAINS THE TREASURED MAP,
THEN COMPLICATIONS START

An expression of hopelessness and frustration swept over Gail's face as he gritted his teeth in rage. What was there to do? Without that map he could not hope to find either Winyah or the golden gods in its palaver house. Who among the hundred or more passengers could have taken it?

Martha squeezed his forearm reassuringly and bestowed a comforting smile upon him.

"After all," she said, "it must be on board this hip, Gail. And since it is here probably you can find it if you try hard enough. You cannot do anything without it, you know."

"Yes, you're right," he agreed grimly. "I will find it. Come, let's take you to your cabin. I've got a lot to do tonight."

They walked silently along the companionway to her door.

"What are you going to do now?" she asked anxiously, as they paused in front of her cabin. "Won't you come in for a minute?"

"No thanks, Martha," he declined in a tone of voice that revealed his preoccupation. "I've got to get off by myself and think. Goodnight!" He looked down into her upturned face and his expression grew soft. Bewitched by her charm, he leaned forward.

"Goodnight, Gail!" she breathed, a mischievous smile playing around her lips, and turning the key in her door she disappeared quickly within, her large black eyes sparkling roguishly. Gail paused for a moment in front of the closed door, and then remembering his tasks, he turned on his heel and made his way to the upper deck.

The sea was calmer and the *Western Hemisphere* was rolling gently. With furrowed brow, Gail trudged back and forth along the deserted deck, thinking furiously. What should he do now? Which way could he turn? Finally he wandered into the aft salon, ordered a Scotch and soda and sat down in a corner of the large

GEORGE S. SCHUYLER

room in a comfortable leather armchair. Several passengers were sitting about playing cards, drinking and conversing.

With dramatic suddenness an idea flashed through his brain. Springing up he almost ran out of the salon and downstairs to the purser's office. The purser, a tall, pleasant-faced Englishman, was put on the point of closing up.

"Hello there, sir," said the purser. "Something I can do for you?"

"Yes," said Gail, lowering his voice and glancing around to see if they were alone. "Now I don't want you to say anything about this to a soul but my cabin has been ransacked and I have been robbed of a valuable document. I haven't the slightest idea who did it but I'm on the lookout. I want you to help me if you will."

"Certainly," agreed the other, his expression grave, "I'll do all I can."

"Well the document is very valuable," continued Gail, "and whoever took it may leave it here with you. If anyone leaves anything here, let me know, will you? The document is about the size of a cigar box cover."

"I'll be glad to help," said the purser, "but of course I should notify the captain and have the ship searched."

"No, I'd rather you keep quiet about it," said Gail, "until I do a bit of investigating on my own."

"Very well, Mr. Reddick."

GAIL RETURNED TO THE AFT saloon, sat down and lit a cigar, puffing thoughtfully. Then he recalled that he had the passenger list in his pocket. He pulled it out and consulted it. Whoever had stolen the map most certainly be going to Monrovia, otherwise the map would be of very little use to him. He turned to the list of the first class passengers deboarding at the Liberian capital. There it was:

Miss Martha Crockett.
Mr. Hans Goebel.
Mr. Peter Johnson.
Mr. Gail Reddick.
Dr. Francis Williams.

There were no second class passengers. He dismissed the four natives on the third class who were scheduled to leave the ship at Monrovia. Leaving out Martha, there were thus three suspects.

He went down again to the purser's office. The pleasant-faced Englishman clad now in pajamas, peered out in answer to his knock.

"Sorry to disturb you, purser," Gail apologized, "but I want some information."

"Certainly, you old chap," said the purser, "what is it?"

"What can you tell me about these three men: Goebel, Johnson and Dr. Williams who are getting off at Monrovia?"

"Well, let me see," said the Englishman thoughtfully. "Goebel is a German trader from Hamburg. He often travels down this way. He's been with us on several trips. I believe he represents Wester & Co. A strange silent chap, he is, typically German. I've never liked him much myself. Johnson is a rubber man going out to the Firestone plantation. It's his first trip. Dr. Williams is the physician in charge of the Firestone hospital. I believe he is returning off his leave to the States. Why, do you suspect one of them?"

"No," said Gail, lying blandly, "I was just curious." He thanked the purser and returned thoughtfully to the salon.

Johnson could obviously be dismissed, he though, and perhaps Dr. Williams, also, but Goebel was different. Gail knew that Webster & Company was a large firm of German exporters and importers with stores in Monrovia and several smaller places in Liberia. Goebel would be the only one of the three white men thoroughly familiar with the Liberian hinterland, and perhaps the only one who might be interested in the leopard skin map. But how could he know about the map? Gail consulted the passenger's list again. Suddenly he noted with surprise that Goebel's cabin was on the same deck with his. The tall Negro's fingers tapped nervously on the arm of his chair. Yes. Goebel might be the thief.

Gail got up, tossed the remnant of his cigar into a cuspidor and descended to his cabin. After replacing his effects, he rang for the steward, a squat, polite Cockney.

"Did you ring, sir?" queried the man a few moments later, peering in the cabin door.

"Yes, come in," said Gail. He glanced searchingly at the steward. No, this fellow was obviously honest. It was needless to suspect him of knowledge of the theft. "What time does Mr. Goebel have his tub in the morning?"

"Seven o'clock sir," answered the steward, evincing some surprise, "right after you, sir."

"Does he go to breakfast, immediately afterward?" asked Gail.

"Why, I think so, sir. Why?" replied the other.

"Well, here's a pound for you, steward," said Gail, handing the man a crisp green bill. "I want you to do something for me. In the morning when Goebel goes to breakfast, I want you to unlock his cabin door with your key. I'll give it back to you later. I have reason to believe that German has stolen a valuable document belonging to me."

"But I couldn't do that, sir," gasped the steward, drawing back.

"Now be sensible, my man," Gail persuaded. "This is a matter of life and death. I'll take nothing belonging to him. This document must be regained. It contains valuable secrets I was carrying to the British consul at Monrovia. It will greatly embarrass England if Germany gets the document. Everything depends upon you, my man. Will you do it? Remember, it's for England, steward!"

"Rather irregular, sir," objected the little man. "I'd lose my job if anything went wrong."

"Nothing will go wrong," insisted Gail. "Here's another pound. Now what do you say? It will only take a few minutes."

The steward was in a brown study. He squinted his eyes, looking first at Gail and then at the crisp pound note held out to him.

"Well, I'll risk it, sir," he agreed reluctantly, "but I don't like such business. It's dangerous, sir." Gail pressed the second bill into the man's itching palm.

GAIL SPENT A SLEEPLESS NIGHT, reading, smoking numerous cigarettes, waiting for the morning that seemed never to arrive. At last came daybreak. Promptly at six-forty-five the steward announced that his tub was ready. Gail rose and went to the bathroom. The little steward winked significantly at him. Fifteen minutes later Gail came back, shaved and then sat down to await the steward's signal.

Around seven-thirty the little Cockney thrust his tousled head into the cabin and whispered, "Very will, sir."

Gail followed him the few steps down the companionway to Goebel's cabin. The door was unlocked. The steward handed him the key. "Hurry, sir!" he admonished.

Gail stepped inside and snapped the catch behind him. Immediately he got to work. He searched Goebel's clothing. Nothing there. He searched Goebel's suitcase and his trunk, both of which were fortunately unlocked. Nothing there. Gail's face grew grim with frustration and rage. Frantically he ransacked every corner of the cabin, replacing everything as he found it. The map was nowhere to be seen. Finally he gave up the search in disgust and letting himself out he locked the door and returned the key to the anxiously waiting steward. Seeing the fright and apprehension on the little Englishman's face, he shoved a ten shilling note in his hand and winked reassuringly.

"Did you get it, sir?" asked the steward.

"No," said Gail bitterly, and turning, strode down the companionway to the dining salon.

Martha was already there looking fresh and verdant in a dark green dress. Her face lit up as he took his seat.

"Any luck?" she whispered, leaning toward him and titillating his nostrils with the odor of faint perfume.

"None," he replied, telling in undertone what he had done, "but I've got one more chance. I'll tell you later. It's my only chance."

They breakfasted in more or less silence. Afterward they strolled along the deck. The ship was rolling a bit more than the night before. Several times they passed a fleshy, bullet-headed, erect man with close cropped hair and military bearing. He flashed a mocking glance at Gail.

"That's Goebel," whispered Martha. Gail studied the man carefully.

Finally, Goebel went below and excusing himself, Gail followed. The German walked swiftly to his cabin with the

GEORGE S. SCHUYLER

Negro in pursuit. He had scarcely entered and fastened the door behind him when Gail knocked on the door.

"Who iss dot?" came a growl from behind the door.

"The steward, sir!" answered Gail, taking out his small automatic.

Grumblingly the German opened the door. Gail pushed his way in and thrust the muzzle of his pistol into the man's stomach.

"Shut up!" hissed Gail. "One peep of you and I'll plug you." The German noted from his tone and expression that the Negro meant what he said. "Put up your hands!" Goebel reached for the ceiling.

Gail quickly searched his pockets. He emitted a chuckle of triumph as he extracted the precious map from the inside pocket of the German's coat and transferred it to his own pocket.

"Sorry to disturb you, Herr Goebel," said Gail with mock politeness, still keeping the German covered, "but I had to get back that map. I wouldn't advise you to say anything about this because I would then have to tell the captain how you ransacked my cabin last night. I'd hate to see you put in the brig."

"It iss mine!" growled Goebel. "Johnny Kpolleh stole it from me. I will get you for dis, you black schwinhunde. I vill get you for dis!"

"Not while my eyes are open, Dutchy," laughed Gail, stepping out of the cabin and slamming the door behind him.

A great load lifted from his mind, Gail retraced his steps to the sunny deck. Martha was there standing at the rail. She turned and scanned his face anxiously as he took his place beside her. He patted the pocket of his coat where the precious map reposed.

"I'm so glad, Gail," she murmured earnestly. "I was fearfully worried."

"Well, so was I," he admitted, "but I've got to watch that fellow Goebel hereafter. He's not the kind that will take it lying down."

"I know it," she admitted. "I can see it in his face. . . Oh! Here he comes with the Captain!"

Faced red with rage, the German strode up to the couple, the plump Captain of the *Western Hemisphere* with him.

"Dot iss him!" he roared to the Captain and pointing with shaking finger at Gail. "I demand dot he be arrested. He robbed me just five minutes ago. Arrest him! Search him! He hass got my map!"

"I'm sorry, Mr. Reddick," said the Captain, apologetically, "but I'll have to ask you to come to my cabin at once."

III

Gail Proves Goebel Stole Map; Summoned By Monrovia's Mayor

N ow, Mr. Reddick," said the plump captain when they were all assembled in his cabin. "Mr. Goebel has made a very serious charge against you. He says that you entered his cabin with a drawn revolver and robbed him of a valuable map just a few moments ago. Is that true?"

"Yess, it iss true!" cried the excited German, glaring hatefully at the tall Negro. "He knows it iss true. I demand dot he be searched!"

Gail smiled indulgently. Seating himself, he pulled out his cigarette case, offered one to the captain, Herr Goebel and Miss Crockett, and then extracting one himself, retracted the case to his pocket. It was all done with irritating calm.

"Herr Goebel is quite correct," admitted Gail nonchalantly. "I did enter his cabin with a drawn revolver—pistol to be correct, and forced him to hand over to me a very valuable map. I have it in my pocket at the present moment."

"I'm very sorry, Mr. Reddick," said the Captain, flushing to a ruddier hue, "but under the circumstances, there is nothing for me to do but to ask you to return the property and to have you placed in confinement until we reach Monrovia. Robbery on the high seas is a very serious offense, as you are well aware."

"First," said Gail, calmly blowing a column of smoke from his lips, "I think it might be well to summon the purser. I want him to tell you what I reported to him last night."

The captain telephoned for the purser and in a few moments the lanky Englishman stepped into the cabin.

"Yes," the purser replied to the captain's questioning. "Mr. Reddick reported last night that his cabin had been robbed of a valuable document. He asked me to be on the lookout in case anyone sought to deposit it in my office. He said it was about the size of a cigar box cover."

"You see, Captain," interrupted Gail, "that it is Herr Goebel and not I that is guilty of robbery, I merely took back what belonged to me, if you will call the cabin steward he will tell you that I also reported the robbery to him. But in case there is any doubt in your mind, I ask you to look at the map itself." He pulled the map out of his pocket, unwrapped it and handed it to the captain, "You will notice, Captain, that my name appears in the upper right hand corner of the map."

The captain took the map, looked at it curiously, noting the name in the designated place. He handed it back to Gail.

"Well, Herr Goebel," he remarked dryly, "it seems to be Mr. Reddick's property, and I'll ask you to excuse yourself. I don't like your kind on the *Western Hemisphere*."

"It iss a lie!" sputtered the German. "Dot map iss mine, I tell you."

"You'd better go, sir," commanded the captain firmly, glancing at the door. Discomfited, the German went out, muttering imprecations.

Accepting the captain's apologies, Gail and Martha went back to the deck.

"Is it really his map?" she whispered when they were at last alone.

"Sure," chuckled Gail, "I think I recognize him now as one of the white men who attached Johnny Kpolleh that night in Harlem. He's doubtlessly the fellow that Johnny stole the map from."

"But how did your name get on it?" she asked wonderingly.

"I wrote it on there soon after I got it," he replied, "and I'm glad I did now. That was a narrow escape."

"Gee," said Martha, in admiration, "you think of everything."

THE REMAINDER OF THE VOYAGE was pleasantly uneventful, Gail kept his eye on Goebel and he knew that the irate German was always watching him. There were dreamy nights on the tropic sea when he and Martha sat side by side in their deck chairs listening to the music in the salons and coming to know each other much more intimately. They talked of Africa, the natives, the missionaries and a hundred other subjects, but always their conversation returned to the golden gods of Winyah.

Gail confessed to himself in the privacy of his cabin that he had never met a girl quite like Martha Crockett. There had been other comely maids in his life, but none so sensible, so encouraging, so sympathetic, and he hoped that she returned to his growing affection and esteem.

"This is a dangerous mission," he told her the last night out before they reached Monrovia, "but I feel that I am going to succeed. This fellow Goebel is likely to try something when we get to Liberia, but I think I'm a little smarter than he is."

"Oh, I'm sure you are, Gail," she breathed, "but you must be careful. He looks like a man who will stop at nothing to gain his ends, I sometimes feel afraid for you."

"Do you?" he asked. "Do you really feel that way about me, Martha. I wish I could believe it, because I've grown very fond of you during this wonderful trip. It has been the happiest period of my life. There are only two things I need now to make me the happiest man in the world.

"And what are they?" she asked innocently, dropping her gaze to the gleaming white deck.

"The golden gods of Winyah. . . and you," he whispered. "If I am successful, Martha, will you. . . will you, er, marry me?"

"Why, Gail!" she exclaimed in confusion. "I didn't know you felt that way. I—I. . ."

"Will you?" he persisted, leaning over her. "I want you so much. It would be a fitting climax to the success of my quest. Will you?"

He gazed into her eyes pleading, allowing his hand to close over hers.

"Yes, Gail," she murmured softly. His hand stole around her and their lips met.

ALL THE NEXT MORNING THE *Western Hemisphere* swam smoothly through the calm blue waters along the Liberian shore. In the distance could be seen the verdure-fringed beach topped by nodding palms and cocoanut trees, with here and there a little fishing skiff bouncing over the slight swells. A few white wisps of cloud hung in the azure sky. Porpoises skipped and frolicked alongside the steamer. Passengers in tropical white hung over the rail conversing animatedly and watching the approaching headland, Cape Measurado. Finally they were able to discern the white houses of Monrovia with their rusty red roofs and long sandbar that skirted the little shallow harbor.

At noon the *Western Hemisphere* hove to in the shadow of Cape Measurado and the great anchor crashed down into the depths. Martha and Gail stood at the rail watching the long Kru boats put out from shore and, skirting the lone sandbar, approach the steamer, the banks of oars wielded by the glistening black Kru men flashing rhythmically.

At last the little Liberian revenue cutter with its soiled flag fluttering lazily, came alongside and a pompous official ran up the ladder puffing and blowing at the unaccustomed exertion.

The five passengers debarking at Monrovia went into the forward salon to have their passports examined and answer the necessary questions. Gail did not fail to note that the customs official greeted Goebel familiarly. A few moments later he noticed the two in earnest conversation. The bespectacled customs official glanced at Gail rather sharply.

"I don't like the looks of that fellow," Gail whispered to Martha. "I think there's something in the wind."

"Do be careful," she whispered.

In a few minutes the mail and baggage were aboard the revenue cutter and the five passengers and the customs officials took seats. A signal from the helmsman and the ten black oarsmen bent their backs, the oars flashed and the long boat pulled away from the steamer toward the distant shore.

The sea that had seemed so calm when they were aboard the steamer, seemed uncommonly rough now. The narrow Kru boat bobbed up and down. The villainous looking helmsman shouted his orders and bent to the tiller. The black oarsmen chanted as they bowed their backs and sent the rakish craft skimming toward the narrow channel in the sandbar.

An hour later the boat pulled up alongside the little dock and the passengers debarked to find themselves the center of a chattering crowd of grinning natives, grave black officials in spotlessly white tropical suits and a handful of white traders and missionaries.

A small brown man with a large brown helmet and pince-nez that kept slipping them from his oily nose, detached himself from the crowd and stepped up to Herr Goebel.

"How are you, Mayor Sanders?" the German greeted him.

"Very good, Herr Goebel," replied the other, extending his hand. "It is good to see you back again. Did you have a pleasant voyage?"

"Well," said Goebel, grimacing and shooting a hateful glance at Gail, "I'll tell you later, Mr. Sanders."

The two men walked off conversing in undertones. The pompous black customs official joined them.

Gail watched them, frowning thoughtfully. He felt there was something in the wind but he didn't know what. Nor did he have time to speculate on it, for just then a kindly looking portly black man in tropical suit and white helmet approached him and Martha.

"Miss Crockett, I believe?" he said, tipping his helmet slightly. "I am Reverend Matney. I came all of the way down from the Voni Jessu mission to meet you." They shook hands. Martha introduced Gail.

"Come along with us to the mission house here, Mr. Reddick," said the missionary. "You know there are no hotels here, except one kept by an old German and I would not advise you to stay there. You've come to a rather primitive place but it's a coming country. Mr. Reddick, a coming country."

Gail glanced around him somewhat disappointedly. He confessed to himself that he had expected Monrovia to look less down at the heels, less nondescript, less trashy. But after all, this was Africa, and one must be prepared for the unexpected.

After the minute inspection of their baggage, they trudged through the gloomy, smelly warehouse, past gangs of sweaty, naked native workers and lolling black officials to an aged Ford sedan. Two husky black fellows loaded on their trunks and suitcases. When all was ready, Gail and Martha got in alongside Rev. Matney, and with the two natives hanging on the running board, the Ford wheezed up the rocky street to the mission house, a few blocks away.

It was a solid enough structure with broad screened verandas set in a grove of banana plants, paw-paw and mango trees with a ragged white picket fence surrounding it. Mission servants barefooted but dressed in khaki shirt and shorts, ran out to meet the new arrivals.

As Gail started to enter the building a barefoot black policeman, important in khaki shorts and brass buttoned khaki coat and cap, came running down the rocky, weed-grown street.

"Missah Reddick!" he called, "Missah Reddick!"

"What is it?" asked Gail, pausing apprehensively.

"De Mayah, Missah Sanders, "he say he want see you small time. You come with me."

Gail glanced significantly at Martha and then at the puzzled Rev. Matney.

"Alright," he said turning to follow the policeman, "I'll see what he wants."

IV

INTERCEPTION BY U.S. CONSUL SAVES GAIL FROM CONSPIRACY

The barefoot black policeman padded on ahead and Gail followed. He wondered what this summons, so soon after his arrival, could mean. Was Goebel up to some trick? After all, the white man had the advantage over him. He was a trader here, acquainted with the Liberian officials, knew the country intimately, while Gail was a total stranger.

They approached a two-story building with verandas up and down. On the lower veranda a number of natives and chiefs in picturesque flowing gowns lolled, conversing in low tones. The policeman went up the steps, entered the building and climbed a flight of rickety stairs to an office at one end of the upper veranda. He knocked respectfully on the closed door. A voice within commanded, "Enter!"

"Massa, heah be mans," said the policeman, throwing open the door and saluting an official seated behind a flat top desk. The officer stepped aside and Gail entered.

"Mister Reddick, I presume," said the official, a plump brown man wearing a silver-rimmed spectacles. His voice was soft and purring, Gail noted hurriedly that the man had a pair of keen, penetrating eyes and was evidently someone of importance.

"Yes, I'm Reddick," Gail replied.

"I am so happy to meet you, Mister Reddick," said the man, suavely. "We are always delighted to meet one of our cousins from American. I have been to America myself. As a matter of fact, I am a graduate of Howard University. Wonderful country, American. I am hoping to make a visit there next year. Oh, pardon me, won't you sit down? Boy! Bring a chair."

A flunky, barefoot man, black and grinning, appeared from nowhere and pulled a chair up close to the desk.

"Sit down, Mister Reddick, sit down," continued the official. "I trust you had a pleasant trip down."

There was a suggestion of a sneer on his lips as he said this. It did not escape Gail's keen eyes.

"Quite pleasant, thanks," Gail answered. The man was eyeing him keenly, the slight sardonic smile still playing about his full lips. It reminded Gail of a lion toying with its prey. He promised himself to be on his guard. "Am I speaking to the mayor?" he asked.

"Oh, no," replied the other. "I'm terribly rude. I should have told you. I am Mister Daniels, the immigration officer. The mayor will be along shortly. He has probably been detailed." Gail felt the man was lying. Something was evidently in the wind.

"DID YOU WANT TO SEE me about something?" asked Gail, after several moments of silence had elapsed.

"Ah, yes, I had forgotten," said the officer, toying with a red fountain pen and making circles on a paper. "Just a few routine questions, Mister Reddick, just a few questions. Er, ah-h, do you plan to be with us long?"

"Perhaps," replied Gail guardedly, watching the man's face. "You see, I am interested in the native life and I'm hoping to see quite a bit of it. I shall probably be here two or three months. I would like to go into the Hinterland, if permissible, on a long trek, perhaps as far as the French Guinea border."

"Well, that's fine!" exclaimed Daniels, tapping on the desk with his fountain pen and smiling slightly. "A very interesting country you'll find there, Mister Reddick. Very interesting, indeed. Of course, it will be necessary for you to have a permit of residence, you know, and also a permit to enter the back country. I understand you have a rifle and an automatic pistol. Is that so?"

"Yes, I thought it well to bring them along," replied Gail.

"A very wise provision, Mister Reddick, a very wise provision," said the other, "but you will have to have a permit to carry them. The government has to be careful about arms going into the Hinterland. In the past some unscrupulous foreigners have sold arms to rebellious natives." The man gazed at Gail challengingly.

"I'll be very glad to comply with all of the necessary regulations," said Gail. "How do I go about getting these permits?"

GEORGE S. SCHUYLER

"I will issue you your permit of residence," said Daniels, "but you will have to get your travel permit from the Interior Department and your firearms permit from the War Department. That can be easily taken care of. The permit of residence will be five dollars. The other permits I shall arrange for you. I always like to favor our colored visitors from the States."

Gail thanked him. Daniels called a clerk to make out the permit. Reddick paid over the necessary fee. He felt much easier. Things seemed to be moving along smoothly enough.

"Is that all?" he asked finally, gazing squarely at the half-smiling official, and rising to go.

"Well, not exactly," said the other, waving him back to his chair. "Mayor Sanders will be wanting to talk to you. A fine fellow, Mayor Sanders. He has also been to America. Ah, here he is now."

Gail turned to face the mayor as he entered, smiling and daubing his perspiring brow with a large blue bandana handkerchief.

The small brown man sat down, took off his pince-nez, wiped his gleaming face, polished his glasses, replaced them, nodding the while to Gail and the immigration officer. He seemed to be playing for time. Gail watched him closely through half-closed eyelids.

Fully three minutes elapsed. Then there came a knock on the closed door. "Enter!" commanded Daniels. The policeman stuck his head in the door and saluted respectfully.

"White man's come," he announced, to no one in particular.

"Alright," said Mayor Sanders, straightening up. "Show him in!"

The police officer stepped away and Herr Goebel entered. Gail's eyes narrowed. Swiftly he studied the faces of the three men. The mayor was stolid. Daniels was smiling slightly. Goebel's face was flushed.

"Ah, Herr Goebel," said the mayor, bobbing up and greeting the German as though he had not seen him in ages, "it is a great pleasure. Won't you sit down? Boy! A chair for Herr Goebel!"

Daniels rose and shook hands with the trader. Gail kept his seat. The German eyed him savagely. After an exchange of pleasantries that Gail thought somewhat forced, the mayor cleared his throat, removed his pince-nez again and addressed Gail.

"I AM TERRIBLY SORRY, MISTER Reddick," he said soothingly, "but Herr Goebel, an old friend of mine, by the way, tells us that you are here to stir up the natives; that you are a member of the Universal Negro Improvement Association, Marcus Garvey's organization. If that is true, Mister Reddick, and I hope it is not, we shall have to incarcerate you until the next boat arrives and deport you. We do not permit members of that organization in the country. It is so written in our Constitution."

"Why, that's absurd," cried Gail, somewhat surprised. "Where did Goebel get that ridiculous notion?"

"It iss true," accused the German, scowling at Gail, "I with mine own eyes, saw him in der Garfey headquarters in New York. He iss come to Liberia to stir up revolution, I tell you. He hass the papers on him. Search him! I warn you as a friend uff Liberia."

The mayor and the immigration officers glanced inquiringly at Gail. Goebel smiled triumphantly. Gail saw through the trick now. He had felt there was something in the wind. He cursed himself for not leaving the precious map behind at the mission.

"I am quite sure, Mister Reddick," said Daniels suavely, toying with his fountain pen, "that Herr Goebel is mistaken. However, this is a very serious charge which we cannot ignore. You understand our position of course?"

"Yes, Mister Reddick," added the mayor, adjusting his pince-nez, "this is a very serious charge."

"It's a damnable lie," shouted Gail, his anger rising.

"It iss the truth," countered Goebel. "He has the papers. Search him!"

"Well, we can settle that very simply," said the mayor briskly. "There were no such papers in Mister Reddick's baggage, so if he has any, they must be on his person." He turned and beamed upon Gail, and suggested, "You will not mind being searched, will you, Mister Reddick? We, too, believe this charge is ridiculous, but our laws are very strict and we must take no chances."

GAIL THOUGHT SWIFTLY. WHAT COULD he do? He was absolutely in their power. If they searched him, they would surely find the leopard skin map. Then his mission would be ended. It would be impossible to find the sacred city of Winyah without that map. Although it seemed to be useless, he decided to play for time. He took out his cigarette case, offered each of the tree men a cigarette, which they accepted, and took one himself. They all smoked quietly, watching each other.

"Gentlemen," said Gail finally, "what's the game? You know very well that I have nothing to do with that ridiculous U.N.I.A. Goebel knows it too. This white man cares nothing about your or Liberia. He's playing a game of his own. Don't let him take you in."

"Tut! Tut!" exclaimed the mayor, pursing his lips. "Be calm, Mr. Reddick. It will do you no good to pretend. Either you are a Garvey agent or you are not, Herr Goebel says you carry papers. We wish to disprove his charge by submitting you to search. Why do you object?"

"The charge is ridiculous," snapped Gail. "I refuse to be humiliated in this manner." He rose from his chair. The others sat quietly watching him. Mayor Sanders stolidly, Daniels smilingly, the white man anxiously. "Good afternoon, gentlemen."

Gail strode to the door and flung it open, then stepped back in surprise. In front of the open door stood two tall, barefoot, black soldiers with bayoneted rifles pointed menacingly at him.

Goebel chuckled. The mayor beamed. Daniels smiled broadly. Gail's heart sank. He gave a gesture of defeat and returned to his chair.

"I observe that you are a man of rare judgement," purred the mayor, removing his pince-nez again and polishing them vigorously. "Will you now submit to search without more ado?"

THERE WAS A COMMOTION OUTSIDE the door. There came the sound of voices followed by a loud knock.

"Enter!" growled Daniels, frowning for the first time. The door opened wide and a tall, slender, fine-looking mulatto in faultless white entered the room. The four men rose.

"What does this mean?" shouted the mayor, shrilly.

"It means, gentlemen," said the newcomer, "that I demand the immediate release of this man in the name of the United States of America. You have no right to hold him. I am here to protect him and I intend to do so. You know what the consequences will be if he is molested in anyway."

"Mein Gott!" gasped Goebel. "Der American Consul."

"Exactly, Mister Goebel," snapped the Consul. "Come with me, Mister Reddick. Your friends told me where you were."

"But you can't do this," cried Sanders, blustering up. "This is not the United States; this is Liberia."

"Oh, can't I?" sneered the other. "Well, take a look at that." He held out a piece of paper with official letterhead. It was an order from the President.

Mayor Sanders slumped into his chair, beaten.

"You have acted a little too hastily, Mister Thompson," said Daniels smiling sweetly. "We were not holding Mister Reddick. There was no need to go to the President on such a routine matter as an interrogation of a newly-arrived alien. The gentleman is quite at liberty to go."

"Very well, then," snapped the young consul. "Come, Reddick. I want to talk to you."

He turned on his heel and Reddick follow him admiringly out of the office, nodding victoriously to the three discomfited men.

"How did you get wind of it?" asked Gail, as he and the young consul strode up the dusty street to the American Consulate.

"Rev. Matney and that pretty girl that arrived today drove over to my place a while ago and warned me. I was lucky enough to find the President in his office. He knew there'd be trouble if anything happened to you, so he acted at once. Of course, he's personally a pretty decent chap, but there are a lot of rascals around him and he has to play ball with them."

Gail liked William Thompson. He was a fellow after his own heart. Over a whiskey and soda at the Consulate he told him of his mission. The consul grew grave.

"Give it up and leave on the next boat," he said earnestly, "or you'll never leave here alive."

V

DESIGNING AFRICAN FORM ANOTHER PLOT TO GET MAP FROM GAIL

Thanks ever so much, Mr. Thompson," said Gail, smiling at the American consul. "I know it's dangerous but I like danger. This is the adventure of a lifetime and I'm going to see it through. Of course I'm unfamiliar with the country, as you say, but I'll get by."

"You don't understand, Reddick," continued the consul, seriously. "These people will stop at nothing to get that map or to prevent you from completing your mission. I've been here five years and I know. Not only will you have the Liberians to contend with but the natives as well. It is very dangerous to fool with the natives' religion, especially with their gods. You'll never get away with it. And once you get deep into this thing, I can't help you."

"Nevertheless," said Gail, obstinately, "I'm going through with it."

"Very well, then," replied the consul, decisively, "that let's me out. Don't say I didn't warn you."

"Okeh, old man," said Gail, rising to go. "Thanks so much, I know your heart's in the right place but I'm going through with it. I've never failed yet in anything I undertook, and I won't fail this time."

"Well, I sure admire your courage," said Thompson, rising and extending his hand. "I'll do wat I can to help you without, of course, laying myself liable."

The two young men shook hands and turning on his heel, Gail put on his helmet and strode out of the consulate.

It was late in the afternoon the sun, a disc of burnished gold, hung poised over the western horizon. It was much cooler now and a slight breeze from the sea was swaying the pawpaw, banana, and mango trees. As he walked along the rocky street, bordered by the picturesque, weather-beaten ramshackle Monrovian villas with their rusty roofs of corrugated iron, he paused here and there to curiously watch a group of strangely clad natives jabbering together around a little fire or to smile at the antics of a family of fat goats fumbling up and down the verandah of a house.

Africa! The home of his forefathers! He breathed in a lungful of the pleasantly scented air, and pausing to go wipe the perspiration engendered by the unaccustomed humidity, he lit a cigarette and puffed hungrily upon it.

Yes, it was good to be in Africa! Somehow or other, one felt at rest and at peace here in the black man's country where black men ruled free from the pressure of arrogant and prejudiced whites. Overhead a cloudless blue sky reflected the golden luminance of the sinking sun. Out on the placid sea which stretched from his feet to the distant horizon where blue met blue, a lone fishing boat, its mutton chop sail bellied out with the evening breeze, slowly approached the entrance to the sandbar.

Africa! It was so quiet. Scarcely a sound. And so verdant! Green everywhere: green trees, green bushes, green grass! Green unrelieved save by the pale red dust of the road, the dull brown and dirty white of the houses, and the pal purple bowl of the sky above. No wonder Africa got into the blood and hearts of all who visited it, fascinating them, captivating them as a voluptuous mistress holds her lover.

As he approached the solidly build, whitewashed mission house, he could not help but notice its contrast with the houses he had passed on the way over from the consulate. Here was order, cleanliness, and plan. After all, he thought to himself, perhaps the missionaries were some good. At least they get an excellent example to the Africans, civilized and otherwise.

Martha, considerably freshened up and wearing a pale green flowing frock that set off her brown beauty most attractively, rose hurriedly from the wicker rocker in which she had been seated and rushed to meet him. She was obviously relieved.

"Oh, Gail!" she cried, touching his arm lightly in that possessive but shy manner of those in love, "I've been so worried. Rev. Matney has been telling me the most terrible and unbelievable things about these people. Oh, I'm so afraid for you! It was his idea to go to the American consul. He suspected those dreadful people were up to something."

"Now calm down," he said gently, smiling and drawing her back to her chair. "Everything's alright. There's nothing to fear."

"Then they didn't get it?" she asked. "Mr. Thompson arrived in time?"

"No, they didn't get it," he replied, "but they almost did. If it hadn't been for Thompson's timely arrival, I would have been done for."

"Oh!" she gasped, her concern reflected in her large black eyes.

"I love you when you look like that," he breathed, leaning close to her. "You are gorgeous."

"Oh, Gail," she snapped in mock irritation, "can't you be serious for a single minute?"

"I am serious," he grinned: "seriously in love with you!"

"Oh, darling," she murmured, "I don't think I could get along without seeing you now. . . And I swore that I wouldn't fall in love until I was thirty." She glanced up at him coyly with laughing eyes.

Quickly he leaned over and kissed her firmly upon her lips. She clung to him a moment, a few seconds of blissful ecstasy and then hastily pushed him away.

"Not here, Gail," she warned, gasping, "Rev. Matney would be horrified. And what would the servants think if they saw us?"

"As if I cared," he replied, grinning broadly.

A burly, barefooted black garbed in white shirt and shorts, opened the squeaking screen door and came onto the verandah. He halted respectfully before Gail.

"Massah, ba' ready!" he announced, grinning wider and exposing two rows of flawless white teeth.

"What's that?" asked Gail, sharply, puzzled.

"Ba' ready," repeated the "boy."

Gail and Martha glanced at each other, then burst into ringing laughter. The native stood irresolutely before them, marveling at their mirth. Just then, Rev. Matney came out and saved the situation.

"This is Sancee," he said, indicating the tall youth, "A very, very good boy. . . Sancee, this is Mister Reddick and Miss Crockett." This "boy" bowed low. "He is telling you," continued the missionary, "that your bath is all ready. You'll come to understand these people's English a lot better as time goes on. Sancee speaks very plainly compared to some you will meet in this country."

Gail followed Sancee into the mission house, through a long airy whitewashed corridor to the room assigned to him. It was a plain enough room. In the center between two large screened windows was a large white iron bed draped with mosquito netting. In one corner, was a white iron washstand, basin and pitcher.

In another corner was piled Gail's trunks and suitcases. On the oiled wooden floor was a large tin tub of warm water with a bath towel hung on the back of a chair nearby and a straw mat in front of the tub. On a small wooden library table in another corner was a kerosene lamp. Gail began to strip off his clothes.

DARKNESS CAME WITH THE DRAMATIC suddenness of the tropics. The acetylene lamps cast their pale, unearthly glow over the verandah. At one end was the white table all set to receive the food and the diners. Around it moved Sancee and his diminutive assistant, Yama, arranging the silver and the dishes. At the other end of the verandah sat Rev. Matney, Martha, Gail and Consul Thompson, conversing.

Outside giant crickets were chirping, making the night alive with sound. Little lizards crawled here and there over the outer surface of the screening. From the native quarter of the town came the first preliminary rumbles of the drums. The moon was rising slowly, a luminous plate moving up over the dark fringe of trees and housetops. Soon its light would bathe the earth in a ghostly glow, making it almost as light as day.

"Oh, how beautiful is it here," Martha exclaimed.

"Yes," Rev. Matney agreed slowly, "Africa is beautiful, and Liberia is perhaps the most beautiful part of it. But Africa is also deadly. It is enervating and its steady attrition wears down the bravest resolutions, breaks the strongest wills, eventually crushes all who oppose its ways."

"You seem pessimistic, Matney," said Thompson, a slightly incredulous smile on his handsome yellow countenance. "I don't find it all that bad, and I've been here five years."

"And I have been here twenty years," said the missionary, quietly. "I think you, Africa finally gets you. I've seen strong, ambitious men come out here determined to do great things, and what happened to them? Gradually they began to slow down, to be satisfied with little, to let well enough alone. They couldn't stand against the vast inertia of this continent: the heat, the ages-old customs so different from those of Europe and America. Unless they went home occasionally, they inevitably succumbed to the blandishments of old Africa. I know. I've seen it happen too often. That's why the white official out here insists on going back home ever so often. Yes, it takes a strong man to stand out against Africa."

There was silence. Rev. Matney spoke with authority. He was one of the oldest foreign residents of Liberia and perhaps the most respected of the missionaries.

"Chopready!" announced Sancee, standing beside the table with its burden of gleaming cutlery and chins.

The four Americans filed down the verandah to take their places at the table. Yama industriously pumped a Flit gun to rid the verandah of the few insects that had in some manner gotten inside the screen.

"It's practically impossible to keep them all out," said Rev. Matney, apologetically. They all sat down.

Out in the kitchen, separated from the mission house proper by a narrow screened passageway, the fat Bassa cook was perspiring over the range, dishing up the savory food. He did not see the form lurking just outside the kitchen door. He filled the last of the platters and tureens and ran hurriedly to the woodpile to get two or three more sticks of the tough wood for his fire.

Like a flash the skulking form beside the door dashed inside. It was a small, evil-looking black man, dressed only in a "G" string, his black skin gleaming in the in the fitful yellow light from the large kerosene lamp overhead.

Glancing over his shoulder at the departing cook, he held his gnarled black hand over the dishes of food and sprinkled over them a fine gray dust. Then he vanished out of the kitchen door into the enveloping darkness. A few seconds later, the Bassa cook came panting up the pathway, a load of sticks in his arm.

He dropped the wood with a loud crash next to the stove and sticking his head out of the inner kitchen door, he called to the "boys" to come after the dinner. Sancee and Yama padded in with their trays and took the food to the dining table.

The diners looked at it hungrily as the aroma of chicken stewed in palm butter and rice and steaming eddoes assailed their nostrils.

Rev. Matney slowly said the grace while the others waited with bowed heads and watering mouths. At last he finished. One by one he served the four plates.

"Your first taste of African cooking," he said, smiling at Martha and Gail. "I hope you like it."

"I'm sure I will," said Gail, "by the way it smells. Watch me go after it." He impaled a portion of tender chicken on his fork and carried it toward his mouth.

VI

Gail Starts Jaunt Into Wilderness On Quest For Treasure

D on't eat it! Put it down!" The command came, sharp and insistent from the outer darkness. Gail lowered his fork. Rev. Matney looked startled and half rose from his chair. Young Thompson frowned. Martha dropped her fork in fright and it clattered noisily on her plate.

A short, slender, fine-looking brown man, dressed in faultless tropicals bounded up on the verandah and came into the circle of light. He removed his white helmet with a sweep and exposed two rows of splendid white teeth in an engaging smile.

"Hello, Mr. Ferguson!" said Rev. Matney, clearly puzzled by the man's action. "What's eating you tonight, old man?"

"Merely keeping a watch over the just," the newcomer declared.

"Oh, Jim," observed the missionary, "this is our new teacher, Miss Martha Crockett. She just got in from the States today. Miss Crockett, this is Jim Ferguson, our leading merchant here. A good politician, too, only he never seems to get elected to office. Rev. Matney paused to grin. The others smiled cordially. "And Jim, this is Mr. Gail Reddick, another American. Mr. Reddick, this is my good friend, Jim Ferguson. I think probably he can help you."

"I'm very glad to meet you both," said the merchant, suddenly growing grave, "but I believe I have already helped Mr. Reddick, to say nothing of the rest of you. I came just in time." He mopped his gleaming brow with a large white handkerchief.

"What do you mean, Ferguson?" asked the missionary, frowning, curious.

"I mean that I just saved the whole lot of you from being poisoned," replied the merchant, pausing dramatically.

"Is that why you yelled like a Comanche?" asked Thompson.

"Precisely, Consul," Ferguson answered. "You know I find out everything that's going on around this town. Oh, my friends, bring me all of the news and gossip, as well as all of the intrigue. I heard all about your experience this afternoon, Mr. Reddick. And more important than that I learned from one of my 'boys' who heard it first hand, that you were all to be poisoned in order that Mr. Reddick could be gotten out of the way. I immediately hurried over here and I arrived just in time."

The others looked at each other incredulously, then at the steaming victuals before them, and then at the merchant who stood solemnly regarding them.

"Oh, it's true," he said, noting a few expressions of doubt. "I'll prove it to you."

He looked around and noticing Rev. Matney's little tan dog, he called him to the table. Taking the plate of chicken from in front of Gail, he sat it down in front of the canine. The dog sniffed at it hungrily and began to eat. Those seated around the table watched the pet, fascinated.

"But Ferguson," objected Rev. Matney, "this is ridiculous. I would trust my cook with my life and no one else has been near this food except Sancee and Yama. And of course," he paused and shot a sharp glance at the two scared servants, "they would have nothing to do with anything like that."

"No," answered the merchant, "and I'm not accusing any of your servants, Rev. Matney. But you just wait, and see, now. . ."

He was interrupted. The little Gola dog suddenly sat back on its hind legs and then fell over on its side in convulsions. Its mouth foamed and its legs kicked more and more feebly. In a few moments its movements ceased and its eyes stared vacantly.

The horrified company sat tight-lipped and grave.

"Boy!" yelled Mr. Ferguson, "Take him away, quick!" Then turning to the silent company about the table, he said: "I would suggest, Rev. Matney, that you bring your guests and come over to my place. I left orders for dinner to be prepared, knowing that in all probability it would be needed. Will you come?"

"I think not, Ferguson," replied the missionary, soberly. "I haven't any appetite now."

"Neither have I," echoed Consul Thompson, pushing back from the table.

"Nor I," added Gail.

"Nor I," Martha almost whispered.

"Well, well," said the merchant, smiling, "I can understand how you feel. However, there are somethings I want to tell you, Mr. Reddick, and if you are wise you will follow my advice." Ferguson sat down in a nearby wicker rocker and the others left the table and joined him.

"What's the advice, Mr. Ferguson?" asked Gail.

"This:" replied the merchant. "In the first place you'd better abandon this proposed trip of yours and get out of the country as soon as possible. I'm telling you now as a friend. I was born in your country, although I have lived out here for more than twenty years and I am a Liberian citizen. I like Americans and I like you. So you know that I am telling you straight. Get out of here before they kill you. Evidently there is some reason for these people wanting to get you out of the way. I can't imagine what it is and I have no desire to pry into your business. But if you are wise you will go quick because you cannot do whatever you are setting out to do. The odds are too much against you. These people have their spies and allies everywhere, even in the remote parts of the jungle. Do you think for a minute that you can escape them by going into the hinterland? Not at all, my boy. Some way, sometime, somehow, they will get you, I have fought with them for a generation, and I know them."

"He's telling you right, Reddick," observed the young consul, gravely. "Don't be a fool. If you had an army with you it would be different, but you've only yourself. Under other circumstances, I'd be glad to go along with you, but the nature of your mission prevents me from doing so. It would mean by job."

"Yes," Rev. Matney agreed, "Ferguson is right. These rascals will get you before you reach Kakata."

Gail frowned. Then he looked over at Martha. He valued her judgement tremendously, even though in this case he knew she had far less knowledge of the conditions than either Thompson, Matney or Ferguson. And yet, a woman's intuition was often more important than the special knowledge of men.

"Well, Martha," he said slowly, "what do you say?"

A full moment elapsed before she replied. Then lifting her face she smiled serenely.

"I believe you can do it, Gail. If you still want to go, go on. I'll be waiting for you," she said.

"Well, gentlemen," Gail announced in a tone of finality, "that settles it. I'm going. I haven't anything to lose but my life, and I believe I can protect that."

"I'm sorry, Reddick," said Jim Ferguson. "It would be wiser for you to give up this quest, whatever it is, but since you won't I'll help you as much as I can." Thompson and Rev. Matney shook their heads in disapproval of Gail's decision.

"Help me how?" asked Gail, evincing interest.

"Well, in the first place," the merchant explained, "you'll have to get out of here early in the morning for the back country."

"Why?" asked Gail somewhat surprised.

"Well, you have your permit to enter the hinterland, so you'd better get away before this crowd gets to the President and persuades him to stop you," Ferguson explained. "Things move along slowly here, so they expect you to spend three or four days, maybe a week, getting your supplies together and assembling your carriers. You can take them by surprise by getting miles away before they even know you're gone."

"But how can he get supplies and assemble carriers in time to get off early in the morning?" asked Thompson. "The stores don't open until seven or eight."

"I'll take care of that," said Ferguson. "You forget that I have a store, Thompson."

"But I was going as far as Voni Jessu with Rev. Matney and Miss Crockett," Gail objected.

"Alright, I'll get their supplies too," said Ferguson. "The point is that if you are going you must leave before daybreak in the morning. Now come with me down to my store and select your stuff. You had better come also, Rev. Matney, if you're going along with him. There's no time to lose. I know Sanders and I know Goebel. They won't easily give up the idea of stopping Mr. Reddick."

"Well, then we'd better be getting busy," observed Rev. Matney, rising. "It's eight o'clock now."

THE FIRST GRAY STREAKS OF dawn were coloring the dark eastern sky when Jim Ferguson's motor truck drew up in front of the Methodist mission. Ten or twelve almost naked carriers leaped down at a swift command from the merchant and hastened to the veranda, where the trunks, chop boxes, valises, and equipment of the party were piled. At the far end of the verandah stood Rev. Matney, Gail and Martha. Mr. Ferguson walked over to them and spoke in a low tone.

"Are you all ready?" he asked.

"All ready," the missionary answered. "Have you got enough carriers?"

"Yes, I think so," Ferguson replied. "Now who is going to be your steward. You need a trusted 'boy' to prepare your meals, you know."

"We're taking Sancee along," said Rev. Matney. "I'd trust him anywhere. But who have you got for a headman?"

"A fellow who has led several parties before," said Ferguson. "He knows all of the trails. Come on, get on the truck. Daylight will soon be here."

They walked down off the verandah. Jim Ferguson took the wheel. The three others squeezed on the wide front seat alongside of him.

The carriers piled on top of the baggage.

"Left Toe!" the merchant called over his shoulder.

A slender, very black man, dressed in a loin cloth, a long black shirt and a black cap came padding to the front of the truck. Ferguson flashed his electric torch in the man's face. The fellow grinned, displaying a row of yellow, discolored teeth. There was something sinister and cruel about his countenance that immediately arrested Gail's attention. Ferguson introduced them to the headman.

"I don't like his looks," whispered Gail to the merchant as the truck lurched over the road headed out of town.

"Oh I guess he's alright," said Ferguson. "He's an experienced headman and knows how to control these carriers. You'll need somebody like that."

"Well, just the same," said Gail, "I don't like his appearance."

They bowled along easily enough over the uneven road. By the time the sun was well up they had reached the Mount Barclay rubber plantation.

"So far so good," observed Rev. Matney, as they sped along. "We should be in Kakata by ten o'clock, maybe sooner."

VII

Gail Runs Into a Snag On Jaunt Into Jungle In Quest of Treasure

Skillfully Jim Ferguson piloted the truck over the rutty road, picking his way gingerly over the rotten plank bridges. Martha and Gail exclaimed at the beauty of the brilliant green African countryside. Here and there they passed a Liberian farmhouse, occasionally a heavily laden column of native carriers bringing rice into Monrovia.

Higher and higher they ascended into the low hills that rolled away like the green billows to the horizon. The dense undergrowth walled in the narrow red road. Gigantic cotton trees extended their friendly branches benevolently over the way, shielding the travelers from the strong ray of the sun. Here and there palm trees reared up lazily out of the rank growth. It was quiet, ever so quiet, and restful too. There was a somnolence about the countryside that invited drowsiness, a peacefulness that lured the traveler to pause and stay for a while. But the heavily laden truck lumbered on, lurching from side to side, shaking up its human cargo.

"Oh, it's beautiful isn't it?" breathed Martha.

"Yes very beautiful," all agreed, and then, in a whisper "but not as beautiful as you." He pressed her hand gently. She looked up at him and smiled.

"There is no more beautiful country in the world," observed Rev. Matney.

"And no richer country, either," aided Ferguson. "Anything will grow here. The soil is amazingly rich. There are diamonds and gold, too, and some have said that there is oil. All it would need is efficient government and intelligent exploitation."

"Yes," agreed the missionary, "with a hundred miles or so of good roads, the future of Liberia would be assured."

THE SUN ROSE HIGHER AND high and every minute it grew hotter. Finally Ferguson brought the truck to a stop near a clear gurgling brook and they all got off for a drink of pure cold water.

"Ordinarily it would be dangerous to drink like this," observed the merchant, "because many of these streams are contaminated, but I happen to know that this one is alright. I advise you, however, never to drink any water unless it is either filter or boiled. Otherwise you are sure to get malaria or yellow fever."

They drank deeply and then stood around while the carriers sated their thirst by making cups of large green leaves and dipping up the water. Gail noticed that Left Toe stayed near the truck and did not drink. He thought this was strange but said nothing about it.

They started again in a few minutes and were soon skirting the edge of the Firestone plantation. The straight rows of young rubber trees stretched in serried ranks to the horizon. Much of the jungle was cleared away. In the distance the high hills were a hazy blue. The higher they ascended the cooler and fresher became the air.

Suddenly the truck lurched to one side and bumped to a stop. With a curse, Ferguson jumped down followed by the others. The left hind wheel had come completely off. The merchant examined it.

"Somebody has been monkeying with this truck," he declared, frowning and scratching his head. "I swear it was alright when we started."

Rev. Matney looked ruefully at the damage. Suspiciously Gail glanced at the group of naked carriers standing apart talking to themselves and eyeing the broken wheel. His eye caught that of Left Toe. The sinister countenance of the head man wore a satisfied smile. Noting that he was being observed the man quickly became grave and concerned. Gail looked away quickly so as not to arouse the man's suspicious but he was convinced that the headman knew something about the accident. He made a mental note to watch the fellow closely thereafter.

"Well, there's nothing to be done," said Ferguson finally, "except take off the luggage and march. It will take two or three days to fix this. The nearest mechanic, in fact, the only one in the country, is at the shops on the plantation. I wouldn't be surprised if Goebel and his friends don't know something about this. You'll have to watch these 'boys' carefully, Reddick, there's a traitor among them."

"That's what I think," observed Gail quietly, cutting his eye again at Left Toe.

The luggage was unpacked. The carriers took down the traveling chairs and soon the party was proceeding on its way, the porters bearing the trunks and boxes on their heads, the carriers jogging along with the chair poles on their shoulders. Ferguson stayed behind with his broken truck.

The way was hot and dusty, the going much slower than on the truck. As the sun grew higher, the odor from the gleaming skins of the hammock bearers was almost suffocating. The only sound was the padding of the bare feet of the porters and the creak of the hammocks and chairs.

It was noon when they came to the end of the road. Before them was wide, shallow stream. They crossed in a dugout canoe which the porters poled along against the swift current. In a few minutes they arrived at the Kakata mission school.

The missionary, a tall, gray-haired bronzed white man, greeted them in a friendly manner. Rev. Matney introduced Martha and Gail to their host, a Rev. Chandler, who invited them to stay for the night.

The thatched, whitewashed native houses with their Spanish verandahs looked cool and inviting, but Gail remembered Ferguson's parting injunction: to put as much space as possible between them and Monrovia before nightfall.

"No, thanks," he declared decisively, "we must push on."

"But you can't reach Kanda's Town," objected Rev. Chandler, "before five o'clock and before you get settled it will be dark. It is not good to get into a town so late, especially when the chief is not expecting you. Come, stay with me and have a good supper. You'll feel more like traveling in the morning."

Rev. Matney agree with Gail that they should push on even though darkness might overtake them. After a light meal and a smoke, they continued on their way with Rev. Chandler's blessings ringing in their ears.

As they marched through Kakata, Gail observed a Liberian officer watching them closely. They were about to pass on when he hailed them from the verandah of his hut and walked leisurely out to the road. The caravan stopped.

"Where are you going?" the officer asked curtly.

"To Voni Jessu," Rev. Matney spoke up. "I am in charge of the mission there. I am Rev. Matney. This is my teacher, Miss Crockett."

"And who are you?" asked the officer, turning to Gail and eyeing him suspiciously.

"I am Gail Reddick."

"Have you got a pass to go into the hinterland?" questioned the officer. "No one may go back country without a pass." He paused with just a faint trace of a triumphant smile on his stern countenance, as though he expected Gail to answer in the negative.

Gail reached into his coat pocket and pulled out the traveling permit. The officer's face fell. He examined the paper closely as if he expected to find some flaw in it. Them imperiously he waved them on.

"Go ahead!" he said, grudgingly. Then turning to Left Toe, who stood to one side, he spoke rapidly to him in some native dialect. The headman answered in the same tongue. The officer turned and eyed Gail. Then he pivoted on his heel and returned to his easy chair on the verandah.

"That's Captain Miller, the Commandant here," Rev. Matney informed them. "A very hard fellow. The natives are in great fear of him, and with good reason."

"I don't like his looks," observed Martha. "He gave me the chills. Why do all of these people stare through you as if you had committed a crime?"

"Left Toe!" Gail called sharply, calling the headman to the side of his hammock. "What did he say?"

"No palavah nuttin,' massa," answered the man. Gail thought he read mockery in the fellow's eyes. He had a feeling in his bones that something was wrong.

THE SUN WAS LOW AND the cool of the evening had begun to descend when they emerged from the jungle-bordered trail and came to the low hill on which Kanda's Town sprawled. The brown thatched roofs of the gray circular mud huts was a welcome sight to travelers weary from the rocking of chairs and hammocks. Through the winding lanes they straggled, past open doorways in which men and women in their picturesque robes and cloths stood peering curiously, while little naked black children with big white eyes and gleaming teeth gazed timidly from a distance.

Left Toe led them to a square, palm thatched pavilion in the center of the town. They descended from the chairs and hammocks, while porters dropped the luggage about the Palaver Kitchen, as the pavilion is known in Africa.

Slowly the natives gathered around, remaining at a respectful distance. After a few minutes, the chief came, a tall, distinguished man with Mandingo leather slippers on his feet, a red fez on one side of his head, a sword in gay scabbard dangling at his side and a billowy blue-striped robe enveloping his stalwart frame.

A flunky brought the elaborately carved chair of the chief and the latter sat down in the corner of the Palaver Kitchen opposite the visitors.

Finally, Left Toe, acting as interpreter, extended the greetings and presents of the visitors, which the chief accepted with a dignified nod. Then he made a little speech of welcome which Left Toe translated into very bad English. The chief gave instructions to one of his officials and the ceremony was over, except for a few questions he asked about news from Monrovia.

In a short time the guest hut with its two rooms and wide verandah had been placed at their disposal, along with rice, chickens, and palm oil, and they were preparing for dinner.

The efficient Sancee did not keep them waiting long. Scarcely an hour had passed before they were sitting down to a toothsome concoction under the light from two big lanterns.

"I don't like this headman of ours," Gail said to Rev. Matney in a low tone as they enjoyed a cigar after dinner.

"I don't think much of him myself," agreed the missionary. "I've seen lots of his kind out here. Half civilized, cunning, unscrupulous, willing to do anything for whoever pays them, you have to watch them closely. However, it's the best we can do."

"I'll keep my eye on him," said Gail. "he talked a whole lot to that officer not to have been saying anything."

"Well Ferguson did the best he could on such a short notice, I guess," observed the missionary. "Be sure and fasten your windows tight. I've told Sancee to sleep outside Miss Crockett's door. We're in the hinterland now. Anything may happen. Or nothing may happen."

It was a moonless night. An encompassing blackness held the little town in its grip. Slowly human sounds subsided. The place became as still as a tomb. Out in the surrounding jungle that pressed like a great black wall against the little island of humanity, strange sounds arose at intervals. Twigs cracked. Leaves rustled. Crickets and frogs chirped and croaked, and finally they fell silent. Once the faint sounds of a struggle deep in the undergrowth were followed by an almost human cry.

Gail lay, thinking. The folds of his mosquito netting encircled him like a gigantic wedding veil. . . or a shroud. At his side was his rifle, loaded and unlocked.

Three more days now and they would be at Voni Jessu and then the great adventure would really begin. He felt the leopard skin map inside his pajama coat and smiled.

Suddenly he grew drowsy. He became conscious of a pleasant odor. It was like the aroma from a spice house. Pleasant. Titillating. Restful. Something told him to rise up and examine the source of the pleasant perfume, but he felt too comfortably drowsy. He fell off into a deep slumber.

A tremendous chorus of feathered creatures greeting the rising sun startled him from his slumber. Coming from all sides, it was almost deafening, and yet there was something exhilarating about it.

He stretched lazily and yawned. He rubbed his eyes. Then for the first time he noticed a huge gash in his mosquito netting. He knew it hadn't been there when he went to sleep. He sat bolt upright, wide awake now. Automatically his hand went to the front of his pajama coat. The leopard skin map was gone!

GEORGE S. SCHUYLER

VIII

GAIL PUSHES ON DESPITE THEFT OF MAP; VISITS AFRICAN PARADISE

G ail sprang up hastily and called for Sancee.

"Yassah, massa," the steward cried, appearing at the door wearing his perpetual grin.

"Sancee, did you see anyone come in here?" he asked. "I've lost something very valuable. Where is Left Toe?"

It suddenly occurred to Gail that the head man might know something about the lost map.

"I not know massa," replied the steward. "I sleep too much."

"So did I," murmured Gail, regretfully. "Find Left Toe."

"Yassah, massa," Sancee disappeared to find the headman.

Gail rose hurriedly, a frown furrowing his forehead. How could the map have been stolen? He had fastened the door of the hut and had closed the windows. Sancee had slept across the door. And yet the precious map was gone. Gail thoughtfully laced his leather boots and proceeded to perform his morning ablutions.

He was wiping his face and hands when Sancee appeared again at the door.

"Well," said Gail eagerly, "did you find him?"

"Nossuh, massa," replied the stewart gravely, "no find Left Toe."

"Just as I suspected," growled Gail, frowning and lighting a cigarette. "Now I am in for it."

He walked across to the other room where Rev. Matney had stayed. The missionary listened gravely while Gail related what had happened.

"I can see it all," he said. "That pleasant odor you smelled was a powerful narcotic drug the native witch doctors use. It undoubtedly caused you and Sancee to fall into a deep slumber which enabled Left Toe to get in and take the map."

"Well, what can we do?" asked Gail impatiently.

"Nothing. Nothing at all," said Rev. Matney, shaking his head solemnly. "That fellow is miles away by this time. It would be useless to try to catch up with him. You don't even know in which direction he went. I'm afraid you're out of luck, Mr. Reddick. I think you'd better give up your adventure. How can you hope to do anything without a map?"

"I didn't know," replied Gail, "but I'm not going to quit now. I've come too far."

Sancee came in a few minutes later and announced breakfast.

"What shall I do, Martha?" asked Gail, as they sat at the table. "I hate to give up now. I hate to have Goebel beat me, and I am sure that he has a whole lot to do with this."

"Well, Gail," she replied, looking across at him, "I hope you're not thinking of quitting. Can't you go on without the map?"

Her confidence in him was sufficient for Gail. Here was a girl after his own heart. He beamed upon her, and, reaching across the table touched her arm.

"No, you're right, Martha," he said firmly. "I'm not going to quit. There's just one chance in a thousand of succeeding now, but I'm going to take that chance."

"Sancee!" he called. "Get everything packed up. We leave right now. You hear?"

"Yassah, massa." The steward hurried out of the hut to rouse the carriers and porters.

"I admire your courage, Reddick," said Rev. Matney in admiration, "but I think you are rather foolhardy. The odd are too much against you. It was a foolish undertaking even when you had the map. Now success is almost out of the question. I've lived up country for years and even I do not know the trail to Winyah. You'd better give it up."

"No, I won't," said Gail decisively. "There's just a chance that my luck may stay with me. I'll get the best of that German yet."

"I believe you will, dear," said Martha quietly. "By all means, try." She smiled upon him and the smile strengthen him.

Twenty minutes later they were following the trail through the bush toward Billifani, the next big town.

GEORGE S. SCHUYLER

ON THE AFTERNOON OF THE fifth day after leaving Kanda's Town, the party climbed the steep bare hill to Voni Jessu. It was a typical native town of around seventy-five huts, neat, clean, orderly, sprawled out amidst a grove of giant cottonwood trees.

It seemed to Gail and Martha as if they were approaching home. Not that they had ever been there before, of course, but because they were approaching the Methodist mission, an oasis of civilization in the sea of primitive savagery.

A crowd of natives turned out to meet them. Dogs barked. Children, frightened by strangers but quite curious, ran before them, peering out from behind huts and trees. Goats scampered away, running neck and neck with chickens and guinea hens.

It was a beautiful place, Voni Jessu. On each side rode high verdure clad mountains, wreathed at their summits with fleecy white clouds. It was much cooler up here than down in the lowlands or on the coast. There was less humidity in the air. The climate was quite invigorating.

"Why, it's wonderful up here!" Martha exclaimed as they viewed the marvelous panorama. "I never dreamed it would be as beautiful as this. And those dear little children—they're wonderful, perfectly sweet. And such beautiful manners."

"Yes, they are little dears," agreed Rev. Matney, "and you'll be surprised to see how smart they are. All they need is education and the message of Jesus Christ. The greatest wealth in Liberia, my dear, is the children. That's the hope of the country."

They marched through the town, after pausing to pay their respects to Chief Yemasseh, a short, broad-shouldered Buzi man with small penetrating eyes, and proceeded to the mission on an elevation beyond the settlement.

The mission was simple enough.

A main Spanish style, glorified native house with three sides facing a large court. Nearby were the little huts where the school children stayed, and two or three larger huts where the teachers lived. In the meadow close at hand several sleepy-eyed cows were munching the grass.

Matilda Matney met them at the door. A buxom brown woman originally from Philadelphia, she seemed like a mother to the young people as she embraced them in turn.

"Oh, it's so seldom we see anyone except natives up this way," she declared. "I just get so lonesome for the sight of Americans, especially our own people! Come, right on in and wash up. I know you must be starved."

Both Martha and Gail were pleasant surprised at the accommodations. Each room was well floored and there were iron beds and washstands, and acetylene lamps on high stands. The windows and doors were securely screened. The place was faultlessly clean. It gave Gail a different impression of missionaries than he had previously entertained.

"Gee," he exclaimed, as Sancee laid out his clothing on the bed, "this is just like home!"

The blazing sun was sinking behind the dark emerald mountains when Gail, immaculate in his whites, came out on the veranda and threw himself luxuriously into a large wicker rocker. Very shortly Martha and Rev. and Mrs. Matney joined him. Conversation soon drifted around to the subject of the sacred city of Winyah.

"There is a great deal of mystery about it," Rev. Matney replied, in answer to Gail's questioning. "The natives refuse to discuss it. Afraid, I guess. I've tried to find out about it but without any luck. They just won't talk. I know it's up there somewhere, but even my most trusted boys will tell nothing."

"We decided years ago that it was dangerous to nose into these people's business," added Mrs. Matney, shaking her head solemnly. "Lots of foreigners have gotten into trouble prying into native affairs. Even the Liberians can't tell you anything Winyah."

"Yes," said Rev. Matney, "we know it's up there and all."

"Well, I'm going to find out for sure," said Gail with determination, glancing across at Martha. "Everything depends upon it."

Martha blushed beneath her smooth dark skin as she read the meaning in his eyes.

THEY HAD SCARCELY FINISHED THEIR dinner when darkness fell with that suddenness typical of the tropics, and Sancee and Yama lit the acetylene lamps. The night was oppressively quiet save for the chirping of crickets. A Stygian darkness enveloped the world outside the radius of pale blue light shed by the hissing lamps. It was so peaceful, and yet mysterious, uncanny.

Suddenly the drums began to sound across the way in the town. Separate, isolated throbs at first; then a steady rhythmic rumble. Torch lights bobbed in the distance, coming closer and closer.

"I guess that will be Yemasseh," observed Rev. Matney, "returning our visit."

"What sort of chap is he?" asked Gail, leaning forward.

"Very, very clever," the missionary answered slowly, "and not to be trusted. Like all of these chiefs, he holds his position at the will of the people in Monrovia, and they can depend upon him to do their bidding. Be careful, Reddick, be very careful in your dealings with him. Watch him every minute. He is no fool. And if he ever suspects your mission, you'll never get out of here alive. I know what I'm talking about. I've dealt with him for years. He hates missionaries, but he pretends to be our friends."

The sound of the drums grew closer. The torches came nearer. Soon the procession from the village entered the large courtyard, led by the squat chieftain. The jungle orchestra: three or four different kinds of drums, pipes, horns and harps, assembled in one corner of the court. Fifty or sixty natives formed a circle, the light from their torches forming weird shadows. A little naked black boy brought the chief's elaborately carved chair and sat it near the missionaries and their guests. Sancee, who knew the Buzi tongue, interpreted. The chief presented a brace of fat guinea hens, a goat, a kainji of rise and a gourd of palm wine. They gave him many presents in return.

The music started up again. In the yellow circle of light, dancer after dancer came forward, leaping fantastically in time with the throbbing drums. A dozen women and girls, led by a black woman of Amazonian proportions, and armed with gourds full of dried seeds and pebbles, sang weird, eerie native songs.

Then, of a sudden, the circle was cleared. The drums beat furiously. The harps strummed. The pipes and horns bleated and blared. The Americans leaned forward expectantly. Chief Yemasseh held up his arm and cried. The ranks parted and through the aisle of humanity came the most beautiful specimen of a black beauty Gail had ever seen. They all gasped in admiration.

"That's Kama," whispered Rev. Matney to Gail and Martha, "Yemasseh's youngest wife. She's only about fifteen."

"God, but she's beautiful," exclaimed Gail. Martha followed his eyes and sniffed jealously with the eternal alertness of the female for rivalry.

The girl was above average height, remarkably proportioned, with skin that shone like black glass, and firm breasts like chocolate avocadoes. A necklace of leopard's teeth circled her slender neck, their whiteness matching her snowy teeth. She was completely nude except for a brief striped cloth at her middle.

She jumped into the circle and danced like mad. One moment she was crouched low like a leopard stalking its prey. The next instant she was leaping high in the air, kicking her slender feet like a ballet dancer, or racing around the circle like a startled deer. It was a remarkable exhibition. When she finally stopped, recumbent in the middle of the open place, her smooth black skin glistening from the exertion, the American loudly applauded.

Rev. Matney sent Sancee into the mission house for leaf tobacco and stalks of it were distributed all around. To the girl Kama, whom he had watched with a mounting fascination, Gail tossed a large mirror and a long necklace of blue glass beads, much liked by the natives.

Long after the entertainment had ceased and the natives had departed, Gail and Rev. Matney sat on the veranda smoking and quietly discussing native beauty. Martha retired early with a very short "Goodnight" to Gail, evidently in a huff. She had not at all liked his open admiration of the beautiful native girl. She felt panicky when she remembered the way he had eyed Kama.

It was almost midnight when the two men decided to turn in. Gail was pleasantly weary from the exertions of the day. He undressed quickly. Then, conscious of a presence in his room, he switched on his electric torch and swung its beam around. His heart stopped still and he caught his breath. There, curled up on his bed, grinning invitingly, was Kama, the dancer, Chief Yemasseh's youngest wife!

IX

Chieftan's Plot to Trick Gail Fails; Sacred City Reached

What are you doing here?" asked Gail sharply. The attractive black girl only smiled, displaying her splendid white teeth. Gail realized that she could not understand what he was saying.

"Get out! Get out!" he cried, motioning. His voice rang loud in the silence. He pointed to the door, but Kama never moved. If anything, she curled up into a smaller knot and grinned at him invitingly.

Well, what should he do? The girl was evidently determined not to leave and, ignorant of her language, he could communicate his desire only by motions of his hands and his facial expression. He frowned in exasperation and bit his lip. He waved his hand again toward the door and jerked his head. She only smiled back at him and buried her shapely head in the pillow.

"Humph! Just as I expected. You're just like the rest." The voice of Martha Crockett came from the door.

He turned swiftly, guiltily, to face the woman he loved. He realized that appearances were against him. Here was a pretty native girl in his bed. Who would believe that he had not invited her? The expression on Martha's face told him that she believed the worst.

"I don't know how she came here," he explained lamely. "I just came in and here she was."

"Yes, I can imagine," Martha retorted sarcastically. Her black eyes were snapped in anger. "Naturally you didn't encourage her. Oh, I hate you! You're just like the other men, and I thought you were different. I trusted you more than I ever have any man, and this is the result."

"I tell you," he said, earnestly, "that I don't know how she came here in my room. I just walked in and found her here."

"Yes, I know," Martha retorted bitterly. "You're innocent, of course."

　　　　　　　　GEORGE S. SCHUYLER

He told himself that he had never seen her look so beautiful as she did in her anger and disillusionment. There was a spot of color in each of her cheeks and her eyes were smoldering with the fire of jealousy.

Kama remained curled in the center of his bed, grinning. Gail shrugged his shoulders hopelessly, Martha's lips curled disdainfully. Rage registered in her facial expression.

A shadow darkened the door. Gail and Martha turned abruptly. There, standing with a cynical, triumphant smile on his lips, was Yemasseh. Behind him, wonder and surprise struggling to dominate his countenance, was Sancee.

There was an awkward silence. The four persons looked at each other and then at the girl curled in the center of Gail's bed.

"What does he want?" asked Gail, addressing Sancee.

The steward spoke rapidly to the chief. Yemasseh spoke, nodded his head vigorously and addressed a few words to his wife. She replied with animation.

"Chief, he say he wife call you name," said Sancee, seriously.

"What does that mean?" asked Gail. "I don't understand."

"Chief, he say you take his wife," Sancee explained. "She say you tell her to come here. It is very bad, massa. Very bad. When womans call you name you must pay many pounds."

"That's a lie," shouted Gail, "I never told her to come here."

"Yes, massa," said Sancee, "but the girl, she say so, and her word goes."

Martha snickered bitterly and turned to go. Just then, Rev. Matney appeared in the doorway.

"What's wrong, Reddick?" he inquired, looking first at one and then at the other.

"This girl," said Gail, "was in my room when I came in here after leaving you. She tells the chief that I persuaded her to come here. Of course I didn't. What am I to do, Reverend?"

"Oh, that's an old African custom," explained the missionary with a smile. "That's the way they take advantage of strangers. The girl comes to your room and then her husband or father appears and she accuses you of taking advantage of her. That's what they dub 'calling your name.'"

"But I found her here!" Gail objected.

"Of course you did," interrupted Rev. Matney. "I know it because you just left me. That's a way these natives have of getting money out of strangers."

He spoke rapidly to the chief in his own language. His voice was sharp and accusative. The chief answered with animation, gesticulating and pointing first to the girl and then to Gail. Rev. Matney spoke more sharply and pointed to the door. The chief finally beckoned to Kama and spoke a few words of command. The girl rose obediently form the bed, walked out of the room and the two disappeared into the outer darkness.

"You had a narrow escape," said the missionary. "They tried that on me when I first came here. If I hadn't come along, they would have had you up for trial in the native court tomorrow and probably fined you six or eight pounds. These rascals are pretty clever. Quite different from the innocent, untutored savage you imagine. You have to be very careful."

"I'll bet that was part of the plot to delay me," Gail observed grimly.

"Of course it was," the missionary agreed. "If it hadn't been for me you would've been in a fix, I'll tell you!"

"Oh, Gail!" Martha exclaimed, her demeanor completely changed, "I was so unfair, so suspicious, so jealous. I'm terribly sort."

"That's alright, darling. I know exactly how you felt. After all, it did throw me in a pretty bad light." He extended his arms and embraced her. Rev. Matney smiled indulgently.

The sun was high when Sancee awakened Gail for breakfast. Martha and Rev. and Mrs. Matney were already up.

During the meal Gail discussed his plans with them.

"I've lost the map," he said, "but I'm not going to let that stop me one minute. I figure that Goebel will soon appear on the scene to start after the golden gods. Perhaps with a little luck I can beat him to it. I'm going to start out today and make a little reconnaissance. Perhaps I'll be fortunate enough to remember the directions on the map and get up to the sacred town. I have studied the map rather closely. At any rate, there's nothing like a trial. Moreover, there's nothing else I can do."

Rev. Matney agreed. An hour later Gail, with Sancee, Yama and a couple of the porters hurried out of town toward the cloud-capped mountains that reared their verdure-clad eminences around Voni Jessu.

For safety, they went around the town to avoid detection. Gail knew now that Yemasseh was an enemy and he did not want him to know of his departure.

After walking briskly for an hour, they struck the forest belt and began to ascend the mountain along the rugged trail. Into the semi-darkness they plunged. It was cooler, although steamy hot. The giant trees reared two hundred feet overhead, their branches interlacing to effectively shut out the rays of the morning sun.

The primeval forest was as still as death; a grotesque maze of black trunks, dark green shrubbery and looped vines, with here and there a troop of brown monkeys gamboling and chattering in the upper branches.

The little party walked steadily upward. Sancee was leading. Gail's rifle slung over his shoulder and the precious canteen of boiled water swinging from his hand. Behind him were the two porters, bearing packages containing gifts (dash). Bringing up the rear was Gail, trying desperately to remember the trail as plotted on the missing leopard skin map, apprehensive, and yet determined to push on.

At noon they were near the summit, but almost completely exhausted from the climb. While they paused to drink at a fresh mountain stream, Gail wondered if he had chosen the right mountain out of the number that encircled the town. Only time would tell.

After a brief rest they pushed. Gail was wet all over from perspiration, his eyes sunken from weariness and fatigue. The trail seemed not to have been trodden for years. This fact led him to believe that he was going in the right direction.

An hour and a half of climbing brought the little party to the summit of the mountain. There in the center of a vast open space was a neat town of about three score huts. They were structures larger than the ordinary African habitation, and surrounding the whole was a high stockade of sharpened tree trunks.

The sun was high. The heat was oppressive. There seemed to be no one in the village. Quietness reigned. No one was to be seen. Gail signaled for the men to halt at the edge of the forest. He sat down at the base of a gigantic cottonwood tree to rest.

Thousands of feet below them stretched the valley and the yellow huts of Voni Jessu. The sky was a clear, dark blue, in which the sun hung like a ball of fire. Gail pulled out a cigarette, lit it and smoked as he made his plans. Sancee sat attentively nearby, watching his master and clutching the rifle. The place was oppressively quiet, a tropical Valhalla apparently uninhabited. But Gail knew that there *must* be someone in this large settlement, for all its quietness. That this was the sacred city of Winyah, for which he had come six thousand miles to reach, he had no doubt.

After a brief rest, he told Sancee to instruct the two porters to wait where they were while he and his steward made a reconnaissance. Carefully, and without exposing themselves to the gaze of a possible lookout, they circled the town.

It seemed very much like any other African town except that it seemed deserted. They saw no chicken, no goats, no humans. The whole scene was as still as death. Not a voice rose from the settlement. Only the tops of the huts were visible above the stockade. There were two large gates, but both were closed.

Having completely circled the town, Gail and Sancee returned to where the porters were patiently, though apprehensively, waiting. Gail decided to wait until the sun began to go down before trying to enter the place, realizing how dangerous it would be in spite of appearances.

They ate some cold food. He knew, as the sun sank lower, that it was now or never. Instructing Sancee to stay with the porters and to follow him only if he blew his whistle twice to show that the coast was clear, Gail finally started for the main gate of the stockade, armed with only a loaded pistol and a length of rope.

He reached the gate safely, only to find that every crevice and aperture was caulked with clay. Moving farther along the wall, he expertly cast the looped rope over one of the pointed tree trunks in the stockade, pulled it taut and climbed hand over hand to the top.

Quickly surveying the crooked lanes of the village and seeing no one, he pulled himself over the stockade and dropped the other side.

X

GAIL FINDS THE HIDDEN AFRICAN TOWN, LOCATES GOLDEN GODS AND THEN—

Winyah was as quiet as death. Gail crouched in the shadow of the stockade, pistol in hand, and looked cautiously around. There was no one in sight. Apparently his jump had not been heard. The afternoon sun was blazing its final farewell of the day, already caressing the dark green mountain peaks to the west.

There were several large structures and a number smaller, and yet larger than the average African hut. Set around indiscriminately and with no semblance of order, they cast weird shadows in the setting sun. In the center of the town was a great rectangular pavilion, at least one hundred feet square, and on a raised platform of hardened clap with a three-foot wall of the same material around it. In the very center of it stood four huge drums in a row. Fifty feet in back of this palaver kitchen loomed a huge circular building with steep palm-thatched conical roof. The upper part of its wall was light gray, the lower half of darker tone. But most remarkable of all about this building was the decoration: an unending, grotesque, savage mural, depicting gods and demons so horribly ugly that they almost made the blood run cold. A single wide closed door was apparently the only means of ingress and egress.

The sun sank lower and lower. Gail hesitated as to his next step. He must do something, and yet what? The place seemed deserted. Still there was smoke issuing from the tops of many of the huts and once or twice he thought he had heard the low sound of voices.

The shadow of the stockade was a fairly safe hiding place, but he had not come here to hide; he had come to locate the golden gods. They must be here, but where? For the first time he realized what the loss of the leopard skin map had really meant. With it he could have gone directly to the building housing the gods, without it he was all at sea.

He intuition told him that perhaps the formidable circular hut beyond the palaver kitchen held the golden gods. Acting upon this hunch, he slowly followed the stockade around to the huge building, stepping softly and watching the doors of the huts. The silence of the place puzzled him. Why was there no conversation? Why were there no lights? Why did no one appear?

Five minutes later Gail stood in the deep shadows between the stockade and the large round hut. He would be safe here, he thought. It was almost dark in this corner already. When the sun had completely set and the Stygian African darkness swathed the mountain top like a great blanket, it would then be time to stir around and effect an entrance to this mysterious circular building.

While he waited he examined his pistol to see that it was completely loaded. He felt his whistle hanging from his neck by a stout cord. The rope he had wrapped about his waist. His hunting knife hung from his belt. The electric torch was in his back pocket.

The sun was almost gone now. The air was losing its warmth and growing chillier. A slight breeze set the surrounding trees to rustling. He was nervous, eager to get going. Each minute he delayed made the danger the greater.

WHEN THE NIGHT HAD GROWN so dark that the huts were scarcely distinguishable. Gail issued forth stealthily. He must work fast. There might be a moon later on, and when there was a moon he knew Africa always danced. If this town of Winyah *was* actually inhabited, it would be a bad place for him.

Keeping close to the wall of the large circular building, Gail made his way softly but swiftly to the great door facing the palaver kitchen. He pressed upon it gently but firmly, his heart almost stopping with suspense. While he held his breath; the solid slab of hewn timber swung inward slowly, with a slight creaking sound. Gail smiled. So far everything was going fine. Quickly he stepped inside and closed the heavy door behind him.

For a full minute he stood motionless in the awful darkness of the place, listening intently. It was as still as a tomb, except for the loud chirping of a cricket in the thatch. A peculiarly stale, moldy, yet spicy odor filled the building. Gail did not wonder that the air was close, as there were no windows or openings of any kind.

He removed his pistol from his holster and, pulling out his electric torch, kneeled down on the clay floor. Then holding the torch as high above his head as possible, he turned it on.

The clay walls yellow and cracked, leaped toward him here and there. The place was all of sixty feet in diameter. From the rafters hung long strings of herbs and necklaces of leopards' teeth. Ranged around the wall were ceremonial drugs; grotesque wooden idols painted yellow, white, blue and red; ugly masks that grinned murderously; log straw garments used by the "devils" in their dances. From the door ran a wide straw mat held down at intervals by a whitened human skull. Gail followed the mat with his eyes. It ended at a three-step platform which had a thick hardened clay wall at each side and a curtain of straw matting in front of it. On each side of the platform was a low, elaborately decorated chair, inlaid with gold, ivory and silver, with a child's skull on each of their posts. The effect was magnificently terrifying. Gail sighed with relief. Thank God, there was no one inside.

But who could tell when there might be someone? Speed was essential. There was obviously no golden gods here. Gail started to open the great door to leave, when faintly from afar off he heard the throb of a drum. Its ominous monotony startled him. It was evidently in Voni Jessu. There was no moon shining, so it could not be the signal for a dance. Placing his ear at the crack of the door, he listened intently. The drum from far below boomed away. He became tense listening to its infernal hypnotic rhythm.

He heard a distinct creak of a door near at hand. Then there was another and another. It was so eery, that screeching sound of doors being opened. He took a chance, cracked open the door just a trifle and glanced out. From the huts surrounding the palaver kitchen figures in long striped blue robes bearing flaming torches were issuing forth and approaching the pavilion. Each figure wore a forbidding mask and carried a weapon of some kind: a bush knife, a shining sword or as iron-tipped spear. In increasing numbers they came from the huts and ranged themselves about the palaver kitchen until the entire court was filled with mysteriously robed beings whose flaming torches made the place almost as light as day.

Not a sound came from them. Nothing could be heard but the crackle of the torches, the distant throb of the drum and the shuffle of many feet. Gail watched entranced and yet apprehensive. Suppose they should enter his hut? His life wouldn't be worth a shilling.

Suddenly, as if by silent command, the ranks parted and down the newly made pathway strode a gigantic figure, shrouded in an indigo blue robe and wearing a grotesque headdress of horns, teeth and feathers, with a mask terrifying in its brutal sensuality. In one hand he held a long staff, in the other a leather bag about the size of a football and evidently full of "medicine." Heads bowed as he walked past, and only the distant but more insistent throbbing of the drum could be heard. The court was so quiet that Gail imagined he could even hear the swift intake of breaths from the assembled multitude.

The shrouded giant stepped into the palaver kitchen and stopped in front of the row of drums. He cupped his hand to his ear and listened intently to the distant drum. Then he straightened up and lifting his long, clay streaked arms over his savage headdress, he spoke rapidly in a shrill voice that belied his tremendous bulk. His speech was a series of shouts and shrieks.

A murmur went up from the assemblage. The robed figures turned to each other and whispered. The giant shrieked again. The ranks broke. The figures scattered in all directions, their torches streaming behind them like banners of flames as they ran hither and thither as if hunting for someone. With rising apprehension Gail watched them, fearing each moment that they might enter his hiding place.

One by one now the robe figures returned reassembling around the palaver kitchen, torches streaming like the tresses of Furies, weapons clanking. In the center of the pavilion the giant figure stood with streaked arms folded, waiting patiently. When all had returned, he snapped out a few shrill sentences. Replies came gruffly from all sides, replies that seemed to be negative.

It suddenly dawned upon Gail that perhaps they had been looking for him. He remembered what he had heard about the jungle telegraph, the mysterious, penetrating language of the drums, that carried for miles through the dense forests and matted underbrush.

HE SLOWLY CLOSED THE DOOR, and switching on his electric torch, surveyed the building for a hiding place. They had searched every structure but this, and this might be next. There was no safe place to hide. The rafters would be too conspicuous. To crawl inside one of the straw garments, or behind one of the big snarling wooden idols would be too risky.

His flashlight played on the straw curtain. Suppose he hid behind there? It was the safest place of all under the circumstances. Putting action to thought, he strode quickly to the curtain. Outside he could hear the crowd murmuring in undertone as the giant "devil" harangued them. Suddenly the great drums in the palaver kitchen began to boom deafeningly, the cacophony harrowing the eardrums. Screams and yells pierced the din.

Gail lifted the straw curtain and hurriedly stepped behind it. With his hunting knife he made a small hole in the straw so he might closely observe whoever entered. No one had yet entered. The boom of the drums and the screams of the "devils" rose in volume. Gail took out his pistol. He was determined to sell his life dearly if he must. There were twenty bullets in his belt in three magazines, and a full magazine in his automatic.

The pandemonium outside was now almost a story. They were working themselves into a frenzy. Gail decided to examine the little alcove in which he stood in the few moments at his disposal. Switching on his flashlight, he turned, and the sight that met his eyes almost made him cry out in surprise and amazement.

There against the wall stood two ebony pedestals. Inlaid with ivory and ebony, about three feet high and a foot square. Standing on each of them was a grotesque golden image, long, slender, ugly—perfect examples of African art, each over two feet tall, brightly polished, hurling back with golden reflection the rays of the electric torch.

For a moment Gail stood breathless, large-eyed, grinning, almost forgetful of the mob of howling fanatics a few feet away. Here was the goal for which he had translated so far, risked imprisonment, poison and the machinations of Chief Yemasseh! He ran his hand affectionately over the surface of the ugly gods, the exaltation of avarice in his heart.

Then for the first time he noticed the pile of bloodstained bones at the foot of the two ivory pedestals. Human bones, they were: hands, skulls, ribs, feet, spines! Brought suddenly back to earth, he remembered that this was cannibal country! He snapped out his light.

The shouting and drumming outside rumbled and crashed like a tempestuous sea on a rocky coast. Suddenly the great door opened with a screech and there framed in the doorway stood the shrouded giant. He stalked into the place, followed by his torch-bearing followers. Soon they filled the circular room. Slowly the huge leader with clay-streaked arms outstretched approached the platform on which Gail stood, automatic pistol in hand, peering out through his peep hole. There was a low hum of voices as the giant advanced. Great bands of perspiration stood on Gail's forehead. The clay-streaked arm reached for the straw curtain. Gail braced himself.

XI

Gail Is Caught In a Trap, Martha Goes In Pursuit, And Then—

From the moment Gail went off filled with self-confidence on his adventurous quest, Martha was worried, She had a premonition of danger. And yet, she knew how resourceful he was. She went about her work with the native children in the classes, but her mind was elsewhere. Every so often she would pause and listen, her beautiful face drawn with concern.

"Oh, I can't stand it," she told Mrs. Matney at lunch. "I'd much rather have gone with him."

"There, there, darling," the older woman soothed, "don't let these men worry you. He's probably getting along alright."

"Well, it's mighty dangerous," said Rev. Matney, shaking his head. "I would hate to be caught up there. How he expects to get into that place and out again with those images is more than I can figure."

"It will be a wonderful thing for our work if he can get them," said Mrs. Matney. "You have no idea the influence for evil that sacred city and those golden gods have. The natives believe the gods have the power to do everything; that in the time of great emergency they take human form again and go forth to slay the enemies of the people."

"Yes," added her husband, "and some of the natives say they have actually seen the gods disappear before their eyes. These witch doctors are pretty clever, you know."

"Oh, that's impossible!" scoffed Martha.

"Don't say that, my dear," said Mrs. Matney. "Strange things happen in Africa. After you've been here a while, you won't be so cocksure."

Martha was lying in one of those hammocks having her siesta when a great hubbuh arose in the village. She sat straight

GEORGE S. SCHUYLER

up and looked to see the cause of it. From the elevation of the mission station, it was possible to see easily over into the town. A long column of porters and hammock bearers were entering the public square and assembling before the palaver kitchen. Two white clad figures got down from their hammocks. Chief Yemasseh greeted them. The town was all astir.

She suspected that one of the arrivals might be Goebel, the German. One of the newcomers did look like a white man but the other, to whom everyone deferred was certainly a Negro. She called one of the most intelligent and Christianized of the mission boys, a tall, gangling lad who still affected the native garb.

"Frank," she instructed in low tones, "go to town. Fine out who those men are. Listen to what they say. I want to know. Hurry!"

"Yessum, Miss Martha," Frank grinned and loped obediently away. She watched him until he was lost in the crowd filling the square, where natives, porters and soldiers of the Frontier Force milled about.

Martha waited impatiently. Finally an hour passed. The sun was dripping toward the west when the mission boy appeared suddenly at her side. She jumped and suppressed a scream, she was that fidgety.

"Frank!" she exclaimed. "You startled me so! Well, who are they? What did you hear?"

"It be white man name Goebel," Frank explained. "The other is District Commissioner Dan Carter, a bad man. He give native man strong medicine. Tax plenty. Make 'em bring plenty rice and palm oil."

"Well, what did they say? Did you hear?"

"Yessum, Miss Martha, I listen. I sit down under window to Chief's guest house and hear talk. White man he say to Mr. Carter that he have map to Winyah. He say golden gods in big round god house and they can go get them through long hole in ground from little hut right behind god house outside wall. White man he cuss big because Mr. Gail he already gone up mountain, but he say Mr. Gail can't find gods without maps. If he go in town, white man say devils kill Mr. Gail."

"Then what happened?" asked Martha, hanging breathless to each word.

"Mr. Carter say don't fear, that devils get Mr. Gail anyhow cause he tell Chief Yemasseh to send message to mountain on drum that Mr. Gail be there. Then he and white man like they go on through night to Pamdeme, but they go and get golden gods through long hole while natives eat Mr. Gail." Frank paused grinning.

"Eat Gail!" screamed Martha. "My God! Do they eat people?"

"Yessum, Miss Martha. But devils eat mans all time when no soldier be around."

Martha made up her mind then and there. She must go to Gail. Practically alone up there, what chance would he have with those cannibals, roused to religious frenzy? There was no time to lose! She would borrow Rev. Matney's rifle and go to help the man she loved.

"Frank, I want you to go with me. Understand. We must help Mr. Reddick. See? Come on."

The mission boy hesitated, fear in his eyes. He glanced up at the towering green mountains behind the mission.

"No, Missy, that's too bad," he objected. "It be dark. I don't know trail good. Buzi devils eat us."

"Oh, come, come!" cried Martha as she and Frank slipped away toward Matney's rifle and plenty of ammunition. "The devils have no guns, have they?"

"Devils have plenty spear, sword and poisoned arrow," he objected.

"Please, Frank," she pleaded, "I can't go alone, but I must go. I'll give you two pounds."

"Two pounds!" exclaimed the boy, his eyes round with avarice and amazement. "Two pounds! Yessum, Missy Martha, I go for two pounds."

AFTER AN HOUR OF ARGUMENT, Martha finally persuaded Rev. Matney to lend her his rifle and ammunition. He denounced the trip as foolhardy and useless. But Martha was grimly determined. So finally, she and Frank slipped away toward the mountains, along the jungle trail.

The sun was sinking in the west. Long eery shadows crept over the jungle. Martha and Frank sped along. They were traveling light. Martha carried the rifle and a pocket of ammunition. Frank carried a long electric torch, extra batteries, several flare sticks and two pocketfuls of ammunition.

Martha's athletic training stood her in good stead because Frank set a stiff pace. Shortly they reached the foot of the great mountain. Then began the tortuous climb to the summit. Frank was vaguely familiar with the trail. Once, before he was Christianized, he had made this journey with his people to the sacred city of Winyah. Over stones and tree roots they stumbled, hiking steadily upward. When darkness settled down and the forest was perfectly black, Frank lit one of the flare sticks and they pushed on. Martha had put on a pair of khaki shorts instead of a skirt. The thorns and branches cruelly scratched her shapely legs, but she pressed on resolutely. She was reluctant even to stop for a rest until Frank insisted.

They were almost to the summit when the boy stopped stock still and listened intently. From below there came plainly the throb of drums.

"Yemasseh send message," Frank explained, reading the drum code. "It be very bad for Mr. Gail now."

"Come on," cried Martha, weary but determined, "we must hurry."

He extinguished the last of his flares, which made too prominent a light, and used the electric torch. They covered the remaining distance in a few minutes, emerging from the forest to see the light of the torches in the stockaded village. Both sank to the ground exhausted, their hearts pounding from the stiff climb.

From close at hand came a hiss. The two sprang to their feet, Martha pointing the rifle in the direction of the sound. They ran quickly behind the snakelike root of a forest giant. The hiss came again.

"Missy?" came a voice. "Missy Martha?"

"Who's that?" called Martha, surprised.

"This be Sancee and Yama," replied the voice, now familiar.

"Come here, quickly, Sancee," Martha could have shouted with joy, and yet her pleasure was marred by the absence of Gail.

"Where is he?" she cried, as Sancee, Yama and the two porters crept over to them.

"Massah Reddick go over stockade," reported Sancee, rather dolefully. "We not know no more, Missy."

Suddenly the great drums within the village boomed deafeningly, the deep reverberations shaking the ground under their feet.

"Come, Missy," cried Frank, plainly agitated, "we go quick. Devils are out. We no can do anything."

"Oh, yes we can," said Martha, grimly. "We've got two rifles here and plenty of ammunition. We're not going to stand by while Gail is killed. Come on!" She led the way out of the forest toward the sacred walled city. The others hesitated only a moment and then followed her.

THE GOD HOUSE OF WINYAH was as still as death. The mass of masked, robbed figures stood silent. The only sound was the crackling of the flaring torches and the sharp intake of breaths.

As the long streaked arm of the chief devil paused before jerking the curtain aside, he shouted a jarron. The massed voices replied in a bellowing chorus. Gri-gri bags, torches, swords and spears were lifted high in salute.

Another shout from the tall shrouded figure before the straw curtain and Gail peering through his peephole, was surprised to see the entire assemblage prostrate itself, burying faces in the clay floor. There were mumbled walls and groans.

Gail thought swiftly. He knew the end was near. He decided to take a chance. There was no one looking except the chief witch doctor. No one would dare to look up until he gave the signal.

Acting speedily, Gail grasped the barrel of his automatic. Then reaching out from behind the curtain, he crashed the butt of his pistol against the back of the witch doctor's head with all the power he could command. The giant sagged and Gail pulled him quickly behind the curtain where he slumped down on the floor of the platform.

His heart pounding with excitement. Gail removed the man's grotesque headdress and had started to take off the shroud preparatory to donning it himself, when the chief devil, now revealed as a grizzled old fellow, screamed at the top of his voice and grappled with Gail.

Immediately the god house was in an uproar. The mass of masked men seethed toward the platform. Gail fought desperately. He knew why his blow had only dazed the chief devil—the thickness of the headdress had stopped it. He cursed his ill fortune even as he fought a losing battle with the frenzied horde.

At last he was led, securely bound and bleeding from several scratches and wounds to the center of the vast circular room. The masked mob of devils screamed and danced in frenzy. The drums boomed in triumph. Willing hands bound him to a great cross-armed stake. This was then thrust into a large holt in the ground, head down. The blood rushed to Gail's head. Faggots were heaped about him. The vast assemblage chanted and shuffled in a wide circle around him. Over him the chief devil, a torch in his hand, stood like an avenging angel.

Gail strained at the cords binding his wrists, ankles and neck, but even as he did so he knew the effort was useless. There was just one chance in a thousand of escaping. That one glimmer of hope sank when the chief devil thrust the burning torch into the pile of faggots and Gail got the first whiff of acrid smoke in his nostrils. He prayed silently and gritted his teeth for the end. He determined to die like a man.

A roar of approval came from the throats of the robed, masked savages, as the twigs began to ignite and crackle. Several drew their swords and knives in anticipation of the coming feast. All eyes were fastened on the doomed man.

Suddenly the crack of a rifle resounded in the god house. Then another and another and another. Screams of rage and pain rang out as several of the savages fell over wounded. Following almost immediately upon this, there was a terrific flash and explosion. The god house for a moment was as light as day. Then suddenly it was dark. The rifles cracked on.

With screams of terror, the devils dropped everything and jammed the doorway, fighting to get out. The rifles cracked away. The moans and groans of the wounded filled the air.

Suddenly Gail felt his bonds severed and he was led quickly toward the rear.

"It's me, darling," said Martha pressing his hand, "come quickly. Are you hurt?"

"Not much, honey," he replied jubilantly. "Gee, but you're a brick."

"Hurry, there's no time to lose," she warned. "They'll get over their fright in a minute and be back here. Come on! Down the hidden passage!"

She lit her flashlight. There stood Sancee and Frank grinning with still smoking rifles. Behind them were the two porters, looking mighty scared. Gail ordered them to take down the hidden passage opening between the two pedestals. He and Martha followed.

"How did you do it?" he exclaimed.

"Flashlight powder put the finishing touch on," she laughed.

"The rifles helped a little too," said Gail. "To think I stood right there and never found this passage."

They groped their way forward and soon emerged into a small hut. The porters sweated and toiled bringing the heavy golden images through the hole in the floor. Then hurriedly they filled with opening with logs and stones to prevent pursuit.

Meantime, Sancee was busily sawing in two the golden images with the small sharp saw brought for that purpose. One was cut in half and the other almost so, when they heard voices outside the hut.

"Massah Goebel!" breathed Sancee. Gail jerked his pistol out of its holster.

XII

GAIL CLEVERLY OUTWITS HIS SCHEMING RIVALS, THEN ESCAPES WITH TREASURE

They waited almost breathlessly.

Sancee and Frank stood on each side of the hut door, rifles in hand. Swiftly the two porters did the severed gods up in four convenient bundles for carrying.

"This is the place," they heard the German say. "Come on. There's no time to lose here. Those devils have broken loose inside. They must have got Reddick. They're liable to be out here any minute." They heard Carter's booming voice answering.

The door was kicked open. The moonlight streamed in. Goebel had stepped to one side as he booted the door. Now he stood framed in the doorway, pistol in hand, and behind him loomed the giant district commissioner.

"Better close that door," warned the German. "Some of your men might see too much." Carter closed the door softly.

"Where's your flashlight?" asked Carter, groping in the darkness."

"Put 'em up, Goebel!" said Gail sternly. "You, too, Carter! Quick! We've got you and we mean business. Throw down that pistol, Goebel!"

The German cursed softly as he felt the muzzle of Gail's pistol at the side of his head, and dropped his weapon on the floor. Martha snapped on her flashlight and picked up the automatic.

"Take all of his bullets," said Gail, "we'll need them. Sancee, you search Carter."

Swiftly the grinning steward relieved the discomfited official of his pistol and bullets and handed them to Gail. The German and the district commissioner were backed against the wall. Gail noted with satisfaction that the two porters had so wrapped the four large blocks of gold that they were not recognizable as such.

"Well, vat are you going to do now?" asked Goebel. "Ve can't stay here mit dem devils all around us."

"We're going Goebel, but we'll leave you and Carter behind. You know how to deal with these primitive folk."

"Ach, Gott! No, dey vill kill and eat us!"

"That's your funeral then, old man," said Gail, grimacing. "You tried to get me. Now take your medicine. Tie them up, Sancee."

"You fool," boomed Carter, "do you think we came up here alone? No young fellow, we didn't We've got ten good soldiers outside this place and all I've got to do is raise my voice and they'll be in here. So now what?"

Gail paused thoughtfully at this news. There was not a moment to lose he realized. Inside Winyah the noise was deafening. Soon the devil men would be outside. He must be off, now or never.

"I'm not beaten by a long shot," he said. "Boys, pick up your bundles. Goebel, you and Carter go ahead and if there's one peep out of either of you I'll plug you if it's the last thing I do. Get me?"

"Gail, what are you going to do?" asked Martha.

"We're going out that door with Goebel and Carter ahead of us, and they're not going to say a word to their men or I'll shoot both of them in their tracks. Then down the mountain for us."

"How far do you think you'll get with the whole district aroused," sneered Carter.

"Get going," commanded Gail grimly. "We'll get a lot farther than you will. Now, not one word out of either of you!"

GAIL THREW THE DOOR OPEN. In the moonlight stood the ten soldiers of the Liberian Frontier Force, jumpy and tense at the noise from the walled city. They in amazement when they saw nine persons emerge from the hut, where only two had entered.

"Keep going," growled Gail, "and say nothing." Sullenly the two captives followed his advice, which he had emphasized by jabbing each in the side with his pistol.

The party walked hastily toward the ring of trees that fringed the plateau in which Winyah sat. They had traversed more than a third of the distance when, above the din of the dreams, they heard the screams and shouts of pursuers.

Gail glanced back and his heart sank. The great gate of the stockade was open and out of it was pouring the robed, clay-streaked horde of devils, brandishing spears and cutlasses, hounding towards the little party, spurred on by religious frenzy. He saw his party would be cut off before it could reach the dubious shelter of the forest.

"Back to the hut!" he yelled.

Turning, he ran back, with Martha at his side, followed closely by the four gold-laden boys. The soldiers were already formed to repel the attack, distributed fanwise around the hut. Gail paused at the door. His brain was working like a dynamo. He knew he had taken a long chance, but there was no alternative. Not only must he escape the natives, but he must also get away from Goebel, Carter and their soldiers with the gold.

With sudden inspiration, he reached out and collared German. Quickly he reached into the inside pocket of the man's white coat for the leopard skin map and found it. Then, pushing Goebel from him, he followed the rest of his party back into the hut. Sancee hastily bolted the door. The district commissioner and the German were left outside.

Already the battle was on between the devil men and the soldiers. Although the natives had no firearms, they outnumbers the Frontier Force men thirty or forty to one. It was impossible for the soldiers to hold out for long. They heard Carter booming out orders, while Goebel beat on the door begging to be admitted.

"Gail! Gail!" cried Martha, reprovingly, "why did you come back in here? We'll be caught like rats in a trap."

"It's our only chance," he replied. "Now everybody get busy and take that stuff out of that hole. We're going back into the town!"

The noise outside was deafening as inside they worked silently, desperately to clear the entrance of the passageway. In a minute or two it was done. Outside the shots were sounding less frequent. Now there was thuds and death screams as the enraged devil men closed with the little band of soldiers.

"Into the passage," Gail commanded. One by one the men followed his direction. "Go on, dear, I'm right behind you."

When Martha had disappeared underground toward the town, Gail struck a match and reaching high up touched it to the dry palm thatch of the hut. The thatched roof ignited quickly. Then, jumping into the hole, he raced after the others.

They were soon assembled in the deserted god house. Under Gail's direction, the porters filled the passageway with whatever they could find.

"Now, let's have a look at this map," he said. Martha held the flashlight while he unwrapped the map. Outside there were still a few shots above the screams and yells of the natives, signifying that some of the soldiers were still alive.

"Yes, here it is!" he cried.

"What?" asked Martha, craning her neck.

"That other trail, the secret trail, known only to the devil men. It starts on the other side of town. Let's get going."

Gail led the way carefully out of the huge god house. The town was deserted. The devil men were absorbed in their fight with the Liberian soldiers. The little party swiftly crossed the moon drenched open space past the palaver kitchen and gained the shadow of the farther houses.

Leaving the party close to the foot of the stockade, Gail ran back to the gate. He swung it shut slowly, creaking on its crude native hinges. Martha ran up and assisted him in placing the stout bar in place.

"What's the idea?"

"They'll be finished with those soldiers anytime now," he explained. "We must detain them as long as possible because they know the jungle better than we do, and we'll need a long start to get away from them."

By the moonlight he consulted the leopard skin map again. Then, going to the foot of the stockade, he paced off some dozen steps to the right. There, sure enough, was a very small gate, not more than three feet wide. It was the beginning of the trail. It was quickly unbarred and the little party passed through and down the mountainside.

GAIL WAS THE LAST TO leave. Already he could hear the murmurings of the mob at the big gate. There were no more shots now. He knew Goebel, Carter and the soldiers must be done for. He quickly followed the others down the steep, narrow trail, sometimes following the bed of gurgling streams, sometimes through seemingly impenetrable jungle.

It was a short, though precipitous trail, obviously the quickest way between Voni Jessu and the sacred city. No wonder the devil men had been able to mystify the simple peasants by passing between the two places so quickly.

They had almost reached the bottom of the mountain when above them they heard the boom, boom, boom-boom-boom of the great drum of Winyah thundering down from the mountain top.

"Massah, that be bad," gasped the perspiring Sancee as Gail paused and shut off his flashlight. "The devil mans tell Voni Jessup peoples golden gods gone. Old Yemasseh meet us an' kill us. Bad to go back: bad to go on. Massah, what you do?"

"You're right, Sancee. It does look bad. How far is it to the French border, do you know?"

"It be far," Frank spoke up. "It be 'bout three hour to Sublima from Voni Jessu; seven hour from Sublima to Boue, an' six hour to Zorzor from there."

"That's sixteen hours," mused Gail. "And how far is the French Guinea border from Zorzor, Frank?"

"No far. Maybe two mile," the boy replied.

"We've just got to make it," said Gail, "before the whole countryside is aroused or we'll never get out."

"Well, what are we to do, dear?" asked Martha, "we can't stand here."

"We're going to Voni Jessu, right now," Gail announced. "It's our only chance."

"But Yemasseh will get us," Martha objected. Gail strode ahead.

Shortly the huts of Voni Jessu loomed darkly in the distance. There was evidently something going on there. Flaming torches were everywhere. There was much bustling about. They slipped into the mission without being observed. Gail roused his carriers to leave at once.

"You can't get away with this, Reddick," said Rev. Matney, shaking his head, "and I can't help you. I'll be lucky if I get out of it myself. These people go stark crazy when you bother with their fetishes."

"I'll have to get away with it, Reverend. There's no other way out."

The sleepy-eyed carriers slowly assembled with chairs and equipment. The gold was put in two of the chairs. Gail climbed into the third and Martha into the remaining one. Two porters carried each chair.

"Martha, dear," said Gail, "you don't have to go. It'll be dangerous. I don't know how I'm going to get out of this."

"I'm going," she said firmly.

Sancee, leading the party on foot, skirted the town and stopped in the thick jungle on the other side. They could hear the witch doctors around the palaver kitchen working the people into a frenzy. Faintly from the mountain top came the persistent boom-boom-boom of the warning drums.

They waited five minutes, then ten minutes, while the din in the town increased in volume: beating of drums, blowing of horns, the squeals of pipes and the screams of the women. Then, with flaming torches streaming, a huge crowd of people, led by a clay-streaked witch doctor, marched out of the town and toward the mountain doubtless to intercept the fleeing party that had stolen the Golden Buzi gods.

"Now go!" commanded Gail. "A pound for every man if we get to the border!"

The party set off at a dog trot for Sublima. It was not yet daylight when they skirted that substantial town and set out for Boue. It was a ticklish job there. The town was very large, its subsidiary half-towns were numerous. It was after one o'clock in the afternoon when they skirted the place and went on to Zorzor. Always in the back of them they could hear faintly the booming of drums arousing the countryside.

It was dark when they approached Zorzor. There was unusual activity in the town. Torches flamed. Drums rattled and boomed. There was shouting.

Gail frowned and urged the tired, reluctant carriers forward. There must be no stopping now with the border almost in sight.

They approached Zorzor cautiously. Sancee did not know of any road around the town and the leopard skin map did not show one. They would have to go straight through the place. There was just a chance in a thousand that they could get by. It would be foolhardy to stop at the Luthern mission nearby. No, they must go straight through.

After much urging, the carriers hesitantly entered Zorzor. When they reached the public square they were surrounded by a threatening crowd of natives brandishing spears and swords.

Gail had Sancee call immediately for the chief. He came in his long striped robe, hand on his sword.

Gail decided on a bold plan. Slowly and deliberately he pulled an old letter out of his shirt pocket and handed it to the elderly chief.

"Book from District Commissioner," Sancee translated. The chief turned the letter over and over, looking alternately puzzled and suspicious. He handed the letter back, indicating that he could not read.

"District Commissioner," Sancee translated, "he say come quick to Voni Jessu with your men."

Gail waved his hand in the direction whence they had come and shook his head dolefully. Then he reached out, took the surprised chief's hand, shook it, and gave the order to march on. While the chief stood gaping uncertainly, the carriers raced away in the darkness, hurrying to cover the short distance to the border and the protection of the tri-color.

Ten minutes later they were challenged by a black French soldier.

"Well, darling," said Gail, as they sat in the French barracks a few minutes later, "we made it."

"Yes, dear," said Martha, "and to think you wanted to leave me behind!"

THE BEAST OF BRADHURST AVENUE:
A GRIPPING TALE OF ADVENTURE IN
THE HEART OF HARLEM

I

Mystery Murder, Beheading Of Girl Stirs Harlem; Probe Is Started

A shriek like that of a tortured soul from the stifling, searing heat of hell aroused the early morning stillness of Bradhurst Avenue. Again and yet again it rent the air, piteous and horrible. Then there was silence. Ominous silence.

Windows creaked as the curious braved the freezing January air to peer out. Up and down the park-bordered avenue that runs from 142nd Street to the 155th Street viaduct, heads appeared. The shriek had ridden far on the clear cold air.

But there was nothing to be seen. Across from the barrack-like row of huge gray apartment houses the little lights in Colonial Park twinkled feebly amidst the encompassing darkness. If there was anything amiss under the bare, gaunt, black branches of its snow-clothes tress, there was no indication of it. Far above the park and the stone-walled cliff that bordered it, rose the vast, more palatial apartment houses of Edgecombe Avenue. They looked down condescendingly upon the shabbier structures seventy-five feet below.

A police siren wailed down the avenue from 145th Street. The little green roundabout crunched to a stop at 150th Street. The Negro policemen jumped out and hurried into the nearest apartment house.

"Did you ring for the police?" one of them asked a scared elevator man.

"Yes. I-I-I did," he stammered. "Somebody must be killed. There was an awful shriek. Then two more. And then everything was quiet."

"Where'd they come from?" asked the other policeman.

"I don't know," said the elevator man more composed. "I was sitting here reading a magazine when the screams started. It sounded like they came from the park, and then they might've come from the court back there. Wherever they came from they sure was loud, believe me."

"Let's take a look around," said the officer in command. "Keep your eyes open, fellah!" This to the elevator man.

"Ain't nobody gonna catch me keepin' around here this night brother," the man replied with emphasis.

The two officers left the lobby and walked a few feet to the square court of the building. The searching beans of their flashlights revealed nothing. They looked into the walls alongside the basement windows. They found nothing. Only old cans filled with refuse, a battered baby carriage and a discarded Christmas tree.

They went back to their runabout and cruised slowly in the direction of the viaduct. Occasionally they stopped and flashed their lights into an areaway or court. In a few minutes they were back. Leaving the car they searched along the winding, tree bordered cement walks of the park. There was nothing there except the upturned iron benches. Disgusted, they returned to their car and scudded off to report.

"Two o'clock!" mumbled one of them, consulting his wrist watch. "Damn, it's cold!"

Sergent Callahan, a burly, red faced, good-humored Irishman, sat behind the desk in the Harlem precinct station.

"Say, Johnson," he called to a Negro officer, "didja hear anymore about that screamin' on Bradhurst Avenue? Anybody found dead or anything?"

"Nope, sergent, we ain't heard a thing. I figured we'd get a call the next morning, but we didn't."

"Something funny about that," boomed the Irishman, "Lotsa people said they heard the hollerin' but nobody's killed or nothin', so what th' hell? I can't make it out."

"Maybe it was some cokey," suggested the colored policeman, "of his junk."

"No," spoke up one of the officers who had answered the call, "everybody says it sounded like a woman."

The mysterious shrieks were the main topic of discussion in the hundreds of apartments whose windows overlooked Bradhurst

Avenue. No one had seen anything, but all had heard the piteous screams.

Two cold nights passed. Then in the darkness of the third morning, the wails of the police sirens again filled the freezing air. From all directions this time came the little dark green runabouts, their radio sets shouting orders as they raced towards Bradhurst Avenue.

They grouped like curious beetles in an irregular arc around a dark object on the icy sidewalk near one of the gateways to Colonial Park. A dozen uniformed officers crowded around the place. Windows creaked open and heads appeared. Early as it was, a knot of curious pedestrians gathered behind the officers.

The object was lifted into a car which immediately drove off. One by one in rapid succession the police cars darted back in the direction from whence they had come.

"Murder!" said one of the spectators, a diminutive Negro. The blood-quickening word was relayed from lip to lip. It flew with the electric speed of bad news from apartment to apartment along Bradhurst Avenue. By seven o'clock the entire neighborhood was repeating that terrible word, murder!

"WELL, SERGEANT," SAID CAPTAIN QUIGLEY, glancing across at Detective Sergeant Walter Crummel, "what do you make of it?"

The tall, powerful, handsome Negro, dressed in neat blue serge civilian clothes, glanced over the proffered report and handed it back.

"Whoever killed her must have been a fiend!" he exclaimed. "Have they found her head yet?"

"No, that's the funny part about it," said the Captain, frowning, "and unless we can absolutely prove that it's missing Marjorie Fenwick, we couldn't convict the murderer even if he confessed."

"But her parents identified her, didn't they."

"No, it's not really an identification, Walter," the Captain explained, "All they could say was that the body looked like that of their daughter and had a scar on the stomach from a childhood burn. But that isn't enough to convict on. There might be a thousand good-looking colored girls seventeen years old, with similar scars on their stomachs."

"Whoever killed her was a pretty clever duck, then," observed Crummel. "He knew it couldn't be pinned on him."

"That's it exactly," agreed the Captain, "but it's even more complicated than that. Did you notice in the medical examiner's report that no blood was found in the body?"

"Very strange," mused Crummel, slowing munching his inseparable gum. "When did this girl's people said she left home?"

"Sunday night about nine o'clock. She said she was going to a dance at the Renaissance, but she didn't go. We couldn't find anybody that saw her there."

"Any other colored girls of her age missing?" asked Crummel.

"None that we know of," his superior replied. "Oh, I don't doubt that this is her corpse, but we can't prove it."

"Well, I don't see how we can prove it," said Crummel, thoughtfully chewing his gum, "unless we find the head."

"Crummel!" said Captain Quigley, leaning forward, "I'm going to put you on this case. I think you're the man for it. And I needn't tell you what it'll mean if you can solve it. I'll give you all the help you need, but we must have results. The Police Commissioner is all excited and the tabloids are plugging it for all its worth. The colored people up here are all excited and hollering for action. So we've got to show some results."

"Yes, sir. I'll get busy right away," said Crummel, rising lazily to his six feet two inches and stretching. "By the way Captain, who found the corpse in the sack?"

"A milkman. You'll find it all in the report there. By the way, who do you want to work with you?"

"Orestes Williams will be enough for the time being."

"A good man," said the Captain, "you can have him. But remember, Crummel, we must have results."

Sergeant Crummel had finished half of his ham and eggs when detective Orestes Williams hustled into the Eureka Coffee Pot on 8th Avenue a short block from Bradhurst.

William was a wiry brown man with mournful eyes that belled his profession.

"I think I've got something, Chief," he exclaimed in a low tone, seating himself across from Crummel. "I think I know where Majorie Fenwick went last Sunday night when she was supposed to go to a dance at the Renaissance. I got hold of one of her girlfriends who says she used to visit an old actor, Sammy Andrus. You know Sammy? Used to be a dancer, but he's all shot now."

"Did you find out where he lives?"

"Sure. On Bradhurst Avenue. Right in the same apartment house."

"Well," drawled Crummel, swallowing the remnants of his coffee and extracting a stick of chewing gum from a package, "maybe we'd better go see Mister Andrus."

The two walked around the corner to the huge ninety-three family apartment house and were whisked up on the elevator to the fourth floor. They proceeded to a door at the end of the corridor and rang with the usual insistence of policemen with the world over.

Several seconds passed. Detective Williams leaned against the bell with his thumb. They waited. There was a creaked of a board in the hall behind the door.

"Who's there?" someone queried.

"Open up!" commanded Crummel, now alert and grimly chewing his wad of gum. "We're police officers."

A key fumbled at the lock. The door opened a few inches. Detective Williams barged into the dim corridor, followed by his superior. A medium size, elderly brownskin man, wrinkled and gray, with pouches of dissipation under his eyes, faced them inquiringly and somewhat apprehensively as he noticed them sniffing the air. This man had once doubtless been handsome but the ravages of age and physical mistreatment had taken their toll. But his eyes were as bright as those of a youth; bright, worldly, shrewd, calculating.

"You Sammy Andrus?" snapped Williams.

"Yes, I'm Sammy Andrus," admitted the old man. "What do you want with me?"

"We'll just take a look around," Crummel put in firmly, striding past the old man and down the hallway.

It was an unusually furnished place. A thick, dark red runner ran down the center of the hall. Bright prints hung here and there. A pair of heavy wine-colored drapes separated the front room from the hallway. The front room was a symphony in dark, rich red. A gorgeous red silk scarf draped the grand piano. Dainty multi-colored little cushions were piled on the large modernistic green and gold sofa. Wine colored drapes bordered the windows looking out Bradhurst Avenue and Colonial Park. Potted palms and rubber trees added to the oriental, luxuriance of the place. Gold fish swam lazily in a green glass bowl perched on a mahogany pedestal.

"Well, what's the idea?" asked Sammy Andrus somewhat irritably, tying the cord of his purple satin dressing gown tighter and throwing himself into a low, brilliantly upholstered modernistic chair.

The officers seated themselves without saying anything, but all the time Crummel was closely studying the man. He pretended to be in no hurry. Chewing his gum slowly he leisurely surveyed the gorgeous room.

"Pretty nice place you've got here, Andrus. Costs a lot to keep up, I guess," said Crummel, more to himself than to the older man. Then—"how much do you have to pay for a place like this?"

"Fifty-five a month," replied Andrus, his irritation increasing.

"Working?"

"No, I'm not working, why?"

"Well how do you keep a place like this, then?" asked Crummel, drawling innocently.

"That's my business," snapped the other.

"Oh yes?" observed Crummel, "we know what your business is. We could tell that when we walked in the door."

"What do you mean?" snarled Andrus straightening up.

"You're selling reefers, Andrus," challenged Crummel, sternly. "That your business, isn't it Andrus? Do you know we can send you to jail for that, Andrus?"

"You've got nothing on me," he growled, glowering at Crummel. "What are you looking for a shakedown?"

"No, Andrus," observed Crummel slowly, "we don't want a shakedown." Then like a flash the words shout out of his mouth, taking Andrus by surprise: "When did you last see Majorie Fenwick, Andrus?"

The elderly man grew ashen and his bright eyes visibly enlarged.

"Not since Sunday night," he blurted out defensively. Then he caught himself and wild panic raced over his face, Crummel smiled. Williams chuckled.

"Come with us, Andrus," said Crummel, rising. "You're under arrest."

DETECTIVES ARREST LOVER OF DEAD GIRL; FIEND STRIKES AGAIN

Detective Williams deftly snapped the handcuffs on the old actors Bony wrist with a swift motion born of much practice. It was an act the wiry, mournful eyed officer delighted in performing. It was the finishing touch, the culminating gesture, the end of a perfect day. It was what he and his kind lived for, the action that justified their existence and maintained them on the municipal payroll. Almost expressionless while carrying out his duty, there was a gleam of satisfaction in his dull, dreary eyes and a certain relaxation of the body that inevitably followed achievement.

"Well, chief, are we ready to go?" he asked, tonelessly, turning to Sergent Crummel, and jerking the ashen, broken, trembling Sammy Andrus to his feet. "This about washes up the case, don't it?"

"Take it easy," commanded Crummel. "Sit down. I want to look around a bit." He strolled lazily around the room, seemingly looking at nothing in particular.

Almost regretfully, Detective Williams permitted the old actor to sit back down in his chair. Seemed to have aged in those few seconds that had passed since Crummel announced his arrest. His hair seemed grayer, his wrinkles deeper. Even his bright eyes seemed duller, as though coated with the film of despair.

"You ain't got nothing on me," he blurted out, suddenly straightening up in his chair and glaring at Sergeant Crummel. "I can prove that she left here Sunday night. I got witnesses. I've got an alibi. I tell you, I was her friend. No, not what you think. I tried to make her do, right. I gave her money when she needed it. Oh, I know you don't believe it, but I'm on the level. I couldn't do anything like that. I liked the kid. Come on, give me a chance, will you? Don't try to pin this thing on me. I didn't do what I tell you. . ."

"Shut up!" growled Williams in his monotonous pushing the old man's head with his gnarled brown fist.

With a futile shrug and an expression of bitterness on his wrinkled sullen face the old dancer sank back against the cushion of the brilliant hued modernistic chair.

DURING THE OUTBURST, SERGEANT CRUMMEL had stood leaning lazily against the wall regarding the excited old man. Beneath drooping eyelids and munching his chewing gum with a deliberation and placidity of a brooding Jersey cow. He studied Andrus for a full minute while William stood impatiently, eager to be off with his prisoner. Then he sat down near the old man tipped his grey fedora on the back of his finely chiseled head and taking a cigarette. Out of a package, lit it and blew a funnel of smoke toward the pale green ceiling. He crossed his legs aimlessly and settled back.

"What're you gonna do?" asked Williams, frowning slightly.

"You go ahead and search this place," directed Crummel with a slight rasp in his voice. "I want to talk to this fellow."

Williams snorted, almost inaudibly, and strolled into the next room.

"Andrus, you're in a tough spot," snapped Crummel with a sudden animation, but retaining his lolling position. "Now tell me the truth and it may not go so hard with you. Come on, what time is it that Marjorie Fenwick came here Sunday night?"

"A little after nine o'clock," replied Sammy Andrus. "She wanted to borrow a dollar off me."

"When did she leave?"

"In about ten minutes."

"Who was here when she came?"

"Billy Dogan and Margie Smith. You know, they're playing at the Apollo on 125th Street this week."

"Were they here when the Fenwick girl left?"

"Yes, sir."

"Have you seen the Fenwick girl since she left? I mean, did she come back later?"

"No, sir, I've never seen her no more."

"What did she say she wanted the dollar for?"

"To buy some liquor."

"Who for?"

"Oh, I don't know." The old man's bright eyes shifted just a trifle.

"You're lying, Andrus," drawled Sergeant Crummel, recrossing his legs and drawing upon his half-smoked cigarette. "I want the truth. This is no time to cover it for anyone. You're in a tough spot, Andrus."

The old dancer drummed nervously with his bony fingers on the arms of his chair and avoided the detectives steady gaze.

"Who was she going to get that liquor for Andrus?" Crummel's voice was sterner now. He straightened up and leaned forward, his eyes hard, his mouth and grimly set until his face was close to that of the uneasy old man. "You'd better tell me, Andrus, if you know what's good for you. Come on! I'm tired of fooling with you now!" Crummel's voice grated.

"She. . . was. . . getting. . . it. . . for. . ." the old man paused, "for that no'count young fella she was runnin' with. He ain't worked in months. I told her to quit fooling with that guy. He ain't no good." The words tumbled from his lips now as he launched into a denunciation of Marjorie Fenwick's lover. Sergeant Crummel listened alertly, attentively.

"What was this fellow's name and where does he live?" answered Crummel, grasping the old actor's arm.

"Ernest Oats. . . He lives on the ground floor." The old man seemed relieved now. He was more animated. He glanced expectedly as Sergeant Crummel, perhaps hoping he might go free.

Detective William strolled back into the front room, bearing a cigar box and a bath towel stained with blood.

"Well, we got the goods on this guy, alright," he growled, his dull eyes brighter with his discoveries. "Look at this!" He thrust the towel in cigar box at Sergeant Crummel.

"Humph!" exclaimed the taller officer. "Referee, eh? I thought we had you right on them, Andrus. Now, how did that blood get on that towel. Come on, open up!"

"Oh that ain't nothing," scoffed the old actor. "I cut my hand this morning. See?" He extended his hand as far as he could with the cuffs on them and revealed a two inch cut at the base of his thumb.

"Did you happen to find anything else?" snapped Crummel to Williams.

"No, sir."

"Is there a telephone in the apartment where Oats lives?" Crummel asks Andrus.

"Yes, sir."

"Alright, go to the phone and call him up. Tell him to come up here; that you want to see him."

"But I ran him outta here a couple of weeks ago," Andrus objected.

"Telephone him!" snapped Sergeant Crummel. "Unfasten those cuffs, Williams."

Andrus went to the telephone in the corner and dialed a number. Crummel stood at his elbow. Someone answered the call and the wrinkled face of Andrus hardened malevolently. He did as he had been bidden.

"Now," directed Crummel, "when he comes in, you make up to him and give him a reefer. But before he gets to puffing it you ask him sort of offhand, whether he saw Marjorie Fenwick Saturday night. If he says 'yes,' then you ask him when she left and where she said she was going. No monkey business now or it'll be too bad. Williams, you hide in the bathroom there. I'll wait behind this drape."

They waited one minute, three minutes, five minutes. Then the doorbell buzzed. Sammy Andrus rose and walked away to the door he only opened. Fellow stands and black trousers stood on the threshold. The two men exchanged a few words. Andrus invited Oats in to have a "weed." The young man accepted. They passed right by Crummel, hidden behind the holds of drapes, entered the front room and sat down.

"What do you want, Sammy?" asked the youth disrespectful of the actor's years.

"It's about Marjorie," said the old man. "You know, I'm worried about her. I'd hate to think it was really her they found this morning like that. . . Here, have a 'weed.'" The youth eyed him suspiciously. "When did you see her last, Ernest?" He passed the reefer to the young man.

"About one-thirty," replied the youth. "She bought me some gin and we had a little party. She was supposed to be at a dance, so she left at about the time she thought the people would be going home. I haven't seen her since."

Sergeant Crummel stepped from behind the wine colored drapes. Oats sprang up.

"Sit down!" commanded the detective. "Williams, we'll take both of them."

Detective Williams came out of the bedroom, handcuffs out. With alacrity he slipped them on the wrists of the two men.

Young Oats flared with anger, cursing Andrus as a stool pigeon.

"Shut up!" growled Williams, threatening them.

"What are you taking me for?" asked the young man, frowning at the detective.

"Because you've got a lot of explaining to do," said Crummel, quietly.

"You were the last one to see Marjorie Fenwick alive, weren't you? How do we know she ever left your room? How do we know that you didn't kill her and put her body in that sack? Yes, you've got lots to explain, young man. The safest place for you is jail. As for you, Andrus, well, those reefers will hold you until we get to the bottom of this. Even if you had nothing to do with it, we'll need you."

"Alright, let's go!" growled Williams in his monotonous voice.

"Better let that old man put on an overcoat," drawled Crummel. "It's cold out there."

An hour later, Detective Sergeant Walter Crummel sat in the Eureka Coffee Pot eating his favorite dish: ham and eggs, straight up with generous portions of french fried potatoes and a dish of sliced tomatoes. He was washing down the last of the meal with a cold bottle of Budweiser when Detective Orestes Williams strolled in.

"I knew I'd find you here," said Williams, regretfully eyeing the array of soil dishes in front of his superior. "I wish I could eat like that, but well, my stomachs all shot. . . Well, that was a quick job, wasn't it?"

"What job? Asked Crummel.

"Why nabbin' that kid for croaking that broad. He ain't got a chance to beat the rap."

"He's not the murderer," said Crummel calmly, picking his teeth.

"Not the murderer!" echoed Williams, scowling incredulously at his superior. "But he admitted he was with her. I heard him and you heard him. We don't need more than that to send him to the chair, do we?"

"He's not the killer," repeated Crummel, taking another deep drink of the amber fluid. "His story was straight. So was the old man's. They don't know anything about it, I'm sure of that."

"Well, what did you haul them in for and shoot all of that crap to the newspaper boys, then?" asked Williams, gesticulating animatedly, his tone losing much of its monotony.

"That's just a stall," said Crummel, lowering his voice almost to a whisper. "I'm convinced that the real murderer is a fiend, a beast. What other kind of creature would cut off the head of its victim and drain last drop of blood from its body? No, Williams. Neither the Oats boy nor old man Andrus knows anything about this. I locked them up to give the real murderer assurance. Make sure Williams, he'll strike again. I've had experience with the type."

"You don't mean. You're going to encourage him to kill some more?" Williams grew unprofessionally excited.

"It's the only way," said Crummel, calmly finishing his bottle of beer. "We're putting fifty plainclothes men along Bradhurst Avenue from 145th Street to the viaduct tonight and they'll stay there every night until something happens."

"Who do you think is going to do anything with cops swarming all over the place?" scoffed Williams, nibbling one of the french fried potatoes Crummel had left.

"I know the type," insisted Crummel. "Wait and see."

Night came. The temperature sank lower. To all appearances, Bradhurst Avenue and Colonial Park seemed no different than usual, but fifty lynx-eyed men watched hour after hour, from as many points from as many points of vantage.

In a vacant apartment on the sixth floor of a large dwelling, Sergeant Crummel sat at the window patiently chewing his gum, his eye glued on the avenue.

Hours passed. Midnight came. It was quite cold. The steam had been turned off. Sergeant Crummel pulled his overcoat closer round his gigantic frame. He began to doze. He lit a cigarette to keep him awake. Save for the feebly twinkling electric lights in the park and the occasional street lamps, the neighborhood was swathed in black darkness. He took out his watch and consulted it. It was almost two o'clock.

Suddenly a piercing, piteous, pulsating scream; a scream of a tormented soul; a scream seemingly close at hand, chilled his blood for a split second and then galvanized him into action. He threw up the window and looked out. Black coated men were running from all directions towards the house in which he was located, shouting, flashing their electric lamps.

He whirled away from the window and dashed out the door of the apartment pistol in hand. The halls and stairways were but dimly lighted. He raced down the final flight of stairs. He was sure the scream had come from inside this house. The ground floor hall was filled with detectives guns in hand, gasping bewildered at each other.

III

Interracial Love Tryst Ends in Disappearance of Brownskin Venus

S urround the block!" ordered Crummel. "Don't let anybody leave until we searched the whole area!" There were four other huge apartment houses in the square block and the tall dark Detective Sergeant selected three of the plainclothes men to search each one.

"Williams, we'll go over these ourselves. We'll go over this house ourselves. Go get the janitor!"

"Ah'm th' janitah," a rotund black fellow spoke up from the crowd of sparsely clad residents who crowded the halls.

"Alright," commanded Crummel, "get your keys. We'll start at the roof. Make it snappy!"

"Why the roof, chief?" asked Williams and his monotone voice.

"Because the scream that came from over where I was watching. I was on the sixth floor. I wasn't two minutes getting downstairs to the lobby. Now, unless the murderer vanished I am sure that it was murderer went over the roofs, he is still in the house."

The corpulent janitor returned with his pass keys, and three men ascended in the automatic elevator to the seventh floor and ran to the stairway leading to the roof. The janitor was leading, Crummel following closely behind, electric torch in hand, service pistol gripped by the other.

The janitor paused on the last building. Before them was a big door leading out on the roof. Crummel flashed his lamp on the door.

"By God! It's hooked!" he exclaimed, stepping past the janitor. The door was indeed hooked from the inside.

Crummel unhooked the door and examined it closely, inside and out. The roof was covered with snow. There were no footprints going to or from the door. He walked out on the roof and looked around quickly. The house was situated on a corner, thus on two sides it would be almost impossible for anybody to leave. At the rear of the house was a court at least forty feet wide, separating it from the adjoining house on Eighth Avenue. The roof of the adjoining house on Bradhurst Avenue was at least ten feet below. Crummel hastened back to the stairway, hooked the door again and with Williams and the janitor, descended to the seventh door. He walked down the long hall to a window opening on Bradhurst Avenue. Pushing up the window, he looked down. Two detectives were posted in front of the house.

"Hey! One of you fellows come up here quick, take the elevator!"

"What do you make of it, chief?" growled Williams.

"Nothing yet, Williams," he replied in a tone that did not encourage conversation.

The elevator door opened and the detectives Crummel had summoned ripped out.

"I want you to stand in front of that stairway going to the roof," Crummel directed, "and let no one up here. Understand?"

"Yes, Sergeant." The man touching his hat touched his hat and turned to his post.

"Now, janitor," Crummel drawled, "we'll start at the end of the hall and will go through every apartment in this house. Something's wrong here, and we must find out what."

THE JANITOR RANG THE BELL of the apartment. A sleepy eyed old lady opened the door a crack. She objected strenuously when told the apartment would be searched. The officers pushed in past her. They searched well.

"Nothing here," muttered Crummel. Then aloud the old lady. "Did you hear a scream a while ago?"

"Yes, I did, and it scared the daylights out of me. It sounded so close. I got up. . ."

"Let's go," interrupted Crummel, hastening out of the apartment. "I knew it must have come from this part of the house."

One by one they searched the apartments down the hall, to the accompaniment of angry objections and curious questions from the occupants. All had heard that piteous scream, seemingly close at hand.

The janitor rang the bell of an apartment near the end of the hall. There was no answer. He rang again. There was no answer.

"Open!" boomed Crummel. The man unlocked door and stepped apprehensively to one side.

Crummel walked in, followed by Williams, and switched on the lights. Both men gasped at the gorgeousness of the furnishings and decorations.

Certainly there was no more strangely or richly furnished apartment and all the great city of New York. The whole was painted in green and gold. On the walls were grotesque African masks, African horns and harps, strings of leopard teeth and a great ivory elephant tusk. The squat chairs, closely resembling African chiefs' royal chairs, were carved from reddish brown wood and inlaid with silver and ivory. The floor of the parlor was highly polished and glistened like plate glass. A narrow bright green rug ran the length of the room, ending at a raised dais about three feet square, on which squatted an amazingly ugly African image about three feet high. It was lacquered a brilliant blue and had eyes made of bits of ivory. A silver cloth was caught around the middle and another of the same color artistically draped over the head and shoulders. On each side of this image stood an African drum. The ceiling was very light blue and in the center was a great oval orange-colored electric light.

"What kind of joint is this?" gasped Williams turning to the rotund black janitor.

"It belongs to uh woman calls herself some kind of Princess M'bula. Says she's from Africa."

Crummel strode into the adjoining room. He snapped on the light. The walls were painted a dark brown and the whole interior was similar to an African hut. The window had a straw mat for a curtain. In one corner was a very low divan with a bright orange canopy over it. The divan was in disarray. The sheets were rumpled up and the pillow was on the yellow mat in front of the divan. Across an ivory inlaid chair was a yellow kimono, elaborately embroidered in red.

"This dame must have been nuts," growled Williams, a puzzled expression on his usually expressionless face.

"She always wears that yellah gown," offered the janitor, pointing to the kimono.

Crummel strode into the next room, the dining room. Like the parlor, it was green and gold with many hassocks and pillows of brilliant hue around the highly polished floor. In the center on a light blue straw mat was a low, highly polished mahogany table inlaid with bits of ivory. A large black clay bowl of oranges, bananas and apples sat on a large yellow dolly in the center of the table. The beautiful table was scarcely more than sixteen inches high. Its legs were four elongated, grotesque African images with long bony arms and legs, narrow heads, and enormous paunches.

"What a layout!" commented Williams.

Crummel walked into the kitchen. It was small, furnished like most other kitchens, and was strikingly neat and clean with everything in its place.

"Nothin' here, chief," said Williams, looking up at Crummel as the taller man looked around the room.

"I'm not so sure," he muttered, half to himself. His eyes were riveted on the spot on the floor.

It was a large damp spot, evidently made by dirty water. Crummel dropped to his knees and examined it closely, taking its dimensions with a pocket tape measure with the space within, the space where at least a dozen pieces of sawdust. He rose and opened the refrigerator. It was well stocked with food, but there was only a piece of ice in it. Crummel paused, puzzled.

"Hadn't we better be lookin' in them other apartments?" asked Williams.

"Just wait a minute," snapped Crummel. He turned on his heel and strode out of the little kitchen and into the smaller bathroom. It was, like the kitchen, scrupulously clean. The green waterproof shower curtain was drawn the length of the tub.

Just to be sure Crummel reached up and shoved it back. It made a clinking, rasping sound as the hooks of the curtain scraped against the nickeled bar on which it hung.

In the bathtub, tied hand and feet, mouth sealed with adhesive tape and a wound on his forehead from which red blood oozed, lay a young light-haired white man. He was clad in blue pajamas with red Mooriah slippers on his feet. His pajama coat was open, revealing his pale white chest.

"And you were in a hurry to go," observed Crummel, glancing pityingly at Williams.

They lifted the young white man out of the bathtub, loosened his bonds, and peeled the adhesive tape off his mouth. He quickly gained consciousness under their ministrations. They helped him into the front room.

"Who are you?" asked Crummel, sitting down close to the young man and lighting a cigarette.

"My name is Ronald Dane."

"Do you live in this apartment?"

"No," replied the other, somewhat hesitant. "I was just spending the night with M'bula, Princess M'bula." He shifted uneasily.

"These ofay boys sure like black women," observed Williams, just the suggestion of a smile on his expressionless face.

"Where is she?" snapped Crummel.

"I—I don't know. We were just about to go to sleep when we heard a noise out in the kitchen. I went out to see what it was. I reached to switch on the light and got an awful wallop on the head. That's all I remember, officer."

"Well, the girl's gone," said Crummel. "You say you two were in bed, about to go to sleep."

"Yes, sir."

"What did she have on?"

"Green silk pajamas."

"Williams, go downstairs and tell the boys what we've discovered. I guess we've got the place alright. Tell them to hunt for this Princess M'bula. What does she look like, Dane?"

The white man's eyes lighted. He brushed back from his eyes a few strands of yellow hair.

"She is beautiful," he said, simply and affectionately. "The most remarkable specimen of pure Negro beauty I have ever seen. And I've been across Africa. About five feet seven inches tall, I would say. Slender, lithe, supple, with small aristocratic hands and feet, long, slender legs and arms. Small waist and beautiful, erect conical breasts. A beauty I tell you. And a brilliant woman too."

"What color?"

"The color of milk chocolate with skin as smooth as old velvet, and her eyes, her almond-shaped black eyes, God!"

"You like her, eh?"

"I worship her," he replied reverently. "Since the first day I saw her come aboard the steamer at old Grand Bassam, I have worshipped her."

"Well, why didn't you marry her then?" sneered Crummel.

Dane's expression became grave. He did not answer the question.

"If you were so crazy about her," continued Crummel, race feeling rising within him. "Why didn't you marry her like you would have married a white princess?"

"Oh, I asked her a thousand times." he blurted, "but she would not. All the way to Europe from Africa I asked her to marry me, then In Paris, in Rome, in Vienna, in London, wherever we went, I asked her. But she wouldn't do it."

"Why wouldn't she marry you?"

"She never told me but once," Dane answered slowly, "and that was tonight."

"Well, what did she say?"

"She said she could not marry me because it would mean that both of us must die. The curse of her god is on all who violate the sacred tribal law not to marry strangers or even embrace them carnally. Tonight we gave physical expression to our love, and now I'm sure she is dead. It is the curse of her gods." He buried his head in his hands and silently sobbed.

Crummel puffed thoughtfully on his cigarette. He was trying desperately to bring together all of the aspects of this mystery. A young woman, Marjorie Fenwick, had screamed aloud at nearly two o'clock Monday morning. Wednesday morning, a body resembling hers had been found on Bradhurst Avenue. Now at two o'clock Thursday morning, another scream was heard and they find this young woman, Princess M'bula, gone. The kidnapper or murderer could not have left the house by any of the windows because the whole section was under surveillance. The door to the roof was hooked from the inside. The door to this apartment was locked from the inside. Where had the kidnapper or murderer gone? Where was the Princess M'bula? Crummel scratched his head, puzzled.

IV

Startling Discovery Is Made By the Slueths In the Mystery Murder Probe

D etective Williams entered. Crummel looked inquiringly into his eyes.

"Nothing doing, chief. They've searched the whole block. Haven't found a thing." Williams' toneless voice seemed strangely out of place in this colorful apartment, and after the strange tale Crummel had heard.

"Tell them to search every corner of his house. I'll be down later. That girl must be in this house. Find her!"

Williams batted his dreary eyes slowly, and turning quickly on his heel, went out. When the door closed, Crummel took off his slouch hat, threw it on a nearby chair and sat down. He lazily extracted his cigarette from a well fitted package and was soon blowing blue coils toward the orange-colored light that illuminated the pale blue ceiling. He crossed his lanky legs and shifted down comfortably into his chair.

Ronald Dane sat across from him in his blue pajamas and red Mooriah slippers his exceedingly light hair tussled in a manner that greatly accentuated his good looks. Williams thought to himself as he appraised the youth from beneath his lowered eyelids, that he had known black women to succumb to much coarser and uglier white men. Dane gazed back at the tall Negro, respectant, curious as to what should follow. There was something so Frank opened and honest about his countenance that Crummel, with his vast knowledge of faces and character, felt certain that this white man had told him the truth.

"Now, Dane," drawled Crummel, flicking the ashes from his cigarette, but not otherwise moving. "When did you first meet this Princess M'bula?"

"Last summer, when I boarded the steamer at the Grand Bassam. Her father, powerful Chief Tania, allowed her to go.

The missionaries at the school where she had been educated had whetted her curiosity about the western world of the white man. We came up on a German boat, and as she spoke only French and her native language, and since I speak French as well, we soon became acquainted and shortly became good friends. As I told you, we travelled together to Paris, Vienna, London, Rome and most of the resorts. Almost everyday I would ask her to marry me. I meant it. But always a frightened look would come into her face, and her eyes would grow troubled."

"And you two didn't do anything until tonight?"

"Not until tonight, then, she told me. About the curse of the gods, but she said she didn't care that if we couldn't be together, she didn't want to live."

"So you really wanted to marry her?"

"Yes," replied Dane simply. "I did. My people would have objected. Like the devil, of course, but I am of age and I have a million in my own name, so they couldn't have hurt me."

"Did any Africans accompany her or ever visit her here?" asked Crummel, drawling the words out insinuating while studying the white man's face.

"There were four African men got on the steamer at Grand Basman. They traveled in the steerage. Twice Princess M'bula went down to visit them. She returned nervous and irritable. Again in Paris one of these fellows, a tall, wrinkled, elderly black man, came in our suite and talk with the Princess a long time. I saw them no more until we reached New York. But I always somehow had the feeling that everywhere we were being watched."

"What happened after you got here to New York?"

"Well, the Princess sold more of the virgin gold she had brought with her opened a bank account and leased this apartment I helped her furnished it in a manner that will remind her of the Ivory Coast."

"How long ago was that?"

"About a month. Ten days ago, the Princess became suddenly detached following a visit from the same tall, elderly man. He sat where you are sitting, but refused to converse with her until

I had left the room last Sunday night. She went out hatless around eleven o'clock and did not return until two or three o'clock on Monday morning. When I asked where she had been, she had shook her beautiful head. Her eyes looked wild, almost fantastical."

CRUMMEL STRAIGHTENED UP HIS LEISURELY manner, gone and tossed aside his cigarette. Marjorie Fenwick had disappeared last Sunday night. Her screams had been heard sometime. Before one o'clock Monday morning, Princess M'bula had returned to her apartment sometime afterward. What was the connection? Was there any connection? He glanced sharply at Dane.

"You say she left here hatless last Sunday night?"

"Yes. I remember telling her she should wear a hat in the cold weather, but she said she was not going far."

Crummel grunted and nervously pulled out his package of cigarettes. The tobacco seemed to soothe him. He leaned back in his chair.

"You could identify this African fellow if you saw him again?" he asked Dane.

"Certainly. I'll remember his evil red eyes to my dying day. The cannibal!"

"Cannibal!" echoed Crummel, straightening up and throwing his freshly lighted cigarette away. "Did you say cannibal?"

"Why, yes, of course, he was a cannibal. Most of the Ivory Coast people are or were cannibals. The French government has made it a crime, but it still goes on. Princess M'bula belonged to the Guro tribe who until very recently were certainly cannibals," explained Dane.

"Yes, go on," urged Crummel, "tell me what you know about that. We may have something."

"Well, there's not so much to tell. They used to take prisoners in their frequent wars. Every prisoner came to be regarded as meat, his flesh used as food, his blood used for drink. Their teeth are all sharpened even today to an acute triangle. They need to leap upon prisoners of war, gnaw at the throat of the wounded with their sharp teeth, drink their blood, and rend them to pieces."

Crummel rose with a suppressed chuckle. Things seemed to be clearing up, so these Guros drank their victims' blood. Marjorie Fenwick's body had been found drained of blood, but her body had not been marred. Since her head had been severed flush with the shoulders it was impossible to say whether or not her throat had been gashed by savage teeth.

Detective Williams, even gloomier of countenance than usual, opened the door and came in.

"We looked everywhere, chief," he said tonelessly. "There's nothing doing. It's a mystery alright."

Crummel grunted acknowledgement of the report. He reached for the green enameled French telephone concealed inside a miniature African hunt.

"Hello; this is Sergeant Crummel. Yes, look out for a tall, wrinkled, elderly black man. Yes, send a broadcast out for him. We want him for questioning. He has teeth sharpened to an acute triangle. He may lead whoever picks him up to some other Africans. We want them all. Yes, sharpened teeth. Probably speaks broken English."

"Got something, eh?" asked Williams, evincing more than usual animation.

"Maybe," muttered Crummel. Then turning to Dane, "Put on your clothes, Mr. Dane. You'll have to go to headquarters with us. Williams, put an officer in this apartment with order to arrest anyone who enters. Keep all of the men posted below. No one must leave their houses until we return. Understand?"

"Okeh, Chief."

"Will they keep me down there?" asked Dane anxiously.

"I think not," said Crummel kindly. "You've been a big help to us."

They went out together, got in a police car. Inspired to headquarters.

AN HOUR AND A HALF later, Sergeant Crummel stopped by the Eureka Coffee Pot to get his breakfast. He was eating his way heartily through a meal of sausage and eggs, buckwheat cakes and honey, and Detective William Strode in. Williams looked sorrowfully at the vanishing food as he ordered a glass of orange juice and two soft boiled eggs. I sure wish I could eat like that, he observed ruefully. But my stomachs all shot. Williams toyed with his fork and water glass while awaiting his order.

"Well, what do you make of it now, Chief?"

"I'm not quite sure, Williams," he confessed. "When we get our hands on those Africans, we'll be surer of our ground. There are still a number of loose threads. For example, that Princess and whoever took her must still be in that house. With all the men we had around the place, it was impossible for anyone to leave. Since they are still there. Where are they? We've got to find them, Williams. They want results downtown and they expect me to get them. Now, are you sure they searched every place in the house?"

"Chief, they searched every apartment, including the janitor's. I went into the basement with them myself. We searched the furnished room, the trunk room, the laundry room, the ice man's storeroom, the coal bins, and the place they rent as a church. . ."

"A church?" interrupted Crummel, setting down his cup of coffee. "What kind of church?"

"The janitor says he doesn't know. They just paid the rent and said they wanted the place for religious meetings. I went in, but the gal wasn't there."

"What king of place was it?"

"Oh, just a bare room. There was a little platform at one end, but nothing on it except a big box sofa. They've got green cloth hanging at the back of the platform."

"No chairs nor benches?"

"Nope. Nothin' except I what I told you."

"We'd better take a run around there when you finish your show. I want to see this church place. . . No benches, no chairs, eh? Yeah, that sounds interesting."

Fifteen minutes later, the two detectives descended to the smelly basement of the ill-fated apartment house, the janitor preceding them. It was a place of dark, labyrinthine passages, of certain turns, and unexpected rooms and corners.

The janitor unlocked the door of the basement church. It was indeed a bare, gloomy place. There was scarcely any light from the outside. Two small electric light bulbs inadequately illuminated the place.

Crummel looked around curiously. On a low platform was a big green box soft. He walked over and examined it, pressing his long slender fingers into the cushion. Williams and the janitor watched him. Then he reached down and pulled out a long shallow linen drawer underneath the cushion. In it, swathed in scores of yards of narrow blue cloth was what seemed suspiciously like a human body. Crummel whipped out his knife and slit the blue binding. The janitor and Detective Williams gasped at the sight that met their eyes as the cloth fell away.

V

Disappearance Of Pretty African Princess Still Mystifies The Police

L ying in the midst of the severed binding of blue cloth was a remarkably carved African idol. It was grotesque, amazingly ugly, jet black in color, about five feet tall. The grinning teeth were bits of ivory. The eyes, which were almond shaped, were made with pieces of yellow shell. The arms were long and slender, the belly protuberant with exaggerated naval. Around the neck were several robes of necklaces made of beads, of shells, and of leopard's teeth, and enormous (blank) with bright red point was revealed when Crummel lifted the striped brown and white cloth that was caught around the idol's middle.

"Now ain't that sumpin'!"exclaimed the janitor.

"Well, I'll be dogged!" remarked Williams remarked.

"Who rents this place?" snapped Crummel to the janitor. Now he had something to work on, he felt. And when Walter Crummel was hot on the trail, he dropped his languid, unhurried manner.

"Some darkies rented it for a church or somethin'."

"How long ago was that?"

"'Bout a month, I reckon."

Crummel smiled to himself, a sardonic smile that wrinkled one side of his brown face. Here indeed was a coincidence. Princess M'bula had rented her apartment a month ago, and this group had rented this basement room for a church a month ago. There was an African idol in the Princess' apartment and one in this room.

"What did the man look like who rented this place?" snapped Crummel, noting again the super-Spartan frugality with which the room was furnished.

"Now, lemme see. . ." The janitor's voice trailed off as he looked up at the ceiling in an effort to recall the man's appearance. "I'm sorry, officer, but I just disremember. He gimmie two months' rent an' I gave him th' keys, an' I ain't seen him since."

"Was he a tall, wrinkled man?" asked Crummel eagerly.

"Yeah, that's right," agreed the janitor almost enthusiastically. "He sure was. An' lemme see, he talked right funny."

"Like a West Indian?"

"Naw, it wasn't that plane. It sounded like somethin' like geechie talk."

"Like an African?" presumed Crummel.

"I ain't never seen no African 'cept that Princess," countered the janitor, "an' she talked right plain. But I 'spect this fellah mighta bin an African. He sure was black enough."

"Did he have red eyes?"

"I jest can't remember, but I know I didn't like th' way he looked at me." The janitor was empathetic on this latter point. "There was something else funny 'bout that man, too, now that I git to thinkin' 'bout hit, but I disremember whut it was."

"Was it his teeth?" asked Crummel, leaning forward eagerly.

"Yeah, yeah, that were hit," agreed the janitor. "That rascal had teeth jest like a dog. I didn't ask 'em but once, but hit sent a chill oveh me."

"How often do these people meet down here?"

"I dunno. I don' watch 'em. Long as they don' make no noise an' pays their rent. I don't pay them no mind."

Orestes Williams extracted a plug of tobacco from his rear pocket and methodically bit off a husk, chewing it swiftly into a mess that rested like a golf ball in his left cheek.

"It's a cinch, chief," he remarked tonelessly, shifting his fedora to the back of his head. "This is where them African fellows meet. Met when the Princess gets fly with this ofay, they enter her joint, knock this Dane fellow on the bean, take the gal down to the dumb waiter and into this joint," Williams shoved his hands deep into his pockets and rocked back on his heels. He'd show the chief that he could dope things out, too. "All we got to do now," he concluded, "is just to wait for these guys to show up and collar them."

"Very interesting, Williams," said Crummel, smiling, "but where is the Princess now?"

"Why they ate her up!" said William triumphantly. "Didn't that white guy say these birds was cannibals and drank blood, and everything? Why it's a cinch, chief."

"Somewhat plausible Williams, but where are the bones? They are certainly not here."

"Maybe they throwed them in the furnace. Let's go look."

"No, that's a little too unlikely in the first place. They would not have had the time. We were searching the house five minutes after we heard the scream, they could hardly have even been in the house because. No one has left—no one could leave—and we've seen everybody in this place."

"Yes," said Williams, obstinately piqued by the reception his theory had been accorded, "but we weren't looking for men. We were looking for the Princess. You didn't even know what this African fellow looked like until you talked with that Dane fellow. Why couldn't a bunch of them eat her up throw the head and bones in the furnace and then scram to different apartments?"

Crummel smiled indulgently and slowly lit a cigarette.

"Have you attended the furnace since the Princess disappeared?" he asked the janitor quietly.

"Yeah, I was there 'bout fifteen minutes ago."

"See any bones or head inside the furnace?"

"Naw sir!" the man replied empathically. "Wasn't nothin' in there but fiah."

"I guess you'll have to look a little further for your bones, Williams," said Crummel, chuckling at the others discomfiture.

"Well, she ain't gone out of this house," maintained his assistance stoutly. "And she ain't in none of these apartments, nor in the basement. So where is she?"

"I confess, Williams," admitted Crummel blandly, "that I do not know. As you suggest, it is likely that she was taken down the dumb waiter. In fact, she was taken down in the sack."

"How do you know?"

"There were marks of it on the floor. Remember when I examined them? They were sawdust there, too, doubtless from the sack."

"But where is she, chief?" asked Williams, frowning. "This is the thing getting my goat."

"I don't know where she is," confessed Crummel. "But we'll find out when we get ahold of these Africans, even if they can't tell us that they can give us some information. We'll watch this place night and day, Williams, until they meet again. That's your job."

The Thursday afternoon newspapers were full of accounts of the strained disappearance of Princess M'bula and he romance, with Ronald Dane the handsome, adventurous scion of the well-known New York family of that name. Photographs of the huge Harlem apartment house, of the exotic domicile, of the Princess and of the murdered Marjorie Fenwick appeared in every sheet. There were editorial comments on the bewilderment of the police, Harlem was excited and enthralled; Bradhurst Avenue was terror stricken, taunt, expectant.

Captain Quigley looked up as Sergeant Crummel walked into his office.

"Well they're giving us hell," remarked the Captain, indicating the afternoon papers on his desk.

"So I see," said Crummel, throwing himself into a chair nearby.

"We've got to have some action, Crummel," warned Captain Quigley. "You know how nervous the Commissioner is about these unsolved murders. Have you got anything yet?"

"I have and I haven't, Captain. Just when I think I've got something, it blows up. It's the strangest case I've ever had anything to do with it. It can't be solved in a few days. Whoever is doing this job is pretty smart."

"Well, let's get somebody in jail," urged his superior, "to keep these guys off my neck, will you?"

"I'll do my best, Chief," said Crummel.

After a minute or so, Detective Sergeant Crummel went out. He was plainly worried. This was the first time in his fifteen years of service that he had been unable to put his finger on even a suspect in a murder case. Several times he had been decorated for bravery and mentioned for his excellent detective work. There was number better record in the department than his, but this having a woman kidnapped and possibly murdered almost under his very eyes was too much. It would not help his record and he was in line for a lieutenancy. He shrugged his shoulders wearily and strode home to get a little sleep.

Thursday night passed. Friday and Saturday went into the limbo of history. Each day Sergeant Crummel had gone to the huge apartment house on Bradhurst Avenue. Each day, Detective Williams, who was assisted by two blue coats, had nothing to report.

"This case has got me stumped," grumbled Williams to Crummel on Sunday afternoon when the latter came around. "Nobody's been around here except the ice man and the janitor and the delivery man. Not an African insight."

"Well, tonight's likely to be the night," cautioned Crummel. "I'll get a dozen men. They can stay out of sight down here somewhere. You and I will watch. They meet. They met last Sunday night, I believe, and they're likely to meet tonight. Did you get that blue coat cloth and wrap? That image up like I told you."

"Yes, it's all fixed."

"Alright, I'll be back here about dark."

"How about that fellow Sammy Andrus? asked Williams. "And that boy, Ernest Oates. Did you turn them out?"

"Yes. We didn't have anything on the boy. We'll keep an eye on him, of course, but he knows nothing. I let Sammy go because we can use him sometime on something else. He thinks I got him off on that 'reefer' charge. As a matter of fact, I never even reported it. He can give us lots of dope on other cases."

"That's right."

Hours passed. Darkness came. Concealed near the door to the basement church, Sergeant Crummel and Detective Williams patiently awaited the arrival of the Africans. They munched sandwiches at ten-thirty. Still no Africans. The basement was very quiet. Only the squeal of the occasional rodent and the intermittent hum of the automatic elevator motor disturbed the silence. Sometimes the janitor shuffled past attend to his furnace. Eleven-fifteen came and they heard the evening news reports announce from the radio and the janitors apartment nearby.

Suddenly the door from the alley opened and four black men entered. They wore overcoats with collars turned up against the cold. Two had on slouch hats the other two wore caps. They hurried to the door of the basement church, unlocked it, and entered. The waiting detectives were about to come from their hiding places when the alley door opened again. Six very black men entered the basement and proceeded silently to the door of the mysterious chamber.

Five minutes passed. Ten minutes passed. Then at least a dozen black men came from the outside and entered the basement in the wake of the others.

"That makes twenty-two," mumbled Williams "didn't know there were that many Africans in New York."

"Hush!" cautioned Crummel.

The alley door opened again, and half dozen more overcoated black men hurried to the strange basement rendezvous. Crummel noted that two of them carried large bundles and one a big battered suitcase.

"That makes twenty-eight," said Williams. "I ain't never. . ."

The words died on his lips in response to Sergeant Crummel's nudge.

Another large plotty of blacks was entering the basement from the alley. They followed the rest into the room.

"That makes forty," said Williams, taking out his service revolver and examining it carefully in the light of his electric torch. Crummel said nothing. They waited all of fifteen minutes.

Suddenly from the mysterious rendezvous they heard a low, rhythmic almost indistinct throbbing of a drum. Soon it was joined by another drum of deeper tones. Had they not been so close to the door, they could not have heard this sound, so muffled was it, but nonetheless hypnotic.

"Let's see what's going on here," said Crummel approaching the door.

VI

SLUETHS SPY ON STRANGE VOODOO CEREMONIES, MAKE STARTLING DISCOVERY

The two detectives tiptoe to the heavy door of the room, each carrying a stool. They placed the stools side by side against the door and stood upon them from the nearby Shadows the doesn't hidden policemen watched, awaiting Crummel's signal to advance.

The two officers took out pocketknives and carefully removed two wads of white cloth from two eye holes they had drilled in the white washed door the drums were throbbing faster now. They put their eyes to the holes a strange sight leaped to meet them.

In a triple row semicircle squatted the Africans, naked, they're smooth chocolate bodies gleaming in the fitful light from the week electric bulbs they were facing the platform staring intently with wrapped attention, their lips moving as if in a silent prayer, their body swing from left to right with the rhythm of the two drums.

The drums were at each end of the semicircle and close to the platform. each was being played with the Hands by a naked black man shining with perspiration from the exertion, although the sound of the drumming was not loud.

On the platform stood the jet black, ugly African idol, it's grinning Ivory teeth and it's almond shaped eyes of yellow shell reflecting the light the beautiful necklaces of beads, shells and leopards teeth only extenuated the images grotesqueness. The stripped brown and white cloth had been removed from the Idol's middle and the brilliant red point of its enormous phallus caught a flash of light.

At its feet, rocking from side to side and mumbling softly, was a strange figure, a man with a pointed straw cap and a straw cape that enveloped the whole body except bear arms loaded with silver studded elephant toe braces and bare feet to one side of the kneeling priest was a white cloth spread on the platform, a freshly laundered cloth. Upon it were two plates, one containing a small trussed chicken that moves spasmodically, the other was heaped with cooked rice. Three green long necked bottles of wine stood at regular intervals, one in the center of the cloth, and the others at diagonal corners of the cloth. Three tapering black candles, as yet unlighted, stood in the glasses half filled with red wine. A large iron ladle and a large pile of spoons were piled together at one side of the cloth.

On his other side on a sheet of galvanized tin stood a brazier of glowing charcoal with a nearby two thirds full sack of the fuel to replenish the fire on the Brazier stood a large copper cauldron.

Crummel and Williams looked questioningly at each other as if to comment on the strange site, but neither said anything they quickly turned their eyes back to the spectacle in the room beyond the door.

THE STRAW COVERED MAN STOPPED rocking back and forth he took the candles one by one out of the half-filled glasses of one and lift them at the charcoal brazier, returning them to their former place he took one of the long green wine bottles and held it to his mouth. He set the bottle down. slowly his head went back and then jerked forward as he spewed the red wine all over the carved wooden image before him. The naked audience rocked back and forth more quickly as the drums increase their tempo. The priest now reached with one long black arm for the plate heaped with cooked rice. He placed it immediately in front of the idol. Now with a swift motion he turned, erect, and face the audience. The two watching detectives with difficulty suppressed and exclamation. The front of the straw hood was cut away the man's face was streaked with yellow and blue clay into a crude design. A magnificent necklace of finger bones and skulls of small animals hung from his neck. he was tall, and In the dim light of the basement room he seemed even more gigantic.

He raised his long, black braceleted arms and the drumming automatically ceased the assemblage of naked black sat tense, motionless. He clasped his hands now and mumbled, his head lowered. From the audience came a tall, wrinkled, stately black man, absolutely naked. He stopped in front of the priest and kneeled, bowing his head. Two other naked men, younger and shorter than the other, came forward and stood on each side of him. The priest handed each one of the green long necked bottles. They put the bottles to their mouths and drink. They returned the bottles to the priest, who replaced them in their former positions on the white cloth.

Now the priest steps to one side. He muttered a command. The three men spat the wine over the black idol. It gleamed with the red wine streaming down it like blood. At the side of it a murmur went up from the watching blacks, a savage murmur like the grumbling of hungry beast.

The priest muttered another command. A stout black man, completely naked, left the semicircle of crouching natives and hastened to the platform bearing a small suitcase. The priest stepped to one side, the three naked men stepped to the other side. The plump black man set the suitcase down on the platform in front of the gleaming, grotesque black idol he fastened it and threw back the cover.

Cupping his hands in front of his mouth he began a strange chant, part song, part whistling, part humming. From the depths of the suitcase rose slowly the head of a large green snake. It's wicked little eyes gleam maliciously. It rose six inches, a foot, and then stopped rigid, fascinated by the weird minor strains.

The priest reached down to the white cloth and picked up the twitching chicken. He stood now alongside the black idol. The plumped Negro stopped the snake chant. The priest reached out the chicken toward the snake quick as a flash the snake turned and lunge at the hapless foul, but even quicker was the priest. He snatched the chicken to one side and the fangs of the green reptile struck the ugly black idol. Once again this repeated. And then once more.

The plump black man began again his chant. The snake grew rigid. The chicken cease to twitch. The priest took the chicken and walked over to the copper cauldron steaming on the brazier of glowing charcoal. He lifted the heavy cover and looked within. Then he replaced the cover.

GEORGE S. SCHUYLER

He held the trussed chicken at the level of his head. The hapless fowl looking at him, terrified. Then quickly the priest opened his mouth, revealing two roles of filed teeth, and thrusting the chicken's head in his mouth, completely bit it off and spat it out on the platform as another deep murmur rose from the naked ranks before him. He stood still and sucked a great mouthful of blood from the chicken.

He cast the twitching carcass of the fowl into a corner and walked to the copper cauldron his cheeks distended with blood. He lifted the cover and spat the blood into the steaming pot. The snake charmer was still chanting. Now he took the rigid snake out of the suitcase. It was all of five feet long. He grasps the snakes tail and with a snapping motion, broke the reptiles neck and wrenched off its head. Then quickly he walked back to the Copper cauldron and cast the snake inside, replacing the cover.

THE DRUMS BEGAN AGAIN NOW. The gleaming black backs moved from side to side. The plump snake charmer return to his place in the audience. The priest stood in front of the idol. The three other men knelt on the platform.

The drums beat faster. The crowd took up a chant. The priest began to whirl and stamp his feet. He flung himself to the floor at the idol's feet, beating the platform with his fist. He rose again, saliva dripping from his mouth, staggered, shrieked, and fell to the platform. The drums beat faster, the chanting grew louder. The crouching blacks rose in a body and swarmed around the priest as he struggled with demonic ecstasy. Finally his limbs grew tense and his bare heels beat a tattoo on the platform.

A huge Negro came with a box of salt and begin sprinkling it over the prostrate form of the straw-clad priest. It was spread quickly. The other blacks kept dipping their fingers into the salt and putting them in their mouths, murmuring the while.

The priest opened his eyes wide and came to a sitting position. The others hurriedly resumed their places. The drums stopped. He stood up now and began groping in a greasy gri-gri bag that depended from his neck. To the tall, elderly, wrinkled negro he handed a chief of hair from a white horse's tail, to the second man he handed a bundle of feathers wound with grass, to the third he handed a nut through which a whole had been drilled and a large Red Feather inserted.

Now the priest produced a hammer and some long slender nails. The drums began again. The audience moved from side to side, chanting. The priests turned to the black idol behind him. Chanting a guttural song, he began furiously hammering the nails into the image while the chorus grew louder and louder. He hammered with amazing speed. Nail after nail fairly flew into the black wood until finally the supply was exhausted.

"What's he doing that for?" whispered Williams in Crummel's ear.

"African voodoo," explained the chief. "They're getting ready to kill someone who is not present. They conjured the soul into the wooden image and then kill it with the nails."

"What was the idea of all that rigamarole?"

"That was to make the god favorable; to appease him. Keep quiet now."

They turned again to their eye holes. The priest was leaning over the three kneeling men, his striped face gleaming diabolically. Suddenly he leaned farther forward and throwing himself upon one of the men sank his teeth into his neck, growling like a famished beast. The sound of drums and the chanting was now a din.

The attacked man screamed and then they still on the platform. The priest arose. He attacked and turned the second and third man, sinking his teeth into each neck and drinking their blood. All three lay in a heat before him, their bodies jerking, their blood trickling down to the platform. The priest turned to the crowd and snored like a tiger, showing his pointed, bloodstained teeth.

It was enough. Snarling like beasts, the men attacked each other, sinking their pointed teeth into each other's neck and shoulders. Forgotten now where the drumming and chanting. Forgotten was everything but the ancient Guru cannibalistic blood-drinking ordeal.

"Come on!" yelled Crummel, jumping off his stool and jerking out his pistol. The blue-coated officers rushed against the door and it fell inward with the crash sagging on its lower hinge.

GEORGE S. SCHUYLER

"Put 'em up! Put 'em up!" shouted Crummel, waving his pistol and back by the others. "One move and I'll drill you! Get over in that corner!"

Slowly, suddenly, reluctantly, the naked blacks, their orgy interrupted so rudely, obeyed. Blood was streaming down the chest and backs of most of them, and smearing their mouths. A not unpleasant odor was coming from the steaming cauldron. The grinning black idol on the platform seemed derisively indifferent.

Crummel turn to the tall, wrinkled old man, who with the two others on the platform, had risen from their recumbent position assumed after the priest cannibalistic attack.

"You speak English?"

"Yes, I speak English," he replied with a decent accent.

"What are you doing here?"

"This is our meeting place. All of the people from our country living in New York come here for religious rights. Why did you break in? What is it to you? You have interfered with the spirits, you fools, and someone whom he might have saved is probably lost."

"Who is that?" snapped Crummel.

"Princess M'bula, our leader. She disobeyed us and permitted the white man to possess her. Juju told us her life was threatened after she disappeared the other night. We might have saved her, but you American fools interfered. But whoever killed her will die!"

"He will die!" chorus the others.

Crummel pondered the situation. Had the Africans not kill their erring princess after all? Were they in fact but seeking to find her? Was he again confronted by a stone wall?

A shout from the basement interrupted his speculations. The janitor burst through the lines of policemen and ran to detective Sergeant Crummel. His eyes were rolling with fright.

"In the alley!" he shouted. "Come, quick!"

"Hold these birds here," Crummel directed the policeman, "and make them get dressed."

With Detective Williams he followed the quaking janitor out of the basement into the droughty court in the rear of the house.

Williams brought his flashlight into play. The janitor pointed with shaking finger.

There against the wall was a large bulging sack tied securely at the neck. Crummel touched the sack. It was wet, cold, clammy. He took out his pen knife and cut the string at the neck and open the sack. Williams flashed his light inside. They both gasped. Inside was the headless body of a woman!

They carried it inside the basement, taking it out of the wet sack and stretching it on some newspapers, hastily spread by the janitor.

It was the body of a young woman, perfectly formed, the head had been neatly severed. Not a drop of blood came from the body.

"Bring out that tall fellow," commanded Crummel. Williams went immediately to fetch the old African.

The man, now fully dressed, came out, stared at the corpse, then let out a wail of distress that was repeated by his brethren within, and had his wrinkled face in his hands.

"What's the matter?" asked Crummel.

"It is the princess M'bula," said the old man, grief stricken.

"How do you know it is?"

"The noble marks," said the African. "See them on her upper arm."

The detectives looked. Sure enough an intricate design had been cut into the skin and died blue it stood out plainly.

"Well, chief," said Williams, "that settles that case."

"No, Williams," replied Crummel, frowning, "the case has just begun.

VII

HEADLESS BODY OF BROWN PRINCESS BRINGS SPURT IN SEARCH FOR THE 'BEAST'

Well, chief," said Detective Williams in his toneless voice, "Where do we go from here?"

Crummel started as if being awakened from a dream. He had been lost in thought, trying to piece together this jigsaw puzzle. He looked at his watch. It was after one o'clock, in fact, nearly two. The African orgies had lasted longer than he had imagined. He snapped shut his watch and turned to his gloomy assistant.

"Did you post those men where I told you to?"

"Sure. You said to put one guy on the roof of the house next door and one on the roof of the house across the street, and one on the top of the house across the alley. I did that. Then you said to put one cup on the roof of this house where he could watch the penthouse door and the fire escapes. I did that. Then you said to put a cop on each floor to watch the elevated door and the stairways. That's just what I done, chief, and I'll be dogged if I can savvy how that gal's carcass got out in that alley. We got a bunch of the boys surrounding this house and the whole block. This thing is getting' my goat, chief."

Crummel grunted. He was plainly worried. The case was getting his goat too. He felt tired, baffled, puzzled. He wanted to go home and sleep over the case, to return to it later refreshed and with clearer mind, but he knew he couldn't do that. Captain Quigley was expecting results. The police commissioner was nervous. The newspapers Blaze and forth the second murder as soon as they learned of it, and it could not be kept from them. Harlem would be demanding action and no uncertain voice. Already the churches, fraternal organizations, newspapers and citizens of the section were saying that the police were not really trying to solve the Marjorie Fenwick murder. What would they say now, with the finding of the headless, bloodless body of Princess M'Bula?

"Go upstairs and see if those fellow saw anything, Williams," he finally ordered. "make it snappy, now. We haven't much time to lose."

"Okeh, chief."

Crummel turned to the tall African, who stood sorrowfully looking down upon the headless body of Princess M'Bula.

"What's your name, fellow?"

"G'Mando."

"Are you any relation to the Princess?"

"I am her father's brother."

"What were you following her around for?"

"It was by command of the king of the Guro people, my brother, and the wish of Juju."

"Why did he want her followed?"

"Because she was next in line to succeed him. She carried within her the spirit of the first Guro, Juju himself. She had to be protected."

"Well, why did the King let her go on this journey, if she was so precious?"

"The King loved his daughter, the Princess. She wished to see the world of the white man he let her go, but told me and my men to keep watch over her in order that no harm might come."

"What did you tell her when you visited her two weeks ago here?"

The old man hesitated, and lifted his old, bloodshot eyes and a troubled gaze.

"Come on, G'Mando," snapped Crummel. "You'd better talk freely. This case doesn't look so good for you and your people. You'd better clear yourself, if you can."

"I went to tell her," said the old man slowly, "to beware of that young white man. I reminded her of the warning of Juju that Guro blood must never be mixed with that of a stranger; that for eight hundred rains the Guro blood has been pure."

"What else did you tell her?" Crummel persisted.

"I told her that we had gathered together about fifty of our people living in New York who had come over as Sailors on ships, that we had went to this room here for our ceremonies, and that she must attend an officiate as priestess."

"And she came, didn't she?"

"Yes, she came last Sunday night." The old man's eyes brightened at the memory.

"And she did what the witch man did tonight?"

"Yes."

"What's the idea of drinking each other's blood?"

The lips of G'Mando tightened and he said nothing.

"Come on, old fellow," snapped Crummel, frowning, but winking at one of the policeman standing nearby.

"It is not permitted by Juju that we tell his secrets to the unclean," G'Mando said firmly.

"Call up the station house," Crummel commanded a policeman. "We'll take these birds down for the night at least. We can't take any chances now."

G'Mando grew downcast. His age cheeks sagging, his eyes growing dim.

"It is a terrible disgrace," he murmured, "for a great chief of the Guros. It is better to die."

"Now don't feel like that, old fellow," said Crummel, soothingly, "You won't really be in jail. You'll just have to stay in the station house overnight. Murder is a very serious crime in this country, we must get the guilty ones, we can take no chances."

"Juju will get them," observed G'Mando, confidently.

"What do you mean?"

"G'Mane has spoken. Afterwards have flown, they never return."

Outside the cling of the police patrol bell sounded. The Africans were fully dressed now. The policeman heard them into three large vans and drove away.

Crummel ordered the janitor to lock the door of the room and which the savage orgies had been held.

Detective Williams came striding down the passageway a cut of tobacco tucked in his cheek, his countenance expressionless.

"Well?" questioned Crummel.

"Nobody saw a thing," Williams reported. "I went around, Chief and every guy said the same thing. It sure beats me. I can't make head nor tale of it. Must be one of them miracles."

"There are no miracles, Williams," snapped Crummel, frowning. "There is a rational answer for everything. The answer to these murders is in this house it is up to us to find it."

"But what more can we do, chief? Ain't we searched every apartment in the joint? Ain't we put guys to watch on every floor, on the roof and on all the roofs around about? Ain't we had the whole block surrounded? I can't make it out. I don't see what more we can do!"

"Oh, yes, Williams," said Crummel, smiling into doleful consonants of his assistant. "There's always something more to do and there's always something more to do on this case."

Williams said nothing. There was silence in the basement except for the noise occasionally made by the motor of the elevator as it was started and stopped. Suddenly they heard the sound of someone shoveling cold in the fire room.

Crummel smiled craftily. "Call that janitor," he ordered. Williams obediently walked to the fire room.

"Is there anyway to lock that dumb waiter?" Crummel asked the janitor when he arrived, perspiring from his exertions in the fire room.

"Yas suh!"

"Do you lock it from down here?"

"Yas suh!"

"When do you lock it?"

"Eve'y night at eight o'clock, suh, 'ceptin' on Sat'day night."

"What time did you lock it tonight?"

"Ah guess Ah locked hit 'round seben tuhnight, suh 'cause they hain't no groceries or nuthin' much on Sundays."

Crummel walked over to the dumb waiter. The door was locked.

"Unlock it," he snapped, turning to the janitor.

The man unlocked the door. Caramel took out his flashlight and examined the interior of the box and also the shaft. They were wires leading to the upper floors.

"Ah jes pull down dis wire," the janitor explained, "an' dat unlocks all th' doahs. Wen Ah pulls down dis wire, all th' doahs is locked."

GEORGE S. SCHUYLER

"So when the doors are locked it is impossible for them to be opened from the various kitchens, eh?"

"Yas suh."

"Did you lock this dumb waiter at eight o'clock Wednesday night?"

"Yas suh."

"Well, it wasn't locked when we searched down here early Thursday morning," challenged Williams.

"But the dumb waiter door and Princess M'Bula's kitchen was locked," said Crummel.

"Ah sho locked dis doah down heah," said the janitor.

"Well, it's a cinch somebody unlocked it," Crummel observed. "who else has a key to this dumb waiter?"

"Nobody else, jes me."

"How many other dumb waiter shafts are there?"

"Ten, chief," said Williams. "I counted 'em. But this is the one that goes up to that African apartment."

"Does the same key fit the locks of all the other nine dumb waiters fellow?" asked Williams, turning his gaze on the thoroughly scared janitor.

"Yas suh. That makes hit easier foh me."

"Who else has ever had that key in their hands?"

"nobody but mah wife."

"Who uses the dumb waiter most aside from yourself?"

"Well, lemme see now, dere's th' Chinaman what rents that laundry room. Sometimes he sen' laundry up on th' dumb waiter. Den dere's th' groc'ry boys. Dey comes in heah all hours. An' co'se dere's th' icc man, Karl, he allus sen'in' up ice to de folkses."

"How long has this Chinaman been renting the laundry?"

"Oh, Ah reckon 'bout foh er five yeahs."

"ever had any trouble with him?"

"Nossuh, he sho a good man. He married tuh uh Wes' Indian 'ooman in' got a little kid 'bout three yeahs old."

"How long has this iceman been doing business around here?"

"He ain't been heah but 'bout uh month. He bought out Tony, the Italian, whut was heah uh long time."

"Is he a white man?"

"Yas suh, Ah tink he some kinda Dutchman. Ah know he ain't no Italian, an' mos' ice mens 'roun heah is Italians."

"That's strange," mused Crummel, have to himself. "a German iceman in Harlem. There used to be lots of Germans in Harlem fifteen or twenty years ago. Maybe he's a holdover."

"Well, Karl sho ain't bin in dis country no fifteen yeahs," The janitor offered, "'case he cain't hardly speak English good."

"Looks like it's worth following up, Williams," Crummel observed. Then to the janitor: "does this iceman live in the house?"

"Yas suh, he live in auh little one-room apartment on th' firs' flo."

"Come on, Williams," said Crummel, now animated, "I want to talk to this Karl. We can't afford to sleep any bets now. Take us up to his apartment, janitor."

"Yas suh."

The janitor turned toward the elevator followed by the two detectives.

Suddenly a piercing scream tore through the sepulchral quiet of the basement laborious; papaya scream that made the three men shudder. It could have come from any direction in those twisting stone corridors. Again it rented the early morning quiet, a long, mournful, terrible scream. Now it seemed to be nearby. Crummel and Williams turned and dashed in the direction from which they believed it came.

Then was startling, dramatic suddenness every light was extinguished and they were left in the Darkness. The Beast had struck again. Somewhere in that blackened basement the fiend was lurking, crouched over his helpless human prey.

GEORGE S. SCHUYLER

VIII

Another Murder Shocks Harlem As Sleuths Find New Clue to Killings

The basement was as black as death. The very air was charged with some awful, mysterious, sinister spirit. The place was still as an ancient tomb. Standing close to the wall, their pistols in their hands, the two detectives waited almost breathlessly, for some movement of the assassin. There was no move. There was only electric silence. It was as if invisible death had struck through stone walls, steel and plaster to claim a human life.

Crummel snatched out his flashlight. It's conical beam swept a hole through the darkness, down one of the corridors. There was nothing there. Williams did likewise in another direction. The basement seemed deserted.

"Come on," ordered Crummel, addressing the trembling janitor, "get these lights going."

"The switch is in the fire room, chief." said Williams, "I'll go and turn it on."

Williams strode away, only to return in a few seconds. "It wasn't turned off," he said.

"Well, a fuse is blown, then. Somebody caused a short circuit here. Are the lights in the basement on a separate and meter, janitor?"

"Yas, suh, them an' th' lights in th' halls. Ah kin git uh new fuse in uh minute, suh."

"Alright. Make it snappy. Take this flashlight."

The janitor went off down the corridor to his storeroom to get the fuse.

"This thing is sure gettin' my goat, chief," observed Williams, as he flashed his light about the basement.

Crummel said nothing. He merely frowned. He was more aroused now than ever. This latest outrage (for what he was sure someone had been killed or kidnapped) was an outright challenge to the police, purposely come almost before his eyes. He could not go back to the station again without results. He would be laughed at, his reputation ruined. As a Negro he would, of course, get more than his share of blame. He was solved not to leave the apartment house until he had solved the mystery of the fiendish killings. He felt sure the solution was there.

The janitor returned, went into the fire room, and soon the lights flashed on.

"Come on," cried Crummel, "those screams came from down this way."

He led the way down the corridor, pistol in hand, stopping at each electric light socket to examine it. Finally, they came to the end of the corridor after making a sharp turn, and came to a door.

"That's wha de Chinaman stay," said the janitor.

Crummel knocked on the door with the butt of his pistol. There was no answer. He knocked again, more insistently. There was a faint cry from within, a hysterical, childish cry, a cry that touched the very heartstrings. Then silence.

CRUMMEL TURNED THE KNOB. THE door opened softly, easily, swinging into the black interior of the room. There was a mingled odor of starched clothing, human effluvia And strange oriental smells. The place was quiet now, as still as a subterranean stream.

Williams found. The electric light switch and turned it on. The place remained in darkness. He exclaimed in dismay.

"I get it now," Said Crummel, sweeping the place with his flashlight and permitting the beam to rest on the empty electric light almost overhead. It was slightly burned and still warm, clear evidence that here the short circuit had been caused. "Get another bowl from outside, janitor. Hurry!"

The janitor Hassen to obey. Meanwhile, the two detectives swept the room with their lights. Across one end was a dark red curtain separating the sleeping quarters from the laundry room, which was beyond in the large bedroom. Was a large bed, greatly disordered, a bureau, two or three chairs, a table, and a small glass stove. The rumpled bed sheets were stained with several splotches of blood.

Williams nudged his chief and pointed under the bed. A bare foot protruded, an almost white foot, a man's foot.

"Come out from under there!" ordered Crummel, training his pistol. There was no reply, no movement of the protruding foot, only silence.

"Pull him out, Williams," said Crummel.

His assistant reached down, grabbed hold of the man's ankle and with a heave pulled him from beneath the bed. The man was dead, his skull crushed in his white pajamas stained with his blood.

"Dat's Wong," announced the janitor, "de Chinaman."

The laundryman's body was still warm. He had been dead but a few minutes. Williams covered the body with a sheet.

From the laundry room came a faint, startling cry. The detective straightened and reached for their pistols. Again it came, a hysterical, sobbing, shrill wails piercing the malignant stillness of the place.

Crummel leaped to the curtain swept it aside. The beam of his flashlight sought every corner of the room. He found the ceiling light and turned it on. The walls of the room were lined with shelves filled with bundles of laundry, all neatly ticketed. There was a counter across the room and beyond it a door leading to the street and a large window on which was painted in Red letters. "Chinese Hand Laundry, Charlie Wong, Proprietor."

AGAIN CAME THE FAINT CRYING, nearer now. There was a large hamper in one corner of the room. Crummel strolled over to it and yanked off the cover. Inside, cowering, tearful, hysterical, was a little brown, straight-haired boy in a pair of white woolen pajamas.

"Come on out, sonny," invited Crummel kindly, holding out his hand.

"Dat's th' Chinaman's kid," volunteered the janitor.

The little boy held back, sobbing. Crummel lifted him out of the hamper and held him in his arms, talking soothingly, assuring him that everything was alright.

"What's the matter, sonny?" he finally asked. "What are you doing in here? Why aren't you in bed?"

Again the child grew hysterical tears, bathing it's chubby, flushed cheeks, its little breasts heaving with emotion. Crummel saw it would be possible to get little or nothing from the child until it had become composed.

"Call up the station," he told Williams. "Here, janitor, Take this kid into your apartment and keep him there. Try to get him to go to sleep. I guess your wife will know how to take care of him."

"Yas, suh, we got uh couple of ouah own. Ah'll jist put little Bebbie right in with them." He took the child in his arms and went out.

Crummel went around the counter and examined the street door. It was securely locked. He next tried the window. It, too, was locked from the inside. He nodded his head in apparent satisfaction.

Suddenly getting down on his knees, he crept over the floor of the entire place, carefully examining every square foot. Near the door into the corridor, he was rewarded. There, clearly marked in gray dust on the rug was the print of a large stockinged foot.

CRUMMEL HASTILY TOOK OUT HIS powerful magnifying glass and studied the print. Then he looked about and found evidence of other prints, but none so distinct as that by the door. He measured the print, and then measured the foot of the dead Chinese laundryman. The print was longer and wider. In the middle of it were three grains of sawdust.

Further search revealed not another single clue. There were no fingerprints on the doorknobs, none on the bedstead, none anywhere. Crummel took out his notebook, consulted its closely written pages, and then added a few brief notes.

He sat down in an easy chair across from the shrouded body of the murdered Mongolian, lit a cigarette, and leaned back luxuriously to lose himself in thought.

The Chinese was dead and his West Indian Negro wife was missing. It was extremely unlikely that she had killed him. That blow that crushed his skull had been delivered by a powerful person. Most likely a large man, as indicated by the footprint on the rug. The murderer had entered from the door and must have left the same way. He had murdered the laundryman and doubtless kidnapped his wife. The child had escaped. Alarmed by the screams of his victims, the murder had then removed the electric lamp and caused a short circuit. In the interval between the extinguishing of the basement lights and turning them on again, the murderer had left the laundry with the kidnapped woman, and after turning the corner in the corridor, must have for a few moments been right close to the detectives. Where then had he gone? Why had they not heard him? How, with the house closely guarded at every entrance and in every hall, could he possibly have gone outside? How, with the policeman station at the head of the stairway leading from the basement, could the murderer have gone upstairs? Obviously then, the killer-kidnapper was still in the basement. But where? He was most certainly not in the furnace room. He was not in the room in which the African orgies had been held. He most emphatically was not here in the laundryman's place. Where, then, could he be? Well, there were left the large storeroom where were kept tenants' trunks and surplus furniture, another large room which was sort of a work room for the janitor, the janitors apartment, and the little room where the iceman stored his cakes of ice.

Williams came in, his face hard and expressionless as usual. "Th' wagon's on th' way," he announce laconically.

Crummel grunted, tossed away his cigarette butt and lit another smoke. "Take the load off your feet," he said, grinning at Williams.

"Say, what's the idea?" asked his assistant. "Hadn't we better be shakin' it up? We ain't got a thing on this case yet."

"Oh, I'm not so sure, Williams," observed Crummel, a mysterious smile curling the corners of his fine mouth, I'm not so sure."

"Just find the woman, eh?"

"What woman, Williams?"

"Why th' Chink's wife. She probably croaked him and scrammed. I always say people oughtta marry their own kind."

"Where did she go after the murder, Williams? Have any of the boys seen anybody? How did she get out without us hearing her? Why would she scream and alarm the place if she was the murderer?"

"Well, I give up," said Williams, a little hopelessly. "What's the answer?"

"The answer is that Mrs. Wong was kidnapped and her husband killed by the same person that murdered Marjorie Fenwick and Princess M'Bula, and the murderer is in this basement, Williams. We're going to find out where he is hiding right now. Come on!"

IX

Search of Basement of House of Tragedy Brings Strange Clues

"Yuh. . . yuh. . . yuh doan want me, does yuh, Chief?" stammered the janitor, His eyes round with concern, as Crummel indicated that he was to go with them on the search of the basement.

"Yes, come along, we may need you to open some doors."

Crummel, followed by Williams and the quaking janitor, strolled down a corridor. Tried the trunk room. The detective tried the door. It was securely locked.

"Do you keep this door locked all of the time?" he snapped.

"Yas suh!" exclaimed the janitor emphatically. "Ah have tuh do dat 'cause all de folkses stuff is in dah. Only time Ah opens dat doah is we'en somebody wants tuh go in dey trunk or put sumpin' lak furniture in heah."

"Nobody in there, I reckon," growled Williams, shifting his chew of tobacco from one side of his cheek to the other.

"Open it up!" Crummel ordered. "We'll take no chances."

The janitor took out his ring of jingling keys. After some fingering. He selected the right one. And inserted it with trembling hand into the lock. The bolt shot back. The heavy door, sheathed in galvanized iron opened out with a mournful creak that seemed even more eery than usual in the dimly-lit draughty, shadowy corridor.

"Alright, turn on the light," ordered Crummel, frowning at the man's hesitancy. "What's eating you?"

The janitor stepped timidly into the blackness of the room, visibly shaking. They could hear. His sibilant breathing shuffle of his feet on the cement floor. Then there was a sharp click. And the dark room was flooded with light.

It was like some great auction room. All around in individual piles were groups of trunks, suitcases, bedsteads, couches, bookcases, floor lamps, barrels, hampers and jugs. They were nearly all covered with a thick coating of gray dust. The vast room was hot and dry, and an odor not unlike that of a warehouse pervaded it. It was illuminated by several powerful 110 watt electric lamps.

Crummel slowly walked down the first lane, peering searchingly at everything. Ever and anon Williams, pistol in hand, would look behind some suspicious pile of goods, only to emerge with the look of disappointment and sheepishness.

The detective was about to leave when he noticed in the last lane, not far from the door, a pile of trunks plastered with foreign steam, ship and hotel labels and almost dustless. His professional curiosity and his mania for overlooking nothing induced him to pause and examine them. His eye quickly ran over such labels as North German Lloyd Hotel Adion, Berlin; Hotel Kaiserhof, Hamburg; Hotel National Leipzig; Royal Hawaiian Hotel, Honolulu; Grand Hotel, Vienna; The Grace Line; British Empire Hotel Melbourne; Hotel St. Francis, San Francisco; Hotel Pierre, New York: The Savoy, London.

CRUMMEL RAN HIS HAND OVER the top of a small steamer trunk. Brilliant, with a plumage of labels from all parts of the world. He looked at his hand. There was scarcely any dust on it at all.

"How long have these trunks been Here, janitor?"

"'Bout uh mont', suh."

"Who do they belong to? Some actor?"

"No suh. Dem belongs tuh de prefesser upstaihs."

"What professor?" snapped Crummel, immediately interested. This must be some Negro he had not heard about. The man had evidently been everywhere.

"Perfesser Grausmann," answered the janitor, a note of great respect in his voice. "He's uh German gentleman."

"A white man?" ask Crummel, again running his eyes over the expensive luggage and seeing the stickers from world famous hotels and steamship lines.

"Yeh, uh w'ite man," admitted the janitor, "but he sho is uh fine man."

"Tips good, eh?" snapped Crummel, shooting a swift glance at the man.

"Well. . . yeah. . . yeh, he do tip good," this somewhat reluctantly.

"When did he tip you last?"

"Jes th' otha day."

"What for?"

"Foh lettin' him in heah tuh go in one uh his trunks."

"What did he get out of his trunks?"

"Oh, sometimes he git clothes, or packages, or bottles, or sumpin' lak dat."

"You say 'sometimes.' Do you mean that he comes down often?"

"Well. . . Ah guess he bin in heah right offen."

"How long has he been here?"

"'Bout a mont'."

"And how often has he been down here?"

"Oh, Ah doan know. Lemme see. . ." the janitor looked up speculatively at the low ceiling. "Ah guess 'bout five er six times."

Crummel took out his notebook and made several notations.

"What did you say this German's name was?"

"Perfesser Grausmann."

"Did he ever tell you what he is doing living up in Harlem?"

"He jes say he studyin' nigguhs—say he gittin' local coloh." The janitor sniggled, the first sign of humor he had displayed. "He, heh, heh! He sho Gawd fine plenty coloh up heah wi dese folkses."

"What does he do?"

"He doan do nuthin' far's Ah kin see, 'coptin' tuh walk 'roun' de streets. He did say how he lak tuh go tuh de Laffeyette en sometime tuh de Savoy en watch dem nigguhs dancin'."

Crummel made a few more notes in his book, shoved it in his pocket and strolled out of the trunk room.

"Well, what do you think of that?" asked Williams, blinking up to his chief.

"Unusual, but not disturbing," said Crummel, laconically. "Let's go into your workroom janitor."

"Dey ain't nuthin' in dah," the man remonstrated.

"I'll find that out for myself," snapped Crummel. He strode off down the shadowy corridor in the direction of the workroom, followed by the others.

"This sure is a funny house," blurred Williams, unable longer to bottle up his curiosity. "colored folks, Africans, white folks, Chinamen! Man's liable to find anything here."

"No funnier than most houses in Harlem," retorted Crummel, lighting a cigarette. "There are Chinese and Africans and white folks to be found in lots of houses up here. This is the city of refuge, my boy."

"You mean the city of refuse dontcha," Said Williams in his droll tone, with just the suspicion of a smile on his dour countenance.

Crummel left. "Well, perhaps it does about amount to that. We've sure got everything in the world up here."

"But what I don't get," observed Williams, "is why a guy that could stay at the Hotel Pierre would come up here to live. Why? I went down there once when I was in uniform, and that's a swell dump."

"Lots of white people come to Harlem to live for a while," said Crummel. "That's nothing unusual."

"Well, they oughtta to stay with their own people," grumbled Williams.

"There you go," replied Crummel, "Just like a darkly for the world. Now if some cracker said that about your folks, you'd want to knock him down."

"Yeah," said Williams, ominous tone in his voice, "And I would too."

THEY WERE IN THE JANITORS work room now. It was not so large as the trunk room and had no door to it. It just opened off the corridor. Thrown around inside were carpenter's horses, Cans of paint, tools, packing cases, several planks and bundles of newspapers neatly tied. There was a carpenter's bench on one side of the room under a basement window. Against the wall stood three or four paint-splattered ladders.

A glance and a poke here and there revealed nothing.

"We'll go into your place now, janitor."

"Into mah place?" echoed the man. "Wha, mistuh, dey ain' no-buddy dah but mah wife en kids."

"Will overlook nothing," announce Crummel with finality. "I guess we'd better look in on that iceman afterwards, eh Williams?"

"Yeah," nodded Williams, "And I'd like to lamp that there. German professor, too."

"Don't worry," chuckled Crummel, "you will."

The janitor let them into his three room apartment. The close air was heavy with the odor of sleeping humans. He snapped on the light. When the officer strolled through the rooms. In the sitting room, kitchen and bathroom, there was no one nor anything of importance in Crummel's eyes.

The janitor indicated the bedroom door. His two children were asleep on a cot. His wife was lying in the bed with little Bobby Wong with her. The child was asleep, But the janitor's wife, a tall, gaunt, sharp faced woman, very dark and with piercing eyes, was sitting up rigidly, gazing at them with an intense steadiness that seemed almost the result of hypnotism.

"Whutcha mean mon breakin' een ma house lakka dis, eh?" she challenged.

"Dese mens is officeha, Lucy," warned the janitor.

"Ah no cah whut dey is! Ah no cah what dey is!" she yelled excitedly. "Ah doan wan no nigguhs comin' in mah bedroom lakka dis."

"Sorry, Mrs. . . er. . ." Crummel looked around helplessly to the janitor.

"Johnson," the man said.

"Mrs. Johnson," continued Crummel. "You see, we've got to search the whole place, And of course we had to come in here. Two. Well, I guess there's nothing here." His voice trailed off.

He was about to leave the room when he noticed on the lower shelf of a table next to the bed, a large red covered book, much the worse for wear. Had it been a black book, he would have thought it a Bible and given no attention to it, But the obvious ignorance of the Johnsons, and the absence of any other evidences of culture, made him pause to examine the tone. He reached for it.

"Tek yoh han offen hit, mon," screamed the janitor's wife. In a flash she was out of the bed, had pushed Crummel backwards and was grasping the big red book to her bosom.

"Doan nevah tech mah tings mon! Doan nevah tech mah tings!" she cried, backing away, trembling with rage.

She seemed like a furry, with her wrinkled white nightgown billowing around her tall, muscular frame, her bony black hands clawing the volume to her, her sunken eyes now blazing with anger, buried deep behind her broad high brow, her entire being emanating malevolence.

"Les go, Mistuh Detectuff," warned the rotund janitor, nervously, "Mah wife she's fum Nawlina, en she doan stan no foolin'."

Crummel could see the title of the red Book, the way Mrs. Johnson held the volume. It read: *Occultism*. Was the woman a witch? Certainly she looked it.

X

JANITOR'S WIFE, UNDER VOODOO 'SPELL', BARES VITAL CLUES TO CRIMES

Doan nevah tech mah tings!" the janitor's wife cried again, her deep set, evil eyes flashing.

"So you do believe in voodoo, eh?" asked Crummel, a smile playing around on his lips.

"Yeh, Ah believe in it," she answered, "kaze it's true."

"I guess you know how to find out things, eh?" Crummel thought he would humor the woman.

"Yeh, Ah know," She answered, "Oh now. Ah know whut's happened 'n' Ah knows how tuh stop it."

She swayed as she spoke, looking for all the world. Like a furry; her white nightgown billowing about her bony frame, her monovalent eyes filmy in half-closed, her book gripped closer, her thick lips twitching.

Williams and Crummel looked at each other and then at the little rotund janitor who gazed, awed and fascinated at his gaunt spouse.

"It's col'," she murmured, and then in louder tones, "Ah say it's col' . . . It's col' 'n' wet. . . Yeh, it's col' 'n' wet. . . Yeh, it's col' 'n' wet. . .'n' it's goin' . . . its goin' up. . . up. . . up th'ough uh hole. . ."

She was swaying back and forth now, her eyes completely closed, her thick lips twitching, perspiration on her brow.

"Th'ough uh hole. . . up th'ough uh hole," she mumbled. "Ah kin see it. . . Ah kin see it. . ."

"Where is the hole?" asked Crummel quickly. He would sleep. No bets, Pass over no clues. Stranger things had happened in history than this. Who knew? But what there might be something to it?

"Take me to it," he insisted firmly. He reached out and touched the woman's hand. "Take me to it," he commanded again.

Mrs. Johnson grasped his hand with a strong masculine grip that surprised him. Her eyes were closed. Beads of perspiration stood out on her brow. She moistened her switching, bulbous lips with her long purple tongue.

"Ah kin see it. . ." she mumbled, almost in a whisper, moving toward the door and still firmly holding Crummel's hand. "Yeh. . . Ah kin see it. . . it's goin' up th'ough a hole."

"Say, chief," whispered Williams, "Do you think there's anything to this dame?"

"I sleep no bets," replied Crummel, grimly. "I've seen some funny things in my time."

Johnson, the janitor, hurriedly opened his apartment door and flattened himself against the wall.

"How long do these spells last?" asked Crummel out of the side of his mouth as the uncomprehending bare foot black woman led him slowly past her husband.

"Sometimes fi' minutes, sometime ten," he whispered.

"It's goin' up. . ." the woman mumbled hollowly, making her way slowly down the corridor. . . "Yeah. . . it's goin' up. . ."

Crummel wished she would hurry. He wanted to continue his search, But years of experience had taught him to never overlook the slightest clue or tip that might help him solve a case. And this was one case that he *had* to solve. It meant everything to him. It meant a great deal to the police commissioner, all Harlem, all New York was aroused by these fiendish murders. Unless they were solved, they would certainly be a police shakeup.

"It's col' 'n' wet," she murmured, as she strode slowly down the corridor between the stone walls. "It's col' 'n' wet. . . Ah kin see it. . . it's goin' up. . . up. . . th'ough uh hole. . . uh hole. . . uh. . . uh. . ."

Her voice trailed off. Suddenly, like a wax figure before a blazing fire, she collapsed on the cement floor, still clutching the big Red book on witchcraft. Crummel picked her up.

"Take me to it," he insisted frantically, but it was too late. Mrs. Johnson's eyes opened wide.

"Whut Ah doin' outchere?" she thundered in her natural voice, twisting out of the detective's grasp. "Whut Ahm doin' outchere?"

"That's alright, Mrs. Johnson," soothed Crummel, "You were just saying that you knew what had happened around here."

"Ah doan know nuthin'," she snapped angrily, flouncing back into the apartment and slamming the door.

"I knew there wasn't anything to that," scoffed Williams. "That woman's just crazy."

"I don't know, Williams," mused Crummel, lighting a cigarette. "You know, there are many strange things in the world that science has never been able to explain. There are some people more naturally gifted than others. There is an undoubtedly something to all this occultism, or else humanity wouldn't have been believing it for so long. Of course, it has been exaggerated, like everything else, but underneath all of the hokum, Williams, I have a sneaking feeling that there's a bit of truth. Anyhow, I'm going to act on that hunch."

"What do you mean, chief?"

"We'll just go down this corridor a ways."

"Does yuh still want me?" asked the janitor, who was following behind.

"Yes, Johnson, you stay right along with us."

Crummel walked away down the stone-lined corridor. The sacks in which Marjorie Fenwick and Princess M'Bula had been found where both cold and wet, he recalled, but what had she meant about them going up through a hole? And where was the hole?

They came to a door on the right of the corridor, Crummel paused.

"That's the iceman's storeroom, isn't it?" he asked the janitor.

"Yassuh, dat's it."

"Open it up."

"Yassuh." The janitor took out his keys and unlocked the door. As he flung it open, a cold, wet, moist air struck their nostrils. Crummel took out his flashlight and swept the little room with its beam.

The place was half filled with large cakes of ice standing on their long Inns and covered with burlap sacks and canvas. Aside from a chair, there was nothing more.

Crummel reached up and turned on the electric light just over their heads. Then, while the other two men watched, he examined the place minutely, going over the stone walls, the cement floor and the wooden ceiling, which was the floor above.

Suddenly he stopped with an exclamation of surprise and satisfaction. He called Williams. There were three or four clearly marked footprints in basement dust on top of the damp burlap sacks covering the cakes of ice. They had evidently been made by a stockinged foot.

"That looks like something," murmured Crummel, half to himself, a slight smile playing around the corners of his mouth. He measured the plainest footprint. He grunted with satisfaction as he put away his tape, and taking out his notebook, made a few notations and comparisons. Then he turned to his assistant.

"It's the same footprint, absolutely the same measurements as the one in Charlie Wong's room, Williams, we found something at last."

"You mean the murderer was in here?"

"Yes, he was in here. He must have had a key. How did he get it? Where did he go? That's all we've got to find out, Williams, and I think I know someone who can tell us."

"He sure didn't go out in the street," said Williams, glancing at the other door leading to the alley, "because as a cop out there."

"That's right," Crummel agreed. "Maybe he left here while we were in the janitors and is hiding somewhere else in the cellar. Go outside, Williams, and get four or five men. We're going to place a man in each one of these rooms and then search the corridors. This guy can't get away now. He's in this cellar and we'll get him."

"Okeh, Chief," said Williams. "Johnson, open this outside door to the alley for me."

The janitor did as he was told. Williams stepped outside after the policeman.

"Johnson," said Crummel, turning to the rotund janitor, "Where does the iceman live? We'll go there next; I want to talk to him."

"He live upstaihs. . . Fact is, heh live right about heah on th' fust flo'."

"Oh, I see," murmured Crummel. "Well, I guess we'd better look in on him when Williams comes back."

"Ah guess you'll fin' 'im tha, alright. He uh funny man; he doan go nowha. Jist stay around' heah."

"Is that so? And how long did you say he had been handling the ice here?"

"Jist 'bout uh munt."

The outer door opened and Williams came in.

"Here they are, chief," he said, indicating the five policemen behind him.

Crummel directed them to completely search the basement. The janitor locked the outer door of the ice storeroom.

"Now," he announced, "will go up and see this fellow, Karl. He may know something."

"I think so, too, chief," added Williams. "He's about the only guy that fools around these dumb waiters. And that African gal was sure brought down on the dumb waiter. Couldn't have come down any other way. And then who else would have had a key to this room?"

"In addition to that," said Crummel, quietly, "This door leads into the alley or court outside, and Princess M'Bula's body was found there. With all of our men about, it must have come from here. Yes, this man, Karl has a lot to explain. Let's go. Williams, station one of those cops inside this room. I'm going to get to the bottom of this thing right now."

Williams called a policeman. Then he followed Crummel and the janitor to the automatic elevator, where they ascended to the first floor. The policeman on guard there saluted as they came out of the lift.

"Seen anything, Sam?" ask Crummel.

"Not a thing," the officer replied.

"Not one came into the hall?"

"Oh, a couple of people came in. . . Oh, yes, and that old white man that lives down the hall came out and asked me what was going on around here. He talked a few minutes and then went on back into his place."

"That must have been this Professor Grausmann," mused Crummel thoughtfully. "Where is his apartment, Johnson?"

"Right down th' hall theah," replied the janitor. "He live in 1-K. Karl live in 1-J."

They walked down the hall to 1-J, pausing before the door.

"Unlock that door," Crummel commanded.

"Deh man's in tha," protested the janitor. "Ah cain't open people's doahs w'en deys inside. Hit's 'ginst deh rules."

"Shut up," growled Crummel, "and do as you're told. I'm making the rules here now. Turn the key. Easy, I don't want to make any noise." He got out his pistol. Williams did likewise.

The janitor inserted one of his keys gently into the lock and softly turned it until there was a faint click. Crummel shoved him to one side and pushed the door inwards, wide, noiselessly.

The interior was black, dark, forbidding, sinister and silent as an Egyptian tomb.

He signaled to Williams to wait, and then softly closed the door behind him. He tiptoed along the carpeted little hall to the curtain that shut off the view of the room beyond. He reached his hand inside the room to feel for the electric light switch that he knew was alongside the door frame.

Suddenly, in a movement, astoundingly swift, his wrist was held in a vice-like grasp. He was yanked into the dark room, and a hard object crashed against his skull. He lurched forward, but was kept on falling by the giant strength of his assailant. Another blow staggered him and he lost consciousness.

XI

SLEUTHS FIND HIDDEN TRAP DOOR
BUT MORE MURDERS FOLLOW

Detective Orestes Williams waited impatiently outside apartment 1-J, frowning and twirling his pistol around his index finger. One minute, three minutes, five minutes, ten minutes past, and yet Crummel did not reappear. What could he be doing? It surely did not take that long to sleuth a one bedroom apartment.

"Hey, Sam!" he called down the hall to the policeman on guard.

"Yes, sir."

"Come down here." The policeman hurried to him. "I'm going in there, Sam. You keep watch outside. Don't let anyone out of this apartment except Sergeant Crummel or me. Savvy? And if that white man next door comes around, tell him to stay in his apartment. That goes for everybody else, too."

"I gotcha," The policeman replied, sitting himself on an ornamental bench upholstered with red paint where he could watch both door, and holding his service revolver in his hand.

"You wait around here, Johnson." Williams directed the janitor. He turned the knob softly, pistol in his other hand, and gently pushed the door wide open. The place was as still as a subterranean cavern. A heavy blue drape at the end of the little carpeted hallway cast off the view of the bedroom. The fact that there was no light inside immediately aroused the detective suspicions. Why should Crummel remain in the dark.

"Chief!" he called softly. There was no reply.

Thoroughly alarmed now, William strolled the brief length of the hallway, thrust the curtain aside and pulling out his flashlight, allowed its beam to play over the interior of the room. There, sprawled out on the floor, was Crummel, unconscious, a great wound on his forehead. There was no one else there.

First aid methods shortly brought Crummel around. His eyelids flickered and very shortly opened. He looked up at Williams and smiled slowly, then winced with pain.

"What a wallop!" he exclaimed, eagerly touching the lump on his forehead. That guy ought to be in the ring with Carnera."

"What guy?"

"The guy that hit me, you sap," hissed Crummel.

"But where is he? He sure didn't come past me, chief, and he isn't in here. You can see that."

"Yes, Williams," said Crummel, "I'm beginning to see everything. Clearly. It won't be long now. Now let me take a look around this place first. Meantime, you go downstairs and see if that sap in the iceman storeroom has to say anything. Make it snappy."

"Okeh, Chief." Williams hurried out.

Sergeant Crummel proceeded to search the little one room apartment minutely. There was a shallow alcove for cooking, a tiny bathroom, a clothes closet and a bedroom. Moving swiftly but methodically, Crummel examined every bit of the floor and wall, every stitch of clothing, every article of furniture. Several times he exclaimed in satisfaction, as he noted what might be a clue. He made several entries in his notebook.

Suddenly the door opened and Williams hurried in.

"Well, what's up?" asked Crummel looking up from a minute examination of the floor.

"That cop, Adams, Somebody got him. You know, that cop we left in the iceman's storeroom downstairs," shouted Williams.

"Got him how?" asked Crummel, straightening up.

"Shot through the head. They took his coat and badge, his cap and his gun. He's dead, chief."

"I thought as much, Williams. Now we've got this case almost covered. I know there was a way out of this room to that storeroom. That's the way he escaped. That's the way he brought those bodies upstairs."

"Well, all we've got to do then is to catch this fellow, Karl, and the case is settled, eh?" asked Williams.

"I don't know about that," Crummel cautiously replied, "There's something more to this than that. Get a description of this fellow Karl from Johnson, the janitor, telephone it to headquarters so they can broadcast it immediately. Tell them the number of that cop shield, too. It will be a cinch to nab him. Make it snappy, now."

With Williams' departure, Crummel continued his hunt for the hidden trap door. There was not the slightest evidence of it, no crack in the highly polished parquet floor.

The detective sat down in one of the two chairs, lit a cigarette, and pulling his gray hat down over his eyes, settled back to think over the case of this trap door. There must be one. Since there was one, there must be a way of opening it. There must be hinges and a catch somewhere. The door would be at most not more than three feet square. He finally decided that it must be a certain part of the room, where one could enter and leave through it swiftly. He knew it was not where he had fallen because he had not been moved by his assailant.

Somewhere within the area he had marked out, there must be a loose board which the iceman had lifted in order to open the trap door, but where was this board, and how had the big German been able to lift the board quickly, or even find it quickly? Crummel rose and strolled around the little apartment. In the bathroom his eye fell upon a red rubber suction plunger with a long handle. Acting on a hunch, he picked it up.

He walked into the area he had marked out and placing the plunger on each little square flooring in turn, press down and pulled upward. Five or six times. He tried it without any results. He tried it a seventh time for luck. He pulled upward in a tightly fitted square of floor and came up with the rubber suction plunger.

Excitedly, Crummel fell to his knees. Grasping the edge of the flooring with both hands, he pulled upward in a section three feet square, lifted noiselessly on folding steel supports. On the second floor below, there was a small knob. He pulled upward in a section of the flooring, swung up toward him. He found himself looking down into the iceman's storeroom.

The detective smiled triumphantly and softly closed the trap door. Yes, the janitor's wife had been right. There was a hole, as she had said, and obviously the bodies of the murdered persons. Had had to be taken through it. His next step now was to lay hands on Karl, the iceman.

WILLIAMS CAME BACK. "IT'S OKEH, chief. Every cop and plainclothes man in town is hunting for that dude. He won't even get off the island. So all we've got to do now is sit tight and wait until they bring him in. He'll sure burn for this."

"He can't burn except for bumping off that cop," said Crummel, puffing on another cigarette. "We have proof that three persons have been murdered, but we can only legally establish the identity of one of them, the Chinese laundryman. We cannot prove in court that these two female bodies were those of Marjorie Fenwick and Princess M'Bula. We cannot yet prove that this Karl killed the Chinaman, at least we can't prove it until we get Karl."

"I don't get you," declared Williams, frowning, "We've got the bodies of the Fenwick girl and met African woman, ain't we?"

"Yes, but we cannot legally identify them until we find their heads, Williams."

"Well, suppose we don't find their heads? What then?"

"We'll just have to try to get a confession, that's all. We actually have no proof legally that he was in this room when I entered; that he attacked me, or that he escaped through the trap door and shot the policeman on watching the storeroom. I didn't see him. No one saw him. No one heard a shot because he probably used a silencer on his pistol."

"Damn!" said Williams. "He must be a clever duck. We really ain't got nothing at all on him, have we?"

"Legally, no," said Crummel, slowly, flicking the ash off his cigarette. "I know he's guilty, but I can't prove it in court, at least not yet."

"But what I can't savvy," Williams went on, "is why he wanted to kidnap and then murder these women, what did he do with their blood and what did he do with their heads? They were never thrown in the trash or garbage cans because we've had them carefully searched ever since that Fenwick girl was killed.

They weren't thrown in the furnace, either. Yeh, that iceman was smart, if you ask me."

"He isn't the brains behind this," said Crummel. "He was just a muscle man. There's some fiend, who planned these murders, Williams, some maniac, who was cunning and resourceful. I haven't got the whole thing pieced together yet, but it's taking form. But I'm convinced there was someone behind Karl, directing and controlling him. Only a fiend Incarnate, some strange madman, some singular pervert would seek the heads and blood of young women; only some strange magnetic monster could force the cooperation of a giant like this fellow Karl."

"You mean to say that when we get this fellow, Karl," cried Williams, "that we won't have the main guy?"

"That's just what I mean, Williams," said Crummel, grimly. "Where are the heads? Where is the blood? Where is the laundryman's wife? They are not in here, and yet, and yet they must be in this house, but where? That's the big question. We'll get that big German, alright, but when we get him our job is not finished."

"Well," sighed Williams, scratching his head, "I'll be damned if this case ain't got me. What are we gonna do now?"

"WE'LL GO OUT AND GET a bite to eat first," said Crummel in a voice booming louder than usual, "Then we'll come back and see that Professor Grausmann. I want to talk to him, living right next door to this fellow, he should have heard something." He tiptoed to the kitchen, got the flour jar off a shelf and lightly sprinkled the entire floor of the room. Then he replaced the jar.

Crummel led the way out of the apartment, followed by Williams, and down the corridor to the front door and out on to Bradhurst Avenue. Day was just breaking. They turned the corner and Crummel stopped.

"What's the idea," asked Williams. "I thought we were going to eat something."

"Not yet, old man," said Crummel, his eyes gleaming with excitement. "The fun's just beginning. We'll wait five minutes and then go back. I'm making an experiment."

The two officers stood in the early morning cold. When the five minutes was up, Crummel led the way into the court and the basement. They ascended the stairs to the first floor and were starting down the corridor to 1-K when a uniformed officer came after them shouting.

"What's up, Sanderson?" asked Crummel, pausing.

"They found another one," yelled the policeman, "right out in the court."

"Another what?"

"Another woman's body," cried the officer, "It's in a sack, and it ain't got no head, just like the rest."

"By God," exclaimed Williams, and started to go back downstairs to the basement.

"Wait, Williams," commanded Crummel, "I'll need you. This is exactly what I suspected; That's why I came back. I thought five minutes would be enough. Sanderson, you come with us." They followed him down the corridor, puzzled, expectant, on edge.

When they reached the door of the missing iceman's apartment, he threw it open and taking out his flashlight, entered. The beam of the light swept the floor of the one room. There, clearly revealed, were footprints in the film of the flour, footprints leading from the wall of the room across the floor to the window.

Noiselessly, Crummel dropped down and measured the footprints. He made a few notes in his book. Then he looked out of the window which opened upon the court below. There a little knot of uniformed police were clustered around a large gunny sack into which they were peering. He knew it was the body of Mrs. Wong, the laundry man's wife.

He went to the door of the apartment and called the policeman who had been guarding the door.

"Sam, I want you to stand in this little hall here with your gun out. You ought to shoot anybody you see in this apartment. Understand?"

"Yes, sir," Sam took his post gun in his hand.

"Now," said Crummel, "we'll drop into 1-K and see the professor."

"What's that old white guy got to do with this?" asked Williams.

"I don't know," Crummel remarked, "but I'm going to find out."

XII

Detective Crummel's Cleverness Triumphs, Murderers Trapped

Walter Crummel was tremendously curious about the occupant of apartment 1-K. The fact that a white scientist should seek residence in a Harlem apartment house was, in itself, singular. What was he trying to find out? Was there. Any connection between him and that other German, the fugitive, Karl? They had both arrived about the same time; their apartments were side by side. Why? Did it mean anything? Or did it mean nothing?

Crummel frowned. Something told him that behind the door of apartment 1-K was some vital clue. It was not just a hunch; It was the result of careful illumination, and how easily it was to be mistaken.

Motioning to Williams, he approached the door of apartment 1-K. He told the janitor to softly unlock the door. Johnson was about to comply when a hubbub arose at the front door of the apartment. Several policemen were entering. In their midst, securely handcuffed, was a gigantic blonde, square headed man with closed chopped hair and pale vacant blue eyes. He was dressed in a ill-fitting policeman's coat. He had evidently been soundly beaten.

"Dat's Karl," said the janitor.

"That's swell!" exclaimed Crummel, turning to meet the approaching group.

"Well, here he is," announce one of his captors. "We got him up in the Bronx. We sure had a scrap. Man's as strong as a bull."

"Good work," said Crummel, "Well, Karl, Are you going to be smart and talk, or do you want the chair.?"

The blonde giant stared vacantly at the Negro detective, but said nothing.

"We've got the goods on you, Karl," continued Crummel. "We know you killed Marjorie Fenwick. We know you killed Princess

M'Bula. We know you killed Charlie Wong and probably his wife. We know you killed that policeman in your storeroom just a while ago. Why did you kill them? Why did you murder them, Karl? Didn't you know that you would burn in the electric chair? Think of it, Karl, the electric chair. . . You walk down a narrow hallway, Karl. There's a bright light at the end of it. You walk down the narrow hallway, coral, and the priest walks behind you. You walk down the hallway, Karl, and then you walk through a little green door into a little room. The big chair is there, Karl, and that's well, they'll make you sit. Understand? You sit there, Karl, while they strap you in and put that big cap on your head. . . and then. . . and then you die. Karl! It's terrible, Karl, with your flesh and blood, your brains and nerves burning to a crisp! Do you want to die, Karl, or do you want to live?"

The big German stood there, the cold sweat broken out on his broad perturbant brow, his hands clenching and unclenching, his tongue moistening, his heavy, sensual lips. He said nothing, but his eyes stared with cold fright as Crummel's searing words tore their meaning through his tortured mind.

"He won't talk," said Williams, in his cold, monotonous tones. "Shall I give him the works?"

"No, take him and lock him up," commanded Crummel, "But don't give him anything to eat until he talks."

The huge white man still stared vacantly at Crummel, as though he had heard no words of what had been said. The officers started to lead him away.

"Wait a minute there. Bring him back." The offers are stopped and returned their steps. Again Crummel faced the Nordic giant.

"Listen, Karl," said the detective, "do you want to carry the heads with you?"

The man's reaction was electric. His Ruddy face drained itself of blood, and his eyes grew as round as saucers.

"No! No!" he cried, recoiling and raising his manacled hands before his face as though to ward off an unpleasant ghost.

"Where are they?" snapped Crummel, coming closer.

The man slipped, trembled as though to speak. Suddenly he

GEORGE S. SCHUYLER

winced in pain and looked bewildered. He began to sway from side to side and then collapsed on the floor like a house of cards.

The astonished officers bent over him, seeking to get him to his feet. It was no use. In a short while, the man was dead.

"Doggone if this ain't getting' my goat," observed Williams, scratching his head and looking down at the prostate giant. "I wonder how come him shuffle off all of the sudden like that?"

Crummel was grim. He knew he was frustrated again, but of one thing, he was convinced: that there was something very peculiar about Karl's sudden death.

It was sometime before the medical examiner arrived, but they all waited patiently for him. He examined the big German minutely. Then suddenly he gasped, followed by a grunt of satisfaction.

"Just as I thought," he said, gingerly, holding up a slender thorn between the thumb and forefinger.

"What is it, doctor?" asked Crummel, eyeing the thorn curiously.

"Dendang," announce the physician, "One of the deadliest poisons. It is used by the Brazilian Indians in hunting and warfare. They smear it on these thorns and blow them through blow pipes. Death is usually instantaneous."

"But there was no one here with the fellow except us," objected Crummel.

"Well, I don't know, Sergeant," said the physician, "but that's the way this man died."

His suspicions were confirmed: there was something peculiar about the big German's death. It had been murder, but by whom and how? He pondered a moment, and then a smile spread slowly over his face.

"Alright, Johnson," He said, turning to the janitor, "unlock the door of 1-K."

Somewhat hesitantly, the frightened man complied. Crummel nodded to Williams and throwing the door of the apartment wide open, entered. A very small entrance hall opened on what was obviously a large apartment. As they walked into the large sitting room, a tall, stoop shouldered white man with sparse gray hair, a long sharp nose and piercing, glittering eyes, appeared in the opposite doorway. He was dressed as a surgeon, completely in white from head to foot.

"Well," He inquired, with a slight German accent, "What do you want?"

"We are officers," said Crummel, flipping his coat lapel to one side and revealing his badge. "We want to look over this place."

"What for?" countered the scientist, his voice rising. "Am I to be annoyed all of the time by stupid people?"

"It just happened, Professor Grausmann," replied Crummel, mustering all of his caritive characteristics, while avidity, "that several people have been murdered around here and we are questioning everybody."

"What have I got to do with that?"

"Just sit down, professor," commanded Crummel, gazing significantly at Williams, "while I look around."

The man scowled and then, with a shrug of resignation, sat down on the sofa. His swiftly moving, glittery eyes, followed the detective as he went about the place.

Crummel walked through the apartment. There were four rooms in all: a sitting room, a bedroom, a steady, a bathroom, and a kitchen. It was not until he reached the kitchen that he discovered anything untoward. There on an operating table, securely pinioned, was a huge black mastiff, under the influence of either. Professor Grausmann had evidently been interrupted as he was about to operate on the animal's head. There were strange jars filled with various colored fluids on the shelves, boxes, cans and strains, apparatus on the floor against the wall. Carefully, Crummel went through everything without finding anything important.

He looked into the bathroom again and made note of two large wet bath towels. He emptied the clothes, hamper and piece by piece, examined the soiled linen. He went into the bedroom and opening the closet door, examined all of the professors shoes and slippers. He measured one of the slippers. And then consulted his little notebook. With a grunt of satisfaction, he replaced the book, and taking the slipper, returned into the sitting room.

GEORGE S. SCHUYLER

"Well, I hope you are through," snapped the German, "so I can finish my operation."

"Are you running a dog hospital, professor?" asked Crummel, suavely.

"No, I am merely practicing some vivisection for the purposes of research."

"Do you generally practice on heads, professor?"

"Just what are you trying to get at, my man?"

"I merely asked the question, since there are three heads missing around this vicinity."

"You're not insinuating. . ." The professor's voice rose.

"What do you think, professor?" said Crummel, smiling.

"Come, come, my man. I have no time for foolishness. I've got work to do."

"I should think you had accomplished efficient for one night," remarked Crummel blandly. "You take it easy now before you get careless. You've already made one serious mistake."

"What do you mean?"

"This slipper, professor," said Crummel, still smiling, but coming closer to the man. "You forgot to wipe all of the flour off this slipper."

The man's jaw fell, and he looked panicky for a minute, Then, with an effort, he pulled himself together, regaining his sureness.

"No, I didn't," he replied confidently, Then he caught himself and stammered: "I. . . I haven't wiped off any slippers.

Crummel whipped out his pistol and covered the man. "Put on the bracelets, Williams."

Quick as a flash, Grausmann's Fist lunged out and caught Crummel flush on the chin. He stumbled back against Williams. In the twinkling, the German dashed into the studio. The two detectives raced after him just in time to see the huge bookcase that took up all. One wall of the room swing on a pivot, and the man disappear into the adjoining apartment, formerly occupied by the dead iceman. There was a bash and an explosion, then another and another, and the fugitive slumped onto the floor, clutching his stomach.

"Good work, Sam," complimented Crummel. "It's a good thing I put you in there, but I had a hunch something like this would happen."

Grausmann was badly wounded. They carried him back into his apartment and stretched him out on the sofa. He glared at them, helplessly. Williams hurried off to summon an ambulance.

"You haven't got long to be here, Grossman," said Crummel, as one of the policemen sought to halt the flow of blood with a towel. "Hadn't you better tell me about this?"

"Swine!" gasped the German. "You have interfered with science. You have stopped my life's work with your damned meddling."

"What's your life's work?"

"To transplant a living human brain to the skull of a great dog. It would have been remarkable, revolutionary! And now you. . ."

"Is that why you needed the heads of young Negro women?"

"Yes, the female Negro brain, because of its small size, was best adapted for my purposes."

"What did you do with the skulls?"

"I have them in my bookcase. Look for them. Most of the books are a blind."

"And why did you drain all of the blood from the bodies. What was the idea of that?"

"Karl. . . He was a huge beast. . . A ghoul, an ex-butcher. I saved him from the axe in Germany. He served me faithfully because I gave him human blood. That was the secret of his tremendous strength. . . He was a great brute. . . a subhuman type, but he served me well."

"Why then did you murder him? I know you shot the dart through the eye hole in your apartment door."

"Ah, you know that too, eh? You are a very canny man. Well, Karl might have talked. He was no more used to me. Self-preservation, you know."

The dying man's face was pale and drawn. He breathed with difficulty. He smiled wearily as the ambulance doctor rushed in.

"It's no use, my good man," he sneered. "You fellows will never drag me through your courts. What are three black women compared to my researches? That is what I hate to see ended."

He shook his head sadly. Then, turning to Crummel, he eyed him curiously, then said: "See here, black man, how did you know that? I failed to wipe the flour off one slipper?"

"I didn't," said Crummel blandly. "That was just good guesswork."

The German grimace, closed his cold grey eyes and then muttered an almost inaudible "Damn!"

The End

THE NEGRO-ART HOKUM

Negro art "made in America" is as non-existent as the widely advertised profundity of Cal Coolidge, the "seven years of progress" of Mayor Hylan, or the reported sophistication of New Yorkers. Negro art there has been, is, and will be among the numerous black nations of Africa; but to suggest the possibility of any such development among the ten million colored people in this republic is self-evident foolishness. Eager apostles from Greenwich Village, Harlem, and environs proclaimed a great renaissance of Negro art just around the corner waiting to be ushered on the scene by those whose hobby is taking races, nations, peoples, and movements under their wing. New art forms expressing the "peculiar" psychology of the Negro were about to flood the market. In short, the art of Homo Africanus was about to electrify the waiting world. Skeptics patiently waited. They still wait.

True, from dark-skinned sources have come those slave songs based on Protestant hymns and Biblical texts known as the spirituals, work songs and secular songs of sorrow and tough luck known as the blues, that outgrowth of ragtime known as jazz (in the development of which whites have assisted), and the Charleston, an eccentric dance invented by the gamins around the public market-place in Charleston, S. C. No one can or does deny this. But these are contributions of a caste in a certain section of the country. They are foreign to Northern Negroes, West Indian Negroes, and African Negroes. They are no more expressive or characteristic of the Negro race than the music and dancing of the Appalachian highlanders or the Dalmatian peasantry are expressive or characteristic of the Caucasian race. If one wishes to speak of the musical contributions of the peasantry of the south, very well. Any group under similar circumstances would have produced something similar. It is merely a coincidence that this peasant class happens to be of a darker hue than the other inhabitants of the land. One recalls the remarkable likeness of the minor strains of the Russian mujiks to those of the Southern Negro.

As for the literature, painting, and sculpture of Aframericans—such as there is—it is identical in kind with the literature, painting, and sculpture of white Americans: that is, it shows more or less evidence of European influence. In the field of drama little of any merit has been written by and about Negroes that could not have been written by whites. The dean of the Aframerican literati written by and about Negroes that could not have been written by whites. The dean of the Aframerican literati is W. E. B. Du Bois, a product of Harvard and German universities; the foremost Aframerican sculptor is Meta Warwick Fuller, a graduate of leading American art schools and former student of Rodin; while the most noted Aframerican painter, Henry Ossawa Tanner, is dean of American painters in Paris and has been decorated by the French Government. Now the work of these artists is no more "expressive of the Negro soul"—as the gushers put it—than are the scribblings of Octavus Cohen or Hugh Wiley.

This, of course, is easily understood if one stops to realize that the Aframerican is merely a lampblacked Anglo-Saxon. If the European immigrant after two or three generations of exposure to our schools, politics, advertising, moral crusades, and restaurants becomes indistinguishable from the mass of Americans of the older stock (despite the influence of the foreign-language press), how much truer must it be of the sons of Ham who have been subjected to what the uplifters call Americanism for the last three hundred years. Aside from his color, which ranges from very dark brown to pink, your American Negro is just plain American. Negroes and whites from the same localities in this country talk, think, and act about the same. Because a few writers with a paucity of themes have seized upon imbecilities of the Negro rustics and clowns and palmed them off as authentic and characteristic Aframerican behavior, the common notion that the black American is so "different" from his white neighbor has gained wide currency. The mere mention of the word "Negro" conjures up in the average white American's mind a composite stereotype of Bert Williams, Aunt Jemima, Uncle Tom, Jack Johnson, Florian Slappey, and the various monstrosities scrawled by the cartoonists. Your average Aframerican no more resembles this stereotype than the average American resembles a composite of Andy Gump, Jim Jeffries, and a cartoon by Rube Goldberg.

Again, the Aframerican is subject to the same economic and social forces that mold the actions and thoughts of the white Americans. He is not living in a different world as some whites and a few Negroes would have me believe. When the jangling of his Connecticut alarm clock gets him out of his Grand Rapids bed to a breakfast similar to that eaten by his white brother across the street; when he toils at the same or similar work in mills, mines, factories, and commerce alongside the descendants of Spartacus, Robin Hood, and Erik the Red; when he wears similar clothing and speaks the same language with the same degree of perfection; when he reads the same Bible and belongs to the Baptist, Methodist, Episcopal, or Catholic church; when his fraternal affiliations also include the Elks, Masons, and Knights of Pythias; when he gets the same or similar schooling, lives in the same kind of houses, owns the same Hollywood version of life on the screen; when he smokes the same brands of tobacco and avidly peruses the same puerile periodicals; in short, when he responds to the same political, social, moral, and economic stimuli in precisely the same manner as his white neighbor, it is sheer nonsense to talk about "racial differences" as between the American black man and the American white man. Glance over a Negro newspaper (it is printed in good Americanese) and you will find the usual quota or crime news, scandal, personals, and uplift to be found in the average white newspaper—which, by the way, is more widely read by the Negroes than is the Negro press. In order to satisfy the cravings of an inferiority complex engendered by the colorphobia of the mob, the readers of the Negro newspapers are given a slight dash of racialistic seasoning. In the homes of the black and white Americans of the same cultural and economic level one finds similar furniture, literature, and conversation. How, then, can the black American be expected to produce art and literature dissimilar to that of the white American?

Consider Coleridge-Taylor, Edward Wilmot Blyden, and Claude McKay, the Englishmen; Pushkin, the Russian; Bridgewater, the Pole; Antar, the Arabian; Latino, the Spaniard;

Dumas, père and fils,the Frenchmen; and Paul Laurence Dunbar, Charles W. Chestnut, and James Weldon Johnson, the Americans. All Negroes; yet their work shows the impress of nationality rather than race. They all reveal the psychology and culture of their environment—their color is incidental. Why should Negro artists of America vary from the national artistic norm when Negro artists in other countries have not done so? If we can foresee what kind of white citizens will inhabit this neck of the woods in the next generation by studying the sort of education and environment the children are exposed to now, it should not be difficult to reason that the adults of today are what they are because of the education and environment they were exposed to a generation ago. And that education and environment were about the same for blacks and whites. One contemplates the popularity of the Negro-art hokum and murmurs, "How-come?"

This nonsense is probably the last stand or the old myth palmed off by Negrophobists for all these many years, and recently rehashed by the sainted Harding, that there are "fundamental, eternal, and inescapable differences" between white and black Americans. That there are Negroes who will lend this myth a helping hand need occasion no surprise. It has been broadcast all over the world by the vociferous scions of slaveholders, "scientists" like Madison Grant and Lothrop Stoddard, and the patriots who flood the treasure of the Ku Klux Klan; and is believed, even today, by the majority of free, white citizens. On this baseless premise, so flattering to the white mob, that the blackamoor is inferior and fundamentally different, is erected the postulate that he must needs be peculiar; and when he attempts to portray life through the medium of art, it must of necessity be a peculiar art. While such reasoning may seem conclusive to the majority of Americans, it must be rejected with a loud guffaw by intelligent people.

A Note About the Author

George S. Schuyler (1895–1977) was an author, journalist, social commentator and somewhat controversial figure. Born in Providence, Rhode Island, Schuyler's formative years were shaped by his time in the U.S. military. Enlisting at age 17, Schuyler rose to the title of First Lieutenant before going AWOL due to a racist encounter with a Greek immigrant. Sentenced to five years for the abandonment, Schuyler was released after less than a year for being a model prisoner. In the aftermath of his release, he lived at the Phillis Wheatley Hotel in New York City, coming to learn the teachings of Black nationalist, Marcus Garvey. Not fully convinced of Garvey's teachings, Schuyler would separate himself from both Garveyism and socialism, contributing articles to the *American Mercury* and embracing capitalism. Embarking on a career in journalism, Schuyler would find success and acknowledgement for his editorial skills as he took on the role of Chief Editorial Writer at the *Courier* in 1926. That same year he would pen a controversial piece, "The Negro-Art Hokum" for *The Nation* which—combined with his advocacy for capitalism—further alienated himself from his contemporaries. The article, which argued that art should not be segregated by race and that Black artist had no true style of their own, would inspire Langston Hughes' famous, "The Negro and The Racial Mountain." Five years after this, Schuyler would try his hand at a long fiction form, producing notable novels such as *Slaves Today* (1931), *Black No More* (1931), and *Black Empire* (1936–1938); and while Schuyler would continue to produce work up until the point of his death, it was his public and explicit conservatism and opposition to the Civil Rights Movement of the 1960s–70s that would push both he and his literary work into obscurity. At the time of his death, his legacy and talent as a writer were so overshadowed by his politics that no one within Black circles wanted to interact with his work at all. Despite this, Schuyler produced some of the first satires by a Black writer and addressed intra-community issues at a time when most Black authors appealed solely to the middle-class.

NOTE FROM THE PUBLISHER

Since our inception in 2020, Mint Editions has kept sustainability and innovation at the forefront of our mission. Each and every Mint Edition title gets a fresh, professionally typeset manuscript and a dazzling new cover, all while maintaining the integrity of the original book. With thousands of titles in our collection, we aim to spotlight diverse public domain works to help them find modern audiences. Mint Editions celebrates a breadth of literary works, curated from both canonical and overlooked classics from writers around the globe.

bookfinity & MINT EDITIONS

Enjoy more of your favorite classics with Bookfinity,
a new search and discovery experience for readers.
With Bookfinity, you can discover more vintage
literature for your collection, find your Reader Type,
track books you've read or want to read,
and add reviews to your favorite books.
Visit www.bookfinity.com, and click on
Take the Quiz to get started.

Don't forget to follow us
@bookfinityofficial and @mint_editions

Printed in the USA
CPSIA information can be obtained
at www.ICGtesting.com
JSHW021019230524
R13534700001B/R135347PG63569JSX00005B/7